Turned

Around

~*A Ryan Turner Novel*~

By Jorrell Otoño Mirabal

JM Publishing
Jorrell Mirabal
PO Box 1168, Magdalena, NM 87825
jorrellmirabal@yahoo.com

ISBN: 9781717208187

At the publication of this book, Turned Around, I want to give a special thanks to the following people: Jaida Valenzuela for the beautiful work she did on the cover and for her great talent; Aunt Carrie-Carrie Sant- for helping me through the editing process and supporting me through this project; Sharon Harris for her undying support and her help with the editing process too. Thank you, from the bottom of my heart to everyone who helped make this book a reality. Turned Around would have never been possible if it weren't for you.

TURNED AROUND

CHAPTER ONE

He shivered violently. Not from the cool air surrounding him, but from the fear and excruciating pain he was experiencing. His chin rested on his chest. No longer able to hold his head up, Pablo Montez was bloodied and battered and still unaware as to where he was now. His legs dangled freely in the air. His ankles were tied together with thick rope. All around him, it was pitch dark, impeding him from seeing the large pool of blood beneath his body. He couldn't move his arms. His hands and wrists throbbed with pain. His head hurt, and he could feel blood pounding behind his ears. He was naked, aside from his underwear. The cool air continuously rushed against his bare skin.

"How is it going up there?" a voice asked out of the darkness.

Pablo attempted to lift his head. He could see nothing in front of him. His eyes failed to adjust to the complete dark. He said nothing.

"Oh, Montez?" the voice called out. "Are you still alive? Please tell me you're still alive and breathing?"

Again, Pablo Montez said nothing. Pain surged through his entire body. He felt as if he was on the brink of death. Suddenly, a small flame began to flicker amid the complete darkness. The flame moved in the dark and came to a stop. It then moved atop a tall candle stick that sat upon a gold base. There were now two flames. The first flame moved again, this time to Montez's right. It stopped again, and another candle, identical to the first, began to flicker. Montez forced himself to lift his head. He looked towards the light to find a figure sitting in a chair. On the floor, a candle was positioned on each side of the chair. The figure before Montez was dressed all in black, and wore a white mask, covering all but two beady eyes. A big gold cross hung from a silver necklace around the individual's neck. Finally, Montez spoke.

"Who are you?" he muttered. "Where am I?"

The figure in black stood up from the chair and picked up the candles off the ground. Holding one in each hand, the individual approached Montez. The person moved with robot-like motions, walking one slow step at a time toward Montez. After a few steps, the individual stopped in front of Montez, and dropped to the floor into a kneeling position. The person in black set the two candles down on the floor, a few feet apart from one another. Pablo's body seized up at the sight of blood.

He could now see the pool of blood beneath him. He could now see that his feet were a foot or two off the ground, tied against a wooden object. A renewed wave of fear surged through his body. He began to yell and tried to move but failed to do so. Aside from his head, he couldn't move a single part of his body. He cried out again.

"Hush, hush," the masked individual said, softly caressing Montez's legs. "Just relax. Breathe. In and out. Everything is going to be just fine."

Shivering, Montez stopped yelling, but quietly began to sob.

"What have I done to you? I don't know you. I am a good man," he cried. "Why am I here? Where am I? Who are you? Please. Please."

"Easy," the figure in black said. "Easy now. You have so many questions, and so little time. Please, one at a time."

There was complete silence for a moment, then Montez quietly asked, "Where am I?"

Now holding a long, jagged blade, the individual answered, "You, Dom, are where you are meant to be. You are where you are supposed to be. You are hanging from a cross. A beautiful, magnificent cross. You are in a place that is of no concern to you. Now, breathe. Deep breaths. In and out. Everything is going to be just fine. You were meant for this moment."

Montez struggled to lift his head high enough to look over at his outstretched arms. The mysterious being in front of him wasn't lying. His hands were nailed to the wood of what he now knew was a cross. He now realized the direct source of where the pain surging through his hands and arms was coming from and began to thrash around.

"Who are you? PLEASE! Why am I here? I don't deserve this! I don't."

Tears streamed down Montez's cheeks. Stroking the knife's blade, the individual dressed in black peered up into Montez's pleading, fear-filled eyes.

"I am The Crucifier. You are right, Dom. You do not deserve this…which is why it must be you."

Before Pablo Montez could mutter another word, The Crucifier shoved the long blade deep into the man's side. Montez whimpered, but no longer had the energy to cry out. Although still breathing, he was already a dead man. It was only a matter of time now before he bled out, or before shock killed him. He no longer had the will to live. He knew he was helpless.

Still holding the blade in Montez's side, The Crucifier whispered, "You are not the first, Pablo Montez. You are not. You are part of something big, something great. This, Pablo Montez, is only the beginning."

The Crucifier then jerked the knife out of the dying man's side. Blood instantly gushed out of the wound. Watching Pablo Montez breathe his last breaths, The Crucifier stepped back, and smiled beneath the white mask. Pablo Montez's head went completely limp. His chest no longer heaved in and out. The Crucifier moved back toward Montez and using Montez's cell phone that had been retrieved earlier, dialed "911", reported the scene, ended the call, and tossed the phone onto the floor. It clattered onto the concrete ground and slid next to the large pool of blood. Then, bending over slightly, The Crucifier kissed Montez's feet.

The killer then took a step back, pointed a finger into the air, and turned away from the body. The Crucifier then exited the cold, dark basement that held Pablo Montez's bloodied, lifeless body.

CHAPTER TWO

Ryan Turner was nervous. He was anxious, and his
body ached from sitting for so long. The relentless heat from
the sun's rays blasted down on Ryan's neck. He took a deep
breath. His heart was racing. His palms were sweaty. His
eyes were locked on the scene in front of him. For the past
hour, his attention hadn't strayed. A bead of sweat ran from
the top of his forehead to the tip of his nose. He didn't even
bother wiping it away. He held his breath. Time seemed to
stand still. He could perfectly see every action and every
movement in front of him. He could hear every single noise.
These were the moments Ryan lived for, the moments he
loved. Ryan Turner leapt to his feet. He crouched down and
covered his eyes, and then peeked through his fingers. His
heart pounded against his chest. He had to let it out. He had
to act now. Ryan couldn't contain himself any longer. He
jumped in the air and clapped his hands together.

"Go! Go! Go!" he cried out, flailing his arms
around.

He then froze as he stared out in front of him. There
was complete silence just before the crowd around him
erupted into cheering. Ryan gave a fist pump as if he was
Kobe Bryant in the 2009 NBA Finals.

"Goal!" Ryan exclaimed.

He flopped back down into his red, fold-up lawn
chair. With a huge smile on his face, he pointed at his

daughter, Kayleen, while she trotted down the soccer field across from him.

"That's my girl!" Ryan yelled.

Wearing a big smile herself, six-year-old Kayleen pointed back at Ryan.

"Gosh, you sure do get riled up," Laura Turner said, placing her left hand on Ryan's right forearm.

"Me?" Ryan asked, winking at his wife. "Never."

Laura chuckled as she massaged Ryan's arm. The two sat in identical chairs at mid-field of the soccer field before them. The field was beautiful and part of the Jackie Robinson Recreation Center. Ryan and Laura looked on as the carefree six-year-old girls attempted to kick the ball back-and-forth while constantly giggling. At times, it was hard for Ryan to tell whether there was an organized game going on or not. Most of the children were more interested in pulling blades of grass up from the field rather than the soccer game itself. Kayleen, on the other hand, took the games seriously and for good reason too. She was good. Really good.

Already, after just three official games, there had been several complaints about Kayleen from other parents. Parents from not just opposing teams, but Kay's own team complained relentlessly that Kayleen "stole the show," "made the other children feel like they aren't any good," and "was a ball-hog." In a few instances, her age was even called into question by snobby parents. All of it really bothered Laura, but Ryan simply ate it up. He honestly loved it. To him, it just confirmed how talented Kayleen really was. It made Ryan swell with pride. At home, he spent every spare moment he could kicking a soccer ball and playing with Kayleen in the backyard of their house. He loved it all almost as much as she did.

Ryan jumped to his feet again.

"Atta girl! Go, Kay, go!"

Ryan crouched down onto his haunches and watched intently as Kayleen stole the ball mid-pass and dribbled it full speed down the field. Ryan's heart pounded with excitement as Kay made her way toward the goal. As she got closer, she started to slow down. It was just her and the goalie. Every other player was trailing far behind Kayleen. She looked poised, cool, and confident as she headed straight for the goalie, running right down the middle of the field. Once she was merely twenty yards away from the goal, Ryan had a feeling she was about to set up to take the shot. Proving his suspicions, Kayleen slowed the ball down and planted her left foot hard into the green turf. She then took a hard swing with her right leg. At first, he felt certain Kayleen had kicked the ball too far to the right. This time he was wrong. He threw his fists into the air as the ball curved to the left and entered into the goal, perfectly to the inside of the right goal post. This time, it was Laura who couldn't contain her excitement. She leapt to her feet.

"Did you see that? Ryan, did you see that?" she asked, grabbing Ryan's arm. "Did you see how she put that spin on the ball? Wow!"

Ryan laughed. "Gosh, you sure do get riled up."

Laura rolled her eyes and punched Ryan in the arm. On the field, a timeout was called, bringing gameplay to a sudden halt. Hearing a faint yip, Ryan looked down at the base of Laura's chair at the little three-legged dog that was tied to it. Tripod. The excitement woke him up and he was suddenly very attentive and barking at the field. Tripod kept his attention on Kayleen's team's huddle. He barked a few times, wagging his tail. The little dog was always aware of Kayleen's location. The two were the best of friends.

Ryan smiled at the little dog. Although he wasn't exactly thrilled when they first got Tripod, he had grown attached to the little animal. He loved the dog. He particularly loved him because the little dog had so much love for Kayleen. The pup had served as a best friend to her and was a service dog to her in a sense. Kayleen really struggled after the whole ordeal of being kidnapped by Cybris Caine, in which she subsequently witnessed the violent though ultimately successful rescue of her family from Caine's evil grip. After everything she went through and saw, Tripod was her outlet, her escape. He brought her happiness. The energetic dog made her smile, laugh, and squeal every day. Kayleen and Tripod slept together and went practically everywhere together.

Ryan reached down and patted the dog on the head. Tripod returned the gesture by licking Ryan's thumb. He then returned his attention more fully back to the game. Kayleen's "Lil Lions" were leading 2-0 with five minutes remaining. Ryan watched as Kayleen stole the ball from an opposing player and dribbled down the sideline toward her team's goal.

"Go, Kay, go!" Ryan said, staying in his seat this time.

Kayleen stopped in her tracks and placed her right foot on top of the ball, bringing it to a halt. Ryan was confused.

What is she doing?

Ryan then realized that Kayleen's eyes were focused on the opposite sideline. Running down the opposite sideline was a little girl trotting down the field. She happened to be one of Kay's teammates.

With her arm, Kayleen motioned toward the goal and yelled, "Go, Maddy!"

The girl across the field picked up speed and ran straight for the goal. Two girls from the other team were right on Kay's heels now but she kept her cool. She began to dribble down the field again, and midstride she sent the ball gliding across the field toward Maddy. The pass couldn't have been any more perfect. Mid-stride, Maddy closed her eyes and kicked the ball hard toward the goal just before losing her footing and landing flat on her back. There was a hush in the crowd as the soccer ball sailed through the air. Ryan held his breath. The ball looked like it would go over the top of the goal; however, it ended up being right on the mark. It sailed right over the goalie's head and into the back of the net.

"Goal!" yelled Ryan while high-fiving Laura.

The entire "Lil Lions" crowd erupted into cheering and screaming. A grin stretched across Ryan's face as he watched Kayleen sprint over to Maddy and lift her up off the ground. Maddy was beaming with joy. Kay lifted her up, spun her around, and then set her down, high-fived her, and threw her arms around her. They embraced in a hug. His daughter's generous heart was the main personal trait which had always made Ryan the proudest of her. Her humility, thoughtfulness, and care and love for those around her is what impressed Ryan most about her every single day.

The moment was interrupted abruptly when Ryan's cell phone started to vibrate inside of his pocket. He grabbed it and looked down at the screen. He glanced at Laura. She shook her head with a slight shrug. Ryan stood from his seat and mouthed the word "sorry" before walking away.

CHAPTER THREE

"Hello, this is Turner."

"Ryan! I mean, Mr. Turner, sir," G-Man replied. "Sorry, sir, I'm still not used to you being Mr. Boss Man. I truly apologize, sir."

Ryan rolled his eyes. "You're hilarious, Gary, just hilarious. 'Ryan' works just fine. What's up?"

Gary Richards cleared his throat. "Well, the prints we ran…from the killing at Majestic Theater? As we guessed, our "Gator" character was responsible. He is now in custody. His name is Flavio Marcona."

Ryan stroked his chin. "Well, well. The newbie, Agent Simmons did well."

"Yes, sir," G-Man said. "He's good, Ryan, really good. He's been very on top of things, very thorough, very punctual. It's been a pleasure working with the guy. I just thought I should let you know what's going on."

"Thank you, Gary. You're the man," Ryan said, peering over at the soccer field to see that the game had concluded.

"You are very welcome, sir. How's your wife holding up?"

Ryan looked over at Laura, who was standing up clapping. "She's doing well," he said. "The baby is healthy,

Laura is healthy, and we're all super excited. Kayleen especially!"

G-Man chuckled. "Glad to hear it. Well, I'll talk to you later, Ryan. Have a good one, my friend."

"You too, G-Man."

Ryan started to walk back to Laura, who was now hugging Kayleen, but he came to a halt as his phone began to vibrate in his pocket again.

"Turner here," he answered.

"Good afternoon, this is Dr. Phillip Hill from the Ryker's Island Prison. I wanted to update you on Cindy Caine and her baby."

"Okay, go ahead, Dr. Hill," Ryan replied.

"Well, the mother is doing great," Hill said enthusiastically. "Cindy has been monitored very closely. The baby is growing perfectly. There have been no complications whatsoever. The little guy is going to be very healthy. We're expecting the baby any day now."

Ryan smiled. "Thank you for the update, Dr. Hill."

"My pleasure!" Hill replied. "Have yourself a wonderful day."

"You as well, Doc. Thanks again."

With that, Ryan ended the call. Kayleen was already running towards him. Tripod trailed right behind her, running as fast as his three little legs could carry him.

"Kay!" Ryan called out, "So, so proud of you, girl!"

Instead of replying, Kayleen stopped in her tracks and looked all around her, then moving her attention back to Ryan she whispered, "Is it okay if I talk to you?"

"Uh, duh!" Ryan said.

Kayleen took a step closer to Ryan. "Are you sure? Like there isn't any top-secret stuff going on here, is there?"

Laughing, Ryan shook his head. "No, you goof!"

Kayleen giggled and threw herself into Ryan's awaiting arms, resting her head on Ryan's shoulder. After a brief hug, Ryan set her down.

"Heck of a game out there! You tore it up, champ!"

Kayleen smiled. "Thanks, Daddy. Did you see Maddy? Did you see her shot?"

"Did I see Maddy's shot?" Ryan placed his hands on his head. "Oh, did I ever! That was awesome! I saw that amazing pass to her too."

Kayleen shrugged. "It was an okay pass. She kicked it so good, though, Daddy! I'm so proud of her."

So humble.

"It was a great kick." Ryan said.

Just then, Maddy and her father walked past Ryan and Kayleen.

"Great job again, Maddy! That was so awesome!" Kayleen yelled out after Maddy.

Maddy stopped walking and spun around. Beads of sweat still covered her forehead.

"Thanks, Kay!" she said. "That was so much fun."

Ryan and Maddy's father made eye-contact; the girl's dad immediately looked away from Ryan and grabbed Maddy by her shoulders.

"Let's go. Come on," he said to Maddy.

The pair turned to walk away, but not before the man muttered something to Maddy under his breath.

"You have nothing to say to that cocky little brat," he said, none too quietly.

Not only did Ryan hear it, but Kayleen did too. Ryan watched as his daughter's bottom lip stuck out and began to quiver. Her eyes welled up with tears. Ryan clenched his fists. It took everything in his power not to come completely unhinged.

"Excuse me, sir?" Ryan exclaimed.

The man continued walking, completely ignoring Ryan. Ryan took a few strides after the man.

"Hey!" he said raising his voice.

This time the man stopped and turned around. Ryan took a few steps to the side and motioned the man over to him.

"What's your name?" Ryan asked as Maddy's Dad walked over to him and stopped directly in front of Ryan.

The two stood face to face.

"Bob," the blonde, overweight man replied.

Ryan placed a hand on Bob's shoulder and leaned closer to the heavyset man.

"Listen, Bob," he said in a hushed tone, "How about we never talk about my little girl like that ever again, yeah?"

Bob smirked, looking Ryan up and down. He looked pretty sure of himself.

Ryan dug into his pocket and pulled out his badge.

"Look that over real quick," he told Bob.

Bob flipped open the badge and froze. His entire demeanor changed.

Ryan smiled a big, fake, cheesy smile and grabbed the badge out of the overweight man's hands.

"Have we come to an understanding? Do you get me?"

Bob nodded and quickly turned away.

"Let's go, Maddy," he said under his breath, as he took his daughter by the arm.

Maddy waved to Kayleen and then waved to Ryan.

"Great job, Maddy," Ryan said. "See you next time."

The little blonde girl looked over her shoulder. "Thank you, Mr. Turner."

Ryan grabbed Kayleen and swung her off her feet, then placed her onto his shoulders.

"Let's go get your mom and head home. How does that sound?" Ryan said.

"Sounds good to me!" proclaimed Kayleen.

"And maybe, *just maybe*, we can stop for some ice cream on the way." Ryan added.

"What?" Kayleen asked. "Just maybe? Oh, come on!"

Pointing to Laura, Ryan said, "It isn't really up to me. You're going to have to run the idea through the boss first."

Immediately Kayleen cried out, "Mommy! Mommy! Can we get some ice cream? Please, please, pretty please! I'll actually clean my room! For real this time, I promise!"

Tripod looked up at Laura and barked, as if to second Kayleen's petition. Laura rose from her chair, turned around and chuckled. Ryan sat Kayleen down and grabbed his and Laura's chairs.

"Hmm," Laura began, "You'll have to ask your dad."

"Ugh!" Kayleen groaned. "You guys always do this!"

Ryan and Laura both laughed.

"I mean, we can. I guess…" Ryan said.

"You rock, Daddy!" Kayleen fist-pumped in the air then scooped Tripod up into her arms.

With the chairs underneath one arm, Ryan wrapped the other around Laura's shoulders.

"Now let's go find us some ice cream," he said. "Who's up for some cherry chocolate ice cream with coconut flakes, sprinkles, hot caramel, whipped cream, and nuts on top?"

"Ewww," Kayleen grimaced, "why do you *always* get that?"

CHAPTER FOUR

Ryan was leaned back in his leather recliner watching a New York Yankees baseball game when his cell phone rang for the third time that day. The first two from G-Man and Dr. Hill had been pretty positive. The third call, however, dealt with a far more important and darker subject. Ryan sat up in his seat and grabbed the cell phone off his lap.

"Ryan, Honey," Laura called out from the kitchen, "what kind of vegetable do you want with this chicken?"

"Give me a sec," Ryan replied, as he accepted the phone call.

"Okay," Laura answered back.

Ryan lifted the phone up to his ear. "Hello, this is Turner."

"Ryan, how are you, my friend?"

It was FBI Director, Trey Felix. Ryan grabbed the television remote and paused the baseball game playing on the tv.

"I'm doing quite well, Mr. Felix. Thanks for asking. How are you?"

Director Felix broke into a coughing fit for a moment.

"My apologies," he said. "Aside from this flu or whatever it is, I'm doing well. Can't complain. I've been busy, but that's nothing new to me."

"You've got that right," Ryan said. "You're a busy guy."

"And Laura?" Felix asked. "How is she doing?"

Ryan glanced over his shoulder at his pregnant wife, who was in the kitchen cooking up a storm. Even after being married for over a year, he still got butterflies whenever he looked at her.

Ryan smiled. "She's doing really good. Even pregnant, she's so easy-going. She's still currently working shifts at the hospital and does what she can there. She's healthy, the baby's healthy, but, yeah, she's doing great."

"I'm delighted to hear that! I bet you two are very excited about the little guy that you're soon going to be blessed with."

"We sure are. We and Kayleen are ecstatic. We can hardly wait."

Felix broke into another coughing fit, and then replied, "And Kayleen? How is she? You know, after everything she went through? I've been worried about her."

Ryan thought about it for a moment. Kayleen was doing well from what he could tell. For months after the ordeal at Gondleton Farms, Kayleen had countless nightmares and woke up screaming and crying. Ryan hoped with all his heart that things would get better for her. He hoped somehow that she could have a normal life. Thus far, Kayleen was doing okay. Very rarely anymore did she have the horrible nightmares, and never did she bring up what had occurred at Gondleton Farms. For Kayleen, having

Tripod had been a really big deal so far; the dog was better therapy than any sum of money could ever buy.

"She's doing well, I think. Doing noticeably better, at least," Ryan finally replied.

"I'm glad to hear that too," Felix said. "No little girl should have to go through something like that."

"Oh, I'm definitely with you on that one."

"So," the Director said, "to get to the reason I called you. I'm sure you know I didn't just call to check on you and the family."

Ryan nodded his head in agreement but said nothing.

"I wanted to inform you about the recent actions carried out by the individual we have labelled as 'The Crucifier'," Felix continued. "It's been over six months since his last hit. As you know, we haven't had any leads, and the killer had gone quiet. That said, unfortunately, The Crucifier struck again last night, killing a man by the name of Pablo Montez. It was a horrific scene. I'm sending some pictures to your phone now."

Ryan pulled the phone away from his ear, keeping his eyes intently locked on the screen. Phone in hand, he rose from his seat and made his way down the hallway behind him, walking past the first set of doors to the bathroom and the master bedroom. At the end of the hallway, he stopped and entered into the office that was straight across from Kayleen's bedroom. Before entering, he took a quick glance to his right to see Kayleen lying on her bed while brushing her doll's hair. Tripod lay curled up next to her, sound asleep.

As Ryan closed the office door behind him, multiple notifications simultaneously appeared on his phone's screen. Ryan put the phone on speaker just before sitting down at the desk in the back of the room. Setting the phone on the desktop, he opened the first photograph. His heart sank.

"Wow," Ryan said out loud.

"Pretty sick, right?"

Ryan said nothing. He continued to gaze down at the photographs. "Sick" was an understatement. The scene was almost identical to the killer's first murder. Pablo Montez hung limp upon a large wooden cross with his chin resting on his chest. Streaks of blood covered his hands and arms. His face, neck, and bare chest were covered in blood too. His hands were nailed to the outstretched "arms" of the cross. Atop the dead man's head sat a crown of barbed wire. The shape of a cross was cut deeply into the man's forehead. A massive knife wound was apparent on his right side, just above the hip. A large pool of blood covered the ground beneath Montez's feet. Two candles were positioned on the ground-one on each side of the cross. The scene was disgusting. It made Ryan's stomach churn. The next couple of pictures were close-ups of the various wounds, pictures of the basement where the body lay, and photos of the candles, the cross, and the barbed-wire crown.

Ryan shook his head. "This makes me sick. Are there any leads? Any evidence?"

"Just like last time," Felix began, "there's nothing so far. Nothing at all. I've put a number of our guys from the D.C. Bureau on the case."

Ryan placed his hands on his head, keeping his eyes locked on the cell phone.

"I see," he said. "And Montez? Who was he?"

"Pablo Montez," Felix began, "he was forty-six years old, single, living alone. Montez was a good man. He had never been convicted of any sort of crime, not even so much as a speeding or parking ticket. The guy graduated from Washington University at St. Louis. After completing his undergraduate degree, he went to medical school. He was an orthopedic surgeon. The guy was an extremely successful surgeon, but only practiced for six years. After those six years, he had a spiritual revelation and felt it was his calling to be more involved in his church. Two years ago, he finished the process toward becoming a Catholic Priest. He became very popular and a household name almost immediately. Since then, well, up until his death, he had traveled worldwide as an inspirational and spiritual speaker. He is very well-known throughout the Catholic world. His friends, family, and colleagues speak very highly of him. From what it sounds like, he was a really good man with a spotless record. His whole life had been dedicated to helping others. So, that is what we know of Mr. Pablo Montez, thus far."

In deep thought, Ryan nodded his head.

"I see, I see," he said. "So, he's much like The Crucifier's last victim? A moral, upright, giving, unblemished person."

"It would seem so," Felix said in reply.

"Then we do know one thing," Ryan said. "This freak is going after good people; people who don't have a bad bone in their body and have dedicated their lives to helping others."

"Yes, this seems to be true. The first victim, Mrs. Tina Rington, was a dedicated Red Cross member. She was born into a wealthy family and dedicated the entirety of her life to assisting the poor, sick, and under-privileged, and also assisted people in times of natural disaster and need. She even ran her own charity organizations. Now, the latest victim is this Montez guy, who was a world-known and beloved priest, who also devoted his life to bettering the lives of others. So, yes, I believe that we have found a correlation and trend. These two people, of all people, didn't deserve this…

"And all in all, we don't really know any more than that, do we?"

"That's correct."

Ryan folded his arms across his chest. "Hmm, and the cross? Has anyone looked into that? Where it might have come from?"

"Great question. I do have an answer! We've looked into that fairly extensively. We've been searching ever since the first murder took place. Still though, no one has had any luck tracing where the past two crosses came from. We've found no place where giant crosses like that are built, and so far, we haven't been able to find anyone who's been asked to specially make any crosses."

Ryan nodded. "Okay. Then unless we do find someone that has ties to the crosses, we can assume they were self-made, which means maybe this Crucifier freak might have a rural place somewhere. I don't know."

"It could be a theory," Felix said, "but we can't be really sure about that. He could have friends, or multiple friends building those things for him. We really don't know."

Ryan scratched his chin. "True. Has anyone spoken with close friends or family of Montez?"

"That's in the works," Felix answered.

"Okay, good. And cameras? Has any security footage been analyzed?"

"Just like last time, lots of footage has been examined. The only times in both instances that the killer was caught on camera, we were not able to determine a facial profile. All we've been able to determine is The Crucifier's height and build. He's a few inches under six feet tall. He has wide shoulders and a broad chest. Overall, he's pretty built, yet slender guy."

"I see," Ryan said. "So, we basically have nothing on this guy?"

Felix sighed. "That's correct."

"Wow…"

Felix cleared his throat. "Ryan, I'd like you to put someone on this case from your branch."

Ryan thought for a second. "I've got some agents in mind."

"Good. Ryan, there's something else I must tell you."

Oh great…

Ryan waited for Felix to continue.

"Since The Crucifier's first hit," Felix continued, "two FBI field agents out of the DC branch, a Minnesota detective, and a DC detective out of the police department have all wound up dead. What did they all have in common? All of them were closely investigating the crucifixions."

Ryan swallowed. "I doubt that's a coincidence."

"My thoughts exactly," Felix added.

Ryan shook his head. "This is one bizarre case…and no one had been able to link anybody to the deaths of those agents and detectives?"

"Nope. All four of them were poisoned. There's zero evidence so far. There hasn't been a single witness or suspect."

Ryan was stunned. "Really? Nothing at all? No security footage? Nothing?"

"Nothing. We should be able to find something soon enough, but as of now we have nothing."

Ryan's heart was pounding. "This is unbelievable."

"You have a great group of men and woman, Ryan," Felix said. "This Crucifier figure is bound to slip up at some point. I trust you and I trust our Agency."

"Thank you. I do too. Now that I'm thinking about it, I might as well tell you. I think I'll send Allen Simmons. He's one of our newer guys. He's smart, dedicated, and has some real talent. I think I'll send him along with Whitney Lee since she's a veteran when it comes to this business. I think they'll make a great duo."

"Oh!" Felix proclaimed. "Agent Lee! She is a very strong asset."

"I'll have her behind the scenes, watching over Allen," Ryan added. "Hopefully we get somewhere on this case. I'll speak to them both first thing in the morning and get them on a flight to DC as soon as I can."

"Perfect," said Felix. "Keep in touch."

"Will do, Mr. Felix. Have a good one."

"You as well," replied Felix.

With that, the conversation ended. Ryan placed his face in his hands and sighed, then returned his attention to the cell phone sitting on the desk before him. He stared at the picture of Pablo Montez hanging from a cross until the phone powered off and the screen went black. Ryan leaned back in his chair and closed his eyes.

"This one is going to be interesting."

CHAPTER FIVE

There was a knock at the door behind Ryan. It was Laura.

"Honey?" she called out.

"Come in," replied Ryan.

Laura cracked the door open and peeked her head inside the room.

"Is everything okay?" she asked.

Ryan turned in his chair. "Yeah…just some things going on with work, but I'm okay."

Laura smiled a little smile. "You better be. John is here for dinner, and the food is ready when you are."

"Go on ahead and start eating. I'll be there in a sec."

Laura nodded. "Okay, love you."

She then closed the door and left.

With a sigh, Ryan picked his cell phone up off his desk and powered it back on. He gazed down at the picture of Pablo Montez.

What kind of person would do this?

Like Director Felix, Ryan had seen a lot of bizarre things and dealt with a lot of bizarre cases in his career, but this was definitely a first. He exited the photo app and typed a group text message to send to Allen Simmons and Whitney Lee.

It simply read: **We need to talk. Get back to me ASAP.**

Ryan pressed "send" and stood up from his chair, placing the cell phone in his pocket. Just as he reached for the doorknob to leave the room, the phone vibrated, alerting him to a text message.

It was Agent Simmons.

'When and where? What's going on?'

Placing both hands on the phone, Ryan typed: **My office. 7am. Tomorrow morning.**

He hit send, then along with the message sent two pictures of the crime scene.

Ryan exited the office and made his way to the dining room where he found John sitting at the head of the table, making goofy faces at Kayleen while she laughed hysterically. Ryan grinned and took a seat at the end of the table, opposite John. Ryan's younger brother had become a huge part of their family. When he moved to New York, he instantly fit right in. John was living next to the Turners, where the Shambles once resided. Because he lived so close, John was over at Ryan's house quite frequently.

Laura's cooking made the room smell incredible. Ryan's mouth watered and his stomach growled. He hadn't realized that aside from the ice cream cone earlier, this was going to be the first time he ate that day. To Ryan's right, Laura reached over and placed a hand on his knee.

"Everything okay?" Laura asked.

Ryan looked into his wife's eyes. He smiled. Laura was always so worrisome. She was always concerned about what was going on in his life. She cared so much for Ryan, and it meant the world to him. He leaned over and kissed Laura on the cheek.

"Everything's good, sweetheart," he replied.

"EW!" Kayleen cried, shielding her eyes with her hands. "Save it for after we eat. Gosh."

John laughed and chimed in himself. "Yeah, what the heck is wrong with you two? Save it for after dinner. Come on!"

Laura shook her head but couldn't help grinning. "You two hush up! Let's eat."

"Amen to that," Ryan said as he piled food onto the plate in front of him.

The dinner consisted of grilled chicken breasts, a green bean casserole, steamed corn, garlic mashed potatoes, and fresh homemade rolls. That was another little thing Ryan absolutely loved about his wife: she could really cook. She enjoyed it too. The smell of the chicken on Ryan's plate filled his nostrils, causing his stomach to rumble again.

"This looks and smells amazing, Laura," Ryan said, reaching for his fork.

Just as he lifted the silverware off the tabletop, the phone in his pocket vibrated twice. Ryan paused. It could have been Agent Simmons or Lee, but for some reason he had a feeling that it wasn't. Suddenly, he had an overwhelmingly uneasy feeling in his gut. He slowly placed his fork back down on the table. He pulled the phone out of his pocket. Ryan Turner no longer felt hungry. Displayed on the screen of the phone were two text messages below the large "8:33" indicating the time.

The most recent message read: '*This is getting out of hand.*'

The other message was a picture-message. The picture was small as displayed on the lock screen of the phone, but Ryan could see well enough what the photograph was. The two messages were from Director Felix.

"Daddy?" Kayleen said.

Ryan zoned her voice out. His heart was racing.

"Daddy?" Kayleen repeated. "Uncle John is wondering when my next game is."

Ryan didn't even hear her. His palms were sweaty, and his head was pounding. Ryan tapped on the picture-message and the phone came to life. The photo enlarged and filled the screen. Laura nudged Ryan.

"Daddy?" Kayleen whined.

"Kay!" Ryan snapped. "Knock it off. One second, please."

The photo was of a man nailed to a cross. His feet were bound together, a cross was cut into his forehead, and the man wore a crown of barbed wire. This man name was not Pablo Montez either. Ryan felt sick. He no longer felt hungry.

Chewing on a bite of chicken, John stared at Ryan.

"Everything good, bro?" he asked.

Ryan nodded slightly, but still said nothing. He rose from his seat and excused himself from the dinner table. He walked down the hallway to his bedroom, texting Agent Simmons and Lee on the way.

He typed: **Change of plans. Sorry. Meet me at my office tonight. ASAP.**

Ryan grabbed a brown overcoat from his closet along with a blue New York Yankees baseball cap. He threw on the coat and cap and returned to the dining room. All eyes were locked on him.

"I'm sorry," Ryan began, "I feel so bad that I have to go, but duty calls. I have to leave. Laura, sweetheart, thank you so much for dinner. Just put my plate in the fridge for me and I'll eat when I get home tonight. I love you."

He kissed Laura on her forehead and turned to leave.

"Anything I can do?" John called out as Ryan reached the front door. Ryan placed a hand on the door handle and turned to look at his brother. He shook his head.

"No," he replied, "not right now. But later I'll get you up to speed on everything that's going on."

John took a sip of water from his glass. "Be safe," he said.

Kayleen stood up on her seat and yelled, "Love you, Daddy!"

"I love you, Kay," Ryan said. "And don't you be staying up too late."

John threw his arms in the air. "But, but, Ryan. We were going to stay up and *par-tay*!"

"Yeah, Daddy, come on," Kayleen chimed in. "We were going to *par-tay*!"

Ryan couldn't help but chuckle as he threw open the front door of the house. Outside, rain was beginning to fall onto the New York City streets.

"You two, behave yourselves," Ryan said before shutting the door behind him, and walking out into the stormy night.

CHAPTER SIX

The two agents walked in one after the other. The first to stroll through Ryan's office door was Whitney Lee. Ryan sat at his desk straight across from the door. He watched as Agent Lee casually walked in. Her long black hair was tied up in a tight bun and was noticeably damp. It could have been from the pouring rain outside; however, Ryan didn't think that was the case. Agent Lee held a folded-up umbrella in her left hand and wasn't wearing any makeup. He assumed that she had showered a short time before leaving to meet with Ryan. Ryan guessed that she was probably getting ready for bed or was already in bed when Ryan sent his last text.

Agent Lee was a short woman of Asian descent. Her parents had moved to the United States when she was eight years old. She wore dark-blue sweatpants, a white long-sleeved shirt, and tiny white slip-on shoes. She wore silver dragon-shaped earrings that she received as a child from her dear grandmother. She wore them every single day. Lee was forty-eight-years-old, single, and living alone. She had never been married, and for twenty years had devoted her life to her career with the FBI. Her father had died of old age, but her mother was still alive. She was very old and frail, and couldn't hardly care for herself, so she lived with Agent Lee. Lee was a loving, loyal, dedicated, hardworking, down-to-earth woman.

Seconds behind her, in walked Agent Allen Simmons. Simmons was twenty-six-years-old and stood a few inches shorter than Ryan. His hair was buzzcut. He always dressed to impress, no matter the time or day. This particular night, even though late and last-minute, Simmons wore starched khaki pants, a white dress shirt, and a dark blue sweater. On his wrist he wore a Rolex watch. Simmons was one of the smartest, most driven people Ryan had ever met.

Originally from Texas, Simmons was a child prodigy. He finished high school at the age of fifteen. At sixteen, he began college at Princeton. After two years at college, his father got in a car accident, nearly killing him. Simmons then returned to the family ranch in Blanco County, Texas to help run it while his father was down. He remained there for two years before returning to school. At twenty-two, he graduated from Princeton with a master's degree in criminology. He then worked as a criminal profiler for the New York City Police Department. Six months ago he joined the Bureau.

Ryan saw tremendous potential in Allen Simmons. He knew the young man would be a huge asset to the FBI for a very long time. Simmons had a girlfriend named Zaya, and they had a three-year-old daughter named Georgia. She was a beautiful little girl who was always full of life. Zaya often brought her by Ryan's house where Kayleen played with and entertained Georgia. They were a cute little family. Ryan wished Allen and Zaya would just get married already, but it wasn't his place to judge or council them on such matters.

Ryan rose from his seat to greet the two agents, then motioned to a pair of chairs positioned directly in front of his desk.

"Have a seat," he said.

He waited for the two to do so, and once they were seated, Ryan spoke up again.

"Sorry to bring you in here so late and with such short notice. I feel bad for that."

"Nah, you're good," Simmons replied. "Whatever this is, it seems to be pretty important. I'm more than happy to be here. Plus, when there's the possibility of having a new case? I'll be there anytime, anyplace, anywhere, sir. This is what I live for."

Lee nodded in agreement, as she anxiously fidgeting with her hands.

"We're all ears," she said.

"Well thank you two," Ryan said. "Today, after Kayleen's soccer game, Director Felix called and told me about The Crucifier's latest strike. The picture I sent you was of a man by the name of Pablo Montez. As you saw, it was virtually the same scene as the first homicide committed by this assailant. Merely minutes afterwards, Mr. Felix contacted me again and sent me pictures of yet another person hung from a cross. The victim's name is Reverend Oscar Mayfield. This man was a Baptist preacher from Oklahoma City, who had been visiting family in DC, where he was eventually found dead."

Both agents in front of Ryan shook their heads.

"Wait," Simmons said, "so you're saying after months of this psychopath remaining quiet and lying low, that in one day, he managed to kill two people? And not just kill them, you know, but murder them in this very gruesome, particular way. Am I hearing that right?"

Ryan nodded. "Sadly, yes. The first homicide was early this morning. The second was late this afternoon."

"And there's still no evidence, no witnesses, nothing?" Simmons asked. "Still no one has any idea who this guy is?"

"That's correct," Ryan replied.

"Incredible!" Simmons said. "Simply incredible…months and months ago, he brutally murdered a woman. No one was able to figure out who this Crucifier guy is. Now, he crucifies two people this way in a single day and still gets away. Unbelievable."

"Yeah," Ryan said, "unbelievable is certainly one word for the whole situation."

Lee finally spoke up.

"These recent victims? Do they match the profile of the original victim?"

Ryan pursed his lips and nodded. "They do. Montez was an eminent Catholic priest and Reverend Oscar Mayfield was a beloved Baptist preacher."

Lee rubbed the back of her head.

"I see," she said.

Simmons leaned forward. "I'm going to guess that you want us on this case, right?"

"Yes," Ryan said, "that's exactly right."

Allen Simmons smiled slightly and clapped his hands together. "Perfect! Because if you weren't going to, I was going to start investigating this case myself. This case is calling my name. I *know* I can find this guy. I mean, if I was on this case months ago, he'd already be behind bars."

Ryan and Lee both chuckled. Simmons sometimes came across as cocky and arrogant, but Ryan liked the confidence he had in his skills. Ryan was confident in the young agent too.

"I want you both on this case," Ryan said. "Are you okay with that, Agent Lee?"

Lee nodded.

Ryan nodded in return. "Good. Agent Lee, you have tons of experience and have had so much success throughout your career working for the Bureau. Mr. Felix has the utmost respect and confidence in you. So do I. Agent Simmons, you have the some of the most raw talent, drive, and ambition that I've seen for a long time. You have one spectacular, young mind, and a case like this is going to need that. The two of you, I feel, will compliment each other perfectly. When Mr. Felix asked me to assign some of my New York City agents to this case, you two were the first that came to mind."

"That means a lot, Mr. Turner," Simmons said. "We won't let you down."

Lee gave one single nod in agreement. "We'll find him."

"I have no doubt in my mind about that," Ryan said. "There is one thing I have to tell you before I send you off." Ryan swallowed. "Every agent, detective, and police officer that has seriously investigated these killings, has wound up dead. Every single one of them."

Lee swallowed, fidgeting with a piece of paper on top of the desk. She kept her eyes on Ryan but said nothing.

Simmons shrugged. "That's terrible. But, I hope this doesn't come across in the wrong way, but that doesn't mean too much to me. Like I said, Mr. Turner, this is what I live for. I'm more than willing to get on this case. That doesn't scare me away or anything like that."

Ryan looked at Lee. She moved her eyes away from Ryan and looked down at her feet, then took a deep breath and turned her attention back to Ryan.

"I'm with Allen," she said. "I'm in."

Ryan clasped his hands together. "Good to have you both on board. This freak we call The Crucifier, his time has come to an end. I plan on sending you two out tomorrow afternoon to DC. In the morning I'll retrieve all the case files we have compiled thus far and get them to you before you leave on your flight. Does that all sound okay with you two?"

Simmons and Lee exchanged glances then they both nodded.

"Perfect," Ryan said. "In the morning I'll work on getting the files and have my assistant get you two a flight out of here. I'll call you both in the morning to tell you the complete plan. Thank you again for coming tonight."

Allen Simmons stood and shook Ryan's hand. "Thank you, Mr. Turner. We'll see you tomorrow bright and early."

Simmons exited. Lee then stood to her feet.

"Are you sure you're okay with all this?" Ryan asked Lee as she stood up.

Lee looked Ryan in the eyes. "Yes. Yes, I'm okay with this. You trust me, Felix trusts me, and Agent Simmons will need a little guidance. I do agree we will make a good team, and I do believe we can bring this killer down. I know it. To be honest with you, Mr. Turner, it is slightly worrisome that the men and women who have investigated this Crucifier so far have all ended up dead…that is a bit troubling to me, but whatever happens, happens. I could very well be killed too. However, I am willing to take that chance in order to find the person responsible for all this. I've dealt with a lot of psychotic killers in my lifetime. This isn't too much different."

"Yes, you have," Ryan said. "I respect and appreciate you so much. Thank you, Agent Lee."

Lee stuck out her hand and Ryan shook it.

"Have a good night, Mr. Turner."

"You too, Lee. You too."

CHAPTER SEVEN

Ryan returned home just after midnight. Laura had already gone to bed and Kayleen and John were crashed out on the living room couch. The credits of a new Scooby Doo movie were playing and Kayleen was lying across John's lap. John's head was rested on top of the couch. His mouth hung wide-open as he snored loudly. Popcorn was strung out all over the couch and the living room floor. Ryan assumed John and Kayleen had participated in their almost weekly popcorn war. He smiled as he entered his home and saw two of the people he loved most in the world crashed out on the couch. The moment he stepped inside, he closed the door behind him and leaned down to pick up a piece of popcorn that was by his feet.

"Ten seconds left," Ryan whispered to himself. "Clock running down. Turner with the ball."

Ryan stood back up straight and began to walk toward the back of the couch. He held the popcorn high above his head.

"The defense is all over him. Turner drives to the basket."

Ryan pretended to cross a basketball over in front of himself.

"Three…two…one…Turner shoots!"

Ryan reached his hand over John's open mouth and dropped the piece of popcorn in.

"And he scores! Ahhhh! The crowd goes wild!"

John snorted and gagged then grabbed at his throat. He spit the popcorn clear across the living room and it hit the television screen.

Ryan struggled to contain his laughter.

John turned around in his seat and rubbed his groggy eyes.

"Nice shot, you jerk," he said in the middle of a yawn.

Walking over to the fridge in the kitchen, Ryan couldn't help laughing. He opened the refrigerator and grabbed a plastic-wrapped plate of food that had a note taped to it.

It read: *I hope everything is okay. Love you!*

Ryan grinned.

Gosh, I love that woman.

He unwrapped the plate and placed it in the microwave, setting the timer for one minute.

"Where the heck did you go, Captain Turner? You missed out on the amazing dinner and on the party, bro."

Ryan rolled his eyes.

"I see that," he said, turning around. "Laura is going to be thrilled to see that mess in the morning."

"Oh, she won't see it." John was digging around in the cabinet beneath the kitchen sink. "I'm fixing to clean it all up, don't you worry there, old man. You eat your food. You don't have to worry about a thing. I'll clean then take my little buddy to her room, and *then* you can tell me about your adventures from tonight."

The microwave beeped, indicating that the food was ready.

"Deal," Ryan said.

CHAPTER EIGHT

Ryan walked over to the sink and rinsed off his dirty plate. He finished drinking the rest of the water in his glass and rinsed it out. He then returned to the dining room table where John sat.

"It's been a long day, I'll tell you that much," Ryan said as he sat down across from John.

"Man, I bet. What all's been going on?"

Ryan blew out a breath and rested his legs on top of the table, crossing one over the other.

"Remember the Crucifier case?"

"Yeah," John replied, "is he back, or what?"

"Yup, he sure is. Killed two people yesterday. One early in the morning and the other late afternoon."

"Wow…two in one day? And I'm guessing they were killed in the same weird way as the others, right?"

Ryan nodded. "They were. Same wounds. Same objects. Same crosses. Same story."

John scrunched up his eyebrows and looked down at the table.

"Someone needs to find this dude," he said.

"That's for sure. Anyways, that's why I left dinner so suddenly. I had already planned on talking to Agent Simmons and Agent Lee about putting them on the case. I was going to speak with them in the morning. This was after the first homicide, and Felix wanted me to send some of our own people to investigate. So, I told him that Simmons and Lee would be perfect on this case. He agreed. That was just before dinner. While we were getting ready to eat, he sent me a new message containing pictures of a new murder scene and said, 'This is getting out of hand.' I was stunned, sickened. I then sent a message to Lee and Simmons telling them to meet with me ASAP. So, I met with them and now here I am. I'm going to get the case files prepared for them in the morning and get them on a flight to DC."

"Whew," John said, "crazy stuff, man. Can I see the pictures of the homicides?"

Ryan retrieved the phone from his pocket and opened the photo app. He selected the first picture of Pablo Montez's body and slid the phone over to John.

"Wow," John said, rubbing his forehead. "You're right, same exact scene as the others."

"That is Pablo Montez. He was a well-known Catholic Priest. He was known and loved throughout the world. He had devoted his life to service. Never been charged with anything or arrested. Never even had a speeding ticket before. The guy was as good as they come."

John scrolled through the phone's photos until he came to pictures from the second homicide scene.

"And who's this?" he asked.

"Reverend Mayfield," Ryan replied. "He's a beloved Baptist preacher from Oklahoma City. Same thing. He was as good of a man as they come. He was visiting family in Washington DC when he was killed."

John slid the phone back across the table to Ryan.

"This crap pisses me off, to be honest. What kind of sick human being does this? And how is he getting away with this time and time again?"

Ryan shrugged. "I don't know…it makes me sick too. And it needs to come to a stop. I just don't know the point or the end game. What's bad is that..."

"Ryan…let me see those pictures again," John said, interrupting Ryan.

Ryan slid the phone back over to John, who gazed intently down at the pictures again.

"Right here!" he said, zooming in on one of the pictures. "This stuff isn't new. This has happened before. I can't believe I had forgotten about it, but I hadn't seen any previous pictures of the first homicide. I hadn't put much thought into this case because I haven't really been involved in it."

"What are you saying?"

"I'm saying that this has happened before. Gosh, it had to have been six, seven years ago. It was when I first got into the CIA. I had a buddy in the agency who was in Germany on vacation at the time. He had family there and was visiting them. While he was there, a Roman Catholic priest was found brutally murdered upon a cross. Legal or not, the case sparked my friend's interest, and he took pictures of the scene. It was just like this one. There were two candles placed beneath the cross. The body was nailed to the cross. The man's ankles were bound together. There was a massive stab wound in the man's side, he had a crown of barbed wire upon his head and had a cross cut into his forehead. Now looking back, there is also one small detail that connects the two."

John slid the phone to Ryan.

"Look closely," he told Ryan. "The guy's right thumb is completely cut off."

"Oh, wow," Ryan said. "It's missing. This was the case for all three of our victims so far. Their right thumbs were cut off. I thought it was a little weird at the time...I had no idea. How did no one link the case in Germany to these others?"

John shrugged. "Who knows. The thing is though, we in the U.S. don't really cover much of what happens in Germany. As the years go by, things like that fade away."

"Did they ever catch who was responsible? Do you know?"

John nodded his head. "Kind of. They found a member of the priest's church dead in his home. He shot himself in the head and left a suicide note. The note said something about not being sorry. It said that the priest was guilty and so was he. At the end of the note was a scripture out of the book of Leviticus, and a scripture from Romans."

"Interesting..." Ryan said. "Do you remember what the scripture said?"

"Sort of. The note was written in German. My buddy spoke pretty good German and was able to translate it. The one in Leviticus said something about sins, being guilty, and being held responsible. The one out of Romans talked about sinning and I don't know what else, honestly. I just don't remember the exact chapters and verses. I think in Romans it was chapter two. Maybe? I don't know. This was a long time ago."

"Hmm," said Ryan. "I have the bible uploaded on my phone. Let me see if I can find that scripture. I've got to say, John, it's impressive you remembered that."

"I do read my holy bible every morning," John answered, bowing his head and putting his hands together in a praying pose.

Ryan shook his head as he typed away at his phone, entering key words into the bible search engine within the app.

"Here we go. Leviticus 5:17?"

John scratched his chin. "I don't know. Read it for me."

Ryan cleared his throat. "And if a soul sin and commit any of these things which are forbidden to be done by the commandments of the Lord; though he wist it not, yet is he guilty, and shall bear his iniquity."

"Yes! That's the one! Try to find the one in Romans."

Ryan searched "Romans, law, sin".

"Romans 2:12. For as many as have sinned without law shall also perish without law: and as many as have sinned in the law shall be judged by the law. Ring a bell?"

"Yes, that's it," John said.

"Interesting."

"There's some freaks out there, man."

Ryan bookmarked both verses of scripture then looked at the pictures of Montez and Mayfield again, zooming in on their right hands.

"Random thought. The case in Germany, did they ever find the thumb?" he asked.

John shrugged. "I honestly couldn't tell you that. I don't remember."

Ryan stared intently at the photograph on his phone of Reverend Mayfield.

"I had never heard about that case in Germany. It looks like we have a copycat killer. I'll work on looking into the murder in Germany and see who I can contact about it."

"That's a good idea," John said. "I mean, it might not help, but we might as well try. It won't hurt to look into it."

Exactly."

"On the same note, but also a little bit of a different note," John began, "how in the world has no one gotten a lead on this guy? We kind of started talking about it earlier before we went out on a limb, but like there have been no leads? No suspects? No evidence? Nada?"

Ryan nodded. "As maddening as it is, no, there haven't been any leads whatsoever."

John was noticeably annoyed. "Dude, that's ridiculous. Who has been investigating? Seriously. Three totally extravagant, disgusting killings and no one has any idea who is responsible. It's unbelievable. After the first one, a murder as gruesome as it was? The entire world should have been on notice."

"It is pretty unbelievable; I'm not going to lie. At the same time, Felix informed me that every single detective, officer, and agent that attempted to investigate these cases has ended up dead. So, to answer your question of *who* has investigated, they are no longer with us."

"Wait, wait, wait," John said. "Hold up. All of them?"

"Yup," replied Ryan. "DC Detectives. FBI agents. All dead."

"Dang. Whoever's responsible sure knows what they're doing. That's insane. And you're going to send Allen and Whitney?"

Ryan shrugged. "I have to send someone. Felix is frustrated, concerned, and all out of options. These deaths have been all over the news for months and the people of this country are becoming scared. They are angered with the FBI too. I trust Agent Lee and Agent Simmons. I've got a good feeling about it."

"Send me, Ryan. Send me with them."

Ryan stared at John. "What? Huh? No. No, not going to happen."

"Why?" John asked. "Because I'm your brother? Or because you don't think I can handle it?"

Ryan scowled at John. "Really, John? Come on, man. Don't pull that. I actually thought about sending you with Lee but decided against it. Agent Simmons just finished up his last case. He's young, fresh, super motivated, and the guy is a genius when it comes to this sort of thing. Lee has been on countless cases. She's a veteran and one of the best agents we've ever had. I'm sending them because I think they give us the best shot in finding the killer."

"Yeah, I get you. I just wish I could personally find this guy because I'd kill him myself. He wouldn't get a trial, I can tell you that much."

Ryan chuckled. "And there lies one good reason I'm not sending you."

John laughed too. "No, I'm joking…kind of. It would be hard for me not to take him out. Our justice system drives me crazy sometimes. People like this Crucifier guy don't deserve to live."

"I can agree with you on that. But we do have rules. Laws. That is what separates us from the bad guys. We have morals and rule of law. As much as we don't wish we didn't sometimes."

"Yeah, yeah, I know," John said looking down at his feet. He pointed at Ryan. "If things go south and Allen and Whitney aren't able to find this guy, I want this case, okay?"

"We'll see," Ryan said. "Like I said, I have faith in Allen and Lee. If push comes to shove, I'll definitely consider it. Director Felix is a big fan of yours too."

"Of course, he is. I'm just a loveable guy, Ryan! Give me some credit."

Ryan laughed. "Yeah, and you're not at all full of yourself either."

John smiled and stood up from his seat. "I'm going to head home. Thanks for letting me hang around, and thanks for updating me on everything. If you need anything, bro, tell me. I want to help in any way I can."

Ryan stood up, shook John's hand and patted him on the back.

"For sure," Ryan said. "We'll keep in touch. Be safe, man."

John retrieved his jacket from off the couch and headed out the front door. Ryan yawned, shut off all the lights nearby, and made his way to his bedroom. Laura was out cold. She was curled up in the fetal position on her side of the bed. Ryan crawled into bed and pulled his wife close to him. She stretched and laid her head on his chest. He moved her hair out of her face and kissed her on the head. Within seconds, he too was sound asleep.

CHAPTER NINE

Just after the clock struck noon, Ryan Turner stood leaned up against his motorcycle in the parking lot of the JFK Airport making small talk with Agent Lee. She had arrived a few minutes before and as the two spoke, Simmons stepped out of a cab in front of them. He approached Ryan and Lee, pulling a large suitcase behind him. Today, he wore a two-piece suit. The suit was a charcoal color and the tie he wore was made up of charcoal and silver stripes. He wore black lizard-skin shoes, and a Rolex watch on his wrist.

"Sorry, took a while to get a cab," Simmons said as he approached Ryan and Lee.

"No, you're fine," Ryan said as he handed a plane ticket to Simmons.

"I already gave Lee hers," Ryan said. "Again, the flight is set to depart at two. When you're ready to come home we'll find you a flight back."

"Perfect," said Simmons.

Ryan handed a folder to Lee.

"These are the files we have," he said. "It isn't a whole lot, but it's what we got so far."

"Thank you," Lee said.

She grabbed the folder and leaned down to place it inside her suitcase.

"I meant to tell you both some new information earlier when I called," Ryan stated. "I talked to my brother, John, last night and he remembered a case in Germany a few years back. There was a murder, and the victim was killed exactly as The Crucifier's recent victims were. That was a few years back, I know. Also, the suspect was pronounced dead by suicide shortly afterward. I don't know how this fits in, or if it even does at all. I thought I should tell you though. We may be dealing with a copycat killer. I am going to look into the Germany crucifixion either today or tomorrow and get back to you with anything I find."

Simmons was stroking the short, scruffy beard on his face.

"Interesting," he said. "Definitely tell us what you find. I'll do some research on the way to DC too."

"Perfect," Ryan said. "I gave you both Mr. Felix's number. He also has each of yours. He and I will be in contact. The two of you and myself will be in close contact as well. I want constant updates. Also, if there is anything I need to know, or anything I can do to help, I want you to call me. That's what I'm here for. You guys stay safe. Have each other's backs. I'll be praying for you. Thanks again for what you're doing."

Simmons stuck out a hand. "Thank you, sir. We won't let you down."

Lee then shook Ryan's hand too.

"We'll be in touch, Mr. Turner," Lee said.

Ryan nodded. "Definitely. Safe travels."

Just as Ryan started to get on his motorcycle, his cell phone rang.

It was Laura.

"Hello?" he answered.

On the other end of the phoneline, Laura took a deep breath. "Ryan, my water broke. I'm-I'm having contractions."

Ryan's heart started to race. "Laura. Oh my gosh! Laura, I'm heading home! I'll be there in twenty. Laura...Laura! Is there anyone close that can take you to the hospital?"

"Yes," she answered before groaning in pain. "Zaya is taking me, right now. She was at the house. She had brought Georgia over to play with Kayleen. She'll take Kayleen to meet us at the hospital."

"Oh, my goodness, Laura! I'm on my way, okay? Hang in there! I'm on my way!"

"Ryan? Everything is okay. Relax. You sound like the one in labor. I'm perfectly fine, trust me. I'll see you in a little bit."

Ryan took a deep breath. "Okay, honey. I love you! See you in a while."

Ryan ended the call, hopped onto his bike, and sped dangerously fast to hospital.

CHAPTER TEN

3:30 p.m. It had been two hours since Ryan had arrived at the hospital. He quietly pushed open the door of Laura's room. Sitting directly outside the room were Zaya, Georgia, and Kayleen. The moment he opened the door, Kayleen leapt to her feet. Her mouth was open, just waiting for Ryan to give them the word.

"Ready to meet your baby brother?" Ryan asked.

Ryan beamed with excitement. Seeing how excited Kayleen was heightened his level of excitement even more.

"Oh my gosh, oh my gosh, oh my gosh!" Kayleen squealed, jumping up and down.

Ryan held the door open. Kayleen ran in. She was beyond excited. She ran straight up to the bed that held her mother and her newborn baby brother. The room was filled with the sound of a baby's cry.

"I love him! I love him so much!" Kayleen exclaimed.

She stared down at her baby brother. Laura was smiling ear to ear. Ryan proudly looked down at his crying son.

"He's perfect, isn't he?" Laura asked proudly.

Ryan smiled. He never thought newborn babies were cute. He had never seen a newborn that he thought was cute. To him, they looked more like wet little aliens than humans. However, in this moment, his mindset was changed.

He agreed with Laura. The little guy was perfect. He couldn't be any more perfect in Ryan's eyes.

"He sure is," Ryan replied.

Tears of happiness streamed down Laura's face. Ryan could feel the tears welling up in his eyes too. Sometimes he really hated his soft side, but it came out quite often. Ryan had done a lot in his life. He had had many struggles and disappointments. He had also experienced much success and triumph. He had achieved his dream job. He married the girl of his dreams. He had gotten to watch Kayleen play and succeed in a sport that she loved. He had taken down Cybris Caine-the most wanted and dangerous man in the world. He had become the Head of the NYC Bureau. He was reunited with his long-lost baby brother, John. Ryan had experienced much triumph and happiness. This; however, was very likely the proudest moment of his life. Staring down at *his* son in the love of his life's arms filled his heart with pride and joy. Along with marrying Laura, this was the happiest moment of his life.

"He's our little blessing," Laura said, kissing the top of the baby's head. "Here, dad, hold him."

Ryan smiled and gladly took the baby into his arms, tenderly cradling him.

"Can I see him, daddy?" Kayleen asked.

"Of course," Ryan replied. "Sit down first and then I'll give him to you."

Kayleen quickly scampered up onto the chair next to the head of Laura's bed. Kayleen giggled as Ryan handed her the baby.

"I just love him," she said before leaning down and kissing the baby on the cheek.

Ryan sat on the bed and held his wife's hand with one hand and cautiously kept the other by Kayleen.

"Have we officially decided on a name yet?" Laura asked.

Ryan shrugged. "You tell me, honey."

"Ben," she replied, "I like Ben."

Ryan smiled. He liked it too. They had originally planned on naming the baby after Ryan by giving him the name of Ryan Jr. After Laura learned about his past, and his past guardians, the couple decided they liked another name. Ben. It was the name of the man who raised Ryan on the big farm in South Dakota. It was the name of the man who was a father to him, and who literally changed and saved his life.

Ryan smiled. "Little Ben it is."

CHAPTER ELEVEN

Kuron walked into the hospital room at 6:00 p.m. Kuron burst through the door with a huge smile on his face. Malaya Taylor followed close behind him.

"And where is the little guy, huh?" he said approaching Laura and Ryan. "Uncle Kuron is dying to see this dude!"

Baby Ben was sound asleep in Laura's arms.

"Shh!" Ryan said, hushing Kuron.

Laura giggled. "Ryan, it's okay."

"Man, big daddy Ryan is already all uptight," Kuron said, grabbing Ryan by the shoulders and shaking him playfully. "Relax, my man, relax."

Kuron started to massage Ryan's shoulders and Ryan shrugged him off.

"Knock it off," Ryan said laughing.

Laura held Ben up for Kuron to take him. Kuron carefully grabbed the baby from Laura.

"He's adorable," he said, looking down at the sleeping baby in his arms. "Malaya, you're not allowed to look at or hold him. I don't want you getting any sort of idea that we need one of these little things. Plus, there's a fifty-fifty chance the poor thing could end up looking like his father, and we don't want that to happen. That's just a life of suffering right there."

Malaya groaned and playfully slapped Kuron in the back of the head.

"Shut up," she said. "Goodness, I can't take you anywhere! How are you feeling, Laura?"

"Good," Laura replied. "The second one was much easier than the first. After the first, I feel like a professional."

"Good, good," Malaya said. "And have you already decided on a name"

"Ben!" Kayleen exclaimed. "Baby brother Ben!"

"Ah," Kuron stated, "Little Ben, huh? I like it. It fits the little guy."

Ben squirmed in Kuron's arms and his small blue cap fell over his eyes. Kuron pulled the cotton cap out of Ben's eyes then handed the baby to Malaya.

"I guess I'll let you hold him," Kuron said.

Malaya rolled her eyes and gladly took the baby.

"Where's John?" Kuron asked. "I would've expected him to be here."

"He should be here any second now," Ryan replied. "I called him as soon as I got here and he said to call again when the baby was actually here. I did, and he was in the middle of a workout." Ryan looked at the clock on the wall across from the bed. "Yeah, it's just after six now. He said he'd be here at about six."

"I see," Kuron said. "Well he can take his time. We already know who Ben's favorite uncle is going to be, isn't that right, Ben?"

Kuron pointed to himself, and then lightly caressed the baby's cheek. As soon as Ben felt Kuron's cold touch, he broke into a crying fit.

"I don't know about that," Kayleen said covering her mouth, giggling.

Malaya handed Ben back to Laura, who held him against her abdomen. Kuron pointed at Kayleen.

"Just watch," he said." Give the little guy some time. I'll for sure be his favorite. How could I not be?"

"Well Uncle John is my favorite un…" Kayleen began to say before Kuron shushed her.

"Nope, nope, nope. None of that nonsense. I don't want to hear it, girl. Shush."

Kayleen giggled again.

"I am way cooler than John. And bigger, and stronger…"

"And dumber," John said as he walked into the room and grabbed Kuron by the back of his shoulders.

"It's true," Kuron said. "And dumber, and better looking too."

"I'm just about certain Malaya is the only person on this planet that agrees with you there, buddy," John responded, leaning on Kuron's right shoulder.

Malaya put her face in the palm of her hand and shook her head. Laura and Zaya did the same thing. In Zaya's arms, Georgia was waking up from a deep sleep.

"There are way too many women around for you two clowns to be stuck in one room together," Ryan said.

Kuron slung an arm around John's shoulders. "Oh, come on, man," Kuron said. "You need to relax, Big Daddy Ryan."

"Yeah, old man," John chimed in, "relax. You're all uptight."

Ryan rolled his eyes.

"Mind if I hold the little guy?" John asked Laura, stepping closer to the bed.

"Of course," she replied with a sweet smile.

John grabbed baby Ben from Laura's arms. Just as he did, Georgia was becoming responsive and aware. She scampered away from Zaya, who was sitting in the sofa on the opposite side of the bed and hurried toward John.

"Aww!" she exclaimed, walking up to John. Proceeding to tug on his pantleg, she then asked politely, "Sir, can I see the baby?"

Her politeness and the use of "sir" with him brought a smile to John's face. "Why, of course!" he quickly replied.

John knelt and showed baby Ben to Georgia.

"Aww!" Georgia squealed again.

John carefully helped Georgia cradle the baby and she squealed with delight.

"I love him so much!" she said, pushing Ben back to John.

She scampered back to her mother then pulled herself up onto the couch. Ryan's heart was full as he looked around the room. With all his heart, he loved every person in the room. There was newborn baby Ben. Ben was his first child by blood. There was Kayleen. She was his first daughter who every day brought him an inexplainable joy. There in the hospital bed laid Laura, who was his beautiful, sweet, amazing wife. Next to him stood John, his beloved brother. They were his family. However, as he looked around the room, he saw more members of that family than just those four. He gazed over at Zaya and Georgia, and then at Kuron and Malaya who were hugging one another. Ryan smiled. Everyone in the room was family to him. These were the people he loved. *This* was his family. This was his world.

CHAPTER TWELVE

It was the following afternoon. Laura and Ben were finally home. Ryan was now sitting in his home office. It was the first time he had a chance to research the murder in Germany that he and John had discussed. Almost immediately, Ryan found a news article concerning the case. The murder had occurred in Berlin. The article he found was in the *Süddeutsche Zeitung,* a Berlin newspaper. The article was factual and very well written. *Süddeutsche Zeitung* was a regional paper whose circulation was big enough to earn the name "National". It was a popular and trusted news source.

Ryan opened a translator app on his computer and then copied and pasted the article into the translator. The computer whirred and buzzed as the app uploaded the article and translated it right before Ryan's eyes. It took a minute or two, but soon the entire page of German words had turned into English.

The heading of the story read: **Adored Priest brutally murdered. Found hanging from a cross. Suspect found dead.**

Ryan continued reading.

Catholic Priest, Aldrik Bach, was a well- loved, and honorable man. He dedicated his life to the Catholic church and founded a charity for cancer research, known by the name of Hoffen (which means "hope" in

German). He was an inspiration, who was loved by all. Bach was murdered Tuesday night, the fourth of May, year 2013. The scene was horrific. Bach was found dead, hanging from a huge wooden cross. He wore a crown of barbed wire, had a cross carved into his forehead, his hands were nailed to the cross, and there was a gashing wound in his side. Aldrik Bach was found dead at approximately 14:20...

The killer's name was 23-year-old Ferdinand Schneider. Schneider lived alone and was pronounced dead by means of suicide at 16:34. A note was left by his body with two scriptures. Leviticus 5:17. Romans 2:12...

John had been right about it all. The story was accurate. However, there was very little detail about the murder itself and the suspect who committed suicide. The meat of the article told about Aldrik Bach's life. The article was mostly a tribute to the man that Bach was. From what the article said, Bach was a well-known, famous German priest for over thirty years. Bach had one brother named Alric, and a sister by the name of Aloisia. His sister had three daughters. His brother had one son. Bach's brother, Alric, got in a car accident alongside his wife and three years old son. Their son, Baron Bach, survived. His wife Gertraud also did. She was in critical condition, though, and was never able to walk again. Aldrik Bach moved in next to Gertraud and Baron. He cared for the two of them. He practically raised Baron as his own son. Seven years following the accident, Gertraud was killed by an armed robber. Aldrik was shattered but stayed strong and continued to care for Baron. Aldrik Bach's parents both passed away from cancer when they were in their early fifties. About a decade before his death, Aldrik Bach had his own charity set up through Germany's Catholic community.

The past year, his charity had raised $600,000 for cancer research.

Ryan shook his head. It was all interesting information. Bach seemed like an amazing man; however, none of his biography was helpful to Ryan in any way. He scrolled to the top of the article to find who had written the story. The writer's name was Godfrey Hackett, who was originally from England. Ryan searched the name online and soon enough found Hackett's personal website. He had become a blogger and a novelist. He wrote non-fiction about German politics and conspiracy theories. He also wrote fiction novels about mystery, suspense, and serial killers.

This is perfect.

At the bottom of the website's homepage was the man's contact information.

Bingo.

Ryan found the man's email and started composing a message within the translator app on his computer. In the message, Ryan introduced himself to Hackett, then informed him of the recent case concerning The Crucifier. He then explained that he was interested about learning more of the similar case in Germany. He then had a thought. Using his phone, he emailed the pictures of Montez to himself so that they would be available to him on his computer. Ryan found the email he had composed and saved the photographs to his computer. He then added the pictures to the message he had prepared, and with the single click of the mouse, had successfully sent the email off to Godfrey Hackett.

CHAPTER THIRTEEN

Ryan exited the office and went into the living room where the rest of his family sat watching tv. Kayleen lay on the couch, cuddling her favorite blanket. Laura sat next to her, holding baby Ben, whom she was nursing. On the television, the show *Jane and Toot* was playing. It was one of Laura and Kayleen's favorites. It was a new animated show about an elderly woman and her granddaughter, who travel the world to fulfill experiences on Grandma Toot's bucket list.

"Jane and Toot, again?" Ryan asked.

"Yes!" Kayleen exclaimed.

She stood and began to dance. Tripod yelped and joined in too.

"You're just in time for her favorite part," Laura said.

Ryan smiled and sat next to his wife. He watched Kayleen dance to the show's trademark song that played at the end of every episode.

"Jane and Toot. Jane and Toot.

"I love you, and you love me.

"Jane and Toot. Jane and Toot.

"We travel the world, searching for places to see.

"Jane and Toot. Jane and Toot.

"I'll dance with you, and you dance with me.

"Jane and Toot. Jane and Toot.

"Together we travel, sea to sea.

"Jane and Toot. Jane and Toot.

"You can become anything you want to be!

"Jane and Toot. Jane and Toot.

"JANE-ely-do and TOOT-ely-dee."

Mid-dance, Kayleen spun around and blew Ryan a kiss. Laura chuckled. Ryan's masculine side didn't always like to admit it, but he was a Jane and Toot fan too. It was good, clean tv. It was educational with good life-lessons and raw, clean humor. It didn't have any of the usual tv drama either.

As Ryan put his arm around Laura, his mind wandered. He started to wonder how Whitney Lee and Allen Simmons were doing. He hadn't heard from either of them since they arrived in DC the evening before.

"Before I get too comfortable," Ryan said, "I'm going to go make a real quick phone call."

"Okay," Laura replied, looking down at Ben.

Ryan stood and walked outside the front door of the house. He dialed Agent Lee's cell phone number, but she didn't answer. He then called Agent Simmons. Again, no answer. The phone rang until Ryan reached Simmons' voicemail. Ryan knew they were probably okay. Everyone misses phone calls. They were probably busy. He convinced himself that they were okay but couldn't shake the feeling of trepidation he suddenly had.

Where are you guys?

CHAPTER FOURTEEN

Lee and Simmons were in a large, dark, cold basement under a run-down building located on the outskirts of Washington DC. The building was an old bank. The basement beneath it was enormous. It was the basement where Pablo Montez was killed.

Neither Simmons nor Lee heard their cell phones ring in their pocket. Both phones were on silent. Neither agent felt their phone vibrate. There was no electricity inside the basement, which meant no lights. Simmons and Lee both held a flashlight. In Simmons' other hand he held a printed copy of a picture that showed Montez's body on the cross.

Simmons moved the beam of his flashlight to the back wall of the basement.

"Here," he said. "This is where the cross was."

Simmons looked at the picture in his hand and stood where he believed the cross had been.

Lee moved over to Simmons' side to look at the picture.

"Yeah," she stated, "that's about right."

"It's too bad the scene has already been cleaned up. I mean, aside from the blood stains here on the floor."

Lee shivered.

"Allen, let's get out of here."

Simmons glared down at Lee. "What? We've been here for, what? Ten minutes? If that?"

Lee shook her head. "It's pointless. We should go to the morgue and examine the body. Then we need to examine cameras around this area. Besides all that, I have a weird feeling, Allen. I have a very uneasy feeling in my gut. This place is making my skin crawl."

Simmons put an arm around Lee's shoulders.

"Whitney," he said, "come on! After all these years you've been in the Bureau, a little ole basement scares you?"

Lee shrugged Simmons' arm off of her.

"I'm being serious," Lee said.

Simmons rolled his eyes.

"Women…" he muttered under his breath. "Well, Whitney, how about this, you can leave and wait outside while I stay here for a few more minutes. Deal?"

Lee sighed. "I'll wait with you. Just hurry."

Lee unbuckled the gun holster on her hip and took her handgun off of safety.

Simmons stuck a hand in the air and waited for a high-five. Lee ignored the motion.

"Gosh, you really need to lighten up, Ms. Agent Lee. This stuff is fun!"

"Usually, I'd agree. But these feelings, like the one I have right now, are never wrong. I just don't know. This place feels real dark. I feel like we are being watched."

Simmons sent his flashlight beam dancing around the basement walls.

"Well, yeah, it is pretty dark in here," Simmons said. "Which is why we have these handy flashlights. And we are not being watched. I can assure you of that."

Agent Lee was right. They *were* being watched. They weren't the only ones in the basement. Someone was watching them from the shadows, dressed in all black and squatting down behind boards along the basement walls directly to the left of the base of the stairway that led into the basement.

He shook his head as he watched the two FBI agents standing around the bloodied floor. They were conversing and arguing now. The male agent started to walk around the basement again. The female agent remained in place as she slowly moved her flashlight's beam across the walls and the ceiling of the basement. The beam would never find him. He was smart. This wasn't a foreign experience to him. He was well hidden.

The man behind the wall smiled.

The woman was scared, and the man hiding behind the walls loved it.

CHAPTER FIFTEEN

Simmons and Lee exited the dark basement. The farther they got up the stairs, the less the flashlights were required. Lee felt better as her surroundings became lighter and she got further away from the basement.

The two agents finished ascending the stairs and left the old building.

"Well that was pointless," Simmons said while they strolled out of the old bank.

"It's okay," Lee replied. "We'll find something. It was good to be there where it happened."

Simmons stopped almost immediately after he stepped outside of the bank. He was looking toward the road in front of him. Simmons was watching a young woman. She was sitting on the side of the road with her knees pulled up to her chest. She had blonde, almost white hair, she was fair-skinned, very petite, weighing maybe a hundred pounds soaking wet.

Lee noticed the woman too.

"What do you think is wrong?" she asked.

"Let's go find out."

The two sauntered over to the woman. Simmons knelt down beside her.

"Ma'am, is everything okay?" he asked.

The woman glanced over her shoulder then put her face back into her knees.

"It's-it's nothing," she stammered.

Simmons shook his head. "No, it doesn't seem like it. Is there anything we can do to help?"

"My car…no, no, it's not your problem. I'm just having a tough time right now. You can carry on with your day. I'll be alright."

Simmons stood and observed the car. "What's wrong with your car?"

The woman lifted her head slightly. "I don't know. It died. It just gave out on me. I know nothing about cars. My daughter, sh-she…she…"

The woman couldn't finish her sentence and began to wail again. Simmons walked around to the driver's side of the car and got in behind the wheel. Lee sat next to the crying woman.

"It's okay," Lee said. "Please, stop crying. Take deep breaths. Tell me, what is going on?"

The woman took a deep breath. "My daughter…my daughter, Hope, was at school…the principal called me to tell me that Hope had-had randomly collapsed in class and was unresponsive. They didn't know what happened. She was rushed to the hospital." The woman began to cry hysterically again. "I don't even know if my daughter is alive! I DON'T EVEN KNOW!"

Lee rubbed the woman's back. Simmons attempted to start the car, but it didn't even turn over. He stepped out of the vehicle and popped the hood.

"Ah!" he proclaimed. "One of the battery cables came loose. There was no relay of power at all. The casing over the end of the cable came off."

Simmons hooked the battery back up and jumped into the car again. He turned the key in the ignition. This time the car came to life.

The crying woman leapt to her feet. "Oh, thank you, thank you!"

She then gasped and froze. She hastily pulled a cell phone out of the purse she held with her. The phone was ringing.

"Hello? Babe! Babe! What is going on?"

The woman's chest heaved in and out as she waited for a reply. Then her shoulders went lax. She took a deep breath.

"Thank the Lord. I'm on my way there now, babe. Love you."

The woman ended the phone call and threw her arms around Lee.

"Thank you two so much!" she said.

Simmons walked up to the woman and Lee, where he too was met with an awkward hug.

"The two of you are absolute Saints. God bless you."

Simmons patted the young lady on the back, then pulled out of the hug. "The phone call? Who was that? Everything better now?"

The woman patted her chest. "Yes, sir. My baby, Hope, is going to be okay. She's stable, breathing, and they said she's going to be fine. That was my dear husband who just called."

The woman put a finger up and dug into her purse. Within seconds, she came out of the purse holding a small photo. She handed the photograph to Lee.

"This is our little family," she said sniffling. "They're my absolute world. She's our only daughter. I'm just always so protective and worried and an emotional mess. I'm so sorry you had to see me like this. I don't know how I could live if anything ever happened to my baby."

"Well I'm relieved to hear she's okay," Simmons said looking down at the photograph Lee had just handed him. "And I'm relieved your dang car is up and running too."

"Yes!" the woman exclaimed. "Thank you so much. I'm sorry I'm not very car savy. These cars blow my mind. I just know how to drive them and put gas in them. That's where my knowledge ends. I'm sorry to have wasted your time too. You in your spiffy suits, I imagine you both had more important things to do than try to comfort a crazy-looking lady."

"You are perfectly fine," Lee stated. "It was our pleasure to be able to help in any way. I'm glad everything is okay."

"May I get your names? Are you two from around here?"

"No, we're from New York. We're here on a business trip. I'm Allen, this is…"

Lee elbowed Allen hard in his side.

"Ow!" he cried out.

Lee let out a big breath and tried to keep from showing her annoyance toward Simmons. Sometimes, she hated how careless and happy-go-lucky he acted.

"I'm Jessie," Lee said, lying, while looking up at Simmons, giving him a dirty look.

"Good to meet you two," the woman said. "I'm Viviana. I know how hard and expensive it is trying to find a place to stay here. My husband and I have a guest house. You are more than welcome to stay with us. I'm not sure when Hope will be released, but you are welcome at our place. It was very generous and selfless of you to stop for me. There aren't many people like that. You seem like some of the few good ones left in this world."

Simmons smiled. Lee could tell he was beaming with pride.

"Thanks for the offer, Viviana," Simmons said, "we have hotel rooms already reserved and paid for though."

Viviana nodded. "I see. Well, I want to do something for you. Can I make you guys cookies? Bring you some food? Something? Where are you staying? How long are you in town? I could take something to the front desk for you sometime."

In the eight sentences she spoke, Viviana didn't take a single breath. Simmons chuckled.

"You're a sweet woman," he said. "It's okay. Thank you, though. That's a kind gesture."

"Yes," Lee chipped in, "that's very kind of you."

Viviana shrugged. "I do make some mean cookies. I hope you aren't staying at the Griffin Inn or the DC Grand Palace? There have been some bad shootings and robberies there recently."

"Oh, no, no, we aren't," Simmons answered. "We got rooms at the Fairmonton."

Lee irritably shook her head.

"Oh, the Fairmonton," Viviana said. "Good choice! Much nicer and safer! Hey, thank you two again. Gosh I get to talking too much. I better get going. God bless you."

Both agents smiled and nodded, and the woman shook their hands before jumping into her car and leaving.

"Your old age really has you uptight, doesn't it?" Simmons asked. "You need to relax, Ms. Lee. Relax."

Lee rolled her eyes. "I have no idea how I am going to be able to put up with you through all this. All I can say is, Lord help me."

"Psh," Simmons said, "You cut me deep there, Whitney. You cut me real deep. Come on, I'm a fun guy, and I'm good at what I do. I'll grow on you; you just wait and see. But enough with the chit-chat, I'm starving! Let's go find something to eat. It's on me."

CHAPTER SIXTEEN

It was an hour later when Ryan received a message from the German journalist, Godfrey Hackett. Ryan was in the kitchen eating a bowl of cereal when he received the email notification on his phone. He quickly scarfed down his cereal then rushed to his home office. He swung into the chair at the desk and powered on the computer.

He clicked on the message from Hackett and found the message was written in English.

It was one of the craziest stories I ever covered for the paper. I still remember it clearly. Please, feel free to call me. I do speak English.

#: 01567-1096554

Talk to you soon, Mr. Turner.

Ryan had forgotten how weird German phone numbers looked to him. They were much different than U.S. phone numbers, that's for sure.

Ryan promptly dialed the number. After four rings, there was an answer.

"Hello, this is Godfrey Hackett."

"Mr. Hackett, this is Ryan Turner from the Federal Bureau of Investigation here in the U.S. How are you?"

"Oh!" Hackett exclaimed. "I am well. How are you?"

"Not too shabby," Ryan replied. "Are you busy?"

"No, not busy. You said you're a detective?"

"Something like that."

"Well," Hackett said, "how can I help you?"

"Like I said in the message, we're looking into a case here that seems to be much like the case you covered years ago in Germany. Did you receive the photos I sent you?"

"Yes, they're terrible. Much alike to the story I covered. How many victims have there been altogether?"

"Three, so far," Ryan answered. "Two days ago, two people were killed in the same day."

"I looked at the photos," Hackett said. "The cross, the different wounds, the crown, it's all the same. Have you got any leads?"

"Nope. None."

"Crazy...the murderer here was found the same day as the homicide itself. The case was closed very quickly."

"It was," Ryan said. "Must have been nice. Listen, so the main reason I decided to contact you was to see if there was a lead detective or police officer on the Germany case. Do you know who the lead was on the case?"

"I think the head guy was a Berlin detective, who's retired now. The name is Danley Dobson. I think he was born in the States, if my memory is right?"

"Do you know any way I can contact him?"

"Hmm, I don't at the moment," Hackett said. "But maybe I can find his contact information for you, if you'd like?"

"That would be great. Thank you, kind sir."

"You're most certainly welcome. Is there anything else I can help with? Any other questions for me?"

Ryan thought about it. "No, not right now. Thank you again. We'll be in touch."

"Goodbye, Mr. Turner."

CHAPTER SEVENTEEN

Ryan got a phone call immediately after speaking with Godfrey Hackett.

It was Simmons.

"Simmons!" Ryan answered. "Everything okay?"

"Yes, sir," Simmons replied. "Sorry that Whitney and I missed your call."

"No, it's all good. You had me slightly worried but not too badly."

"Oh, we're good boss! Where's your faith in us?"

Ryan chuckled. "I've got plenty of faith in you both. It's just a *boss* thing, I guess. When you're in charge you tend to worry all the time. How are things going so far?"

"Good," Simmons answered. "We are finishing up lunch, right now, which was pretty good, wouldn't you say, Whitney?"

Ryan heard Lee mutter something.

"Yeah aside from finding a good place to eat," Simmons continued, "we haven't found much yet. We went to the site of Pablo Montez's murder just to see it ourselves, to get a feel for the scene, and possibly find something. We didn't find anything though. Just a pool of blood. As soon as we finish eating, we plan on checking various security tapes around the old bank where Montez was found. Past investigators haven't found anything of use, but I hope that maybe we'll see something others didn't. Last night we went and checked out the scene where Mayfield was killed. The scene was left as is for us to look at it, which was nice. So, the body was still there. People stayed there before we arrived to keep animals and curiosity seekers away from the body. It was out in the trees on the outskirts of DC. I guess it was a hiker that found the body."

"All sounds good. If you need any help finding or looking at security footage, tell me. G-Man has that new system he created. He calls it La Águila. You find anything of interest where Reverend Mayfield was killed?"

"Ha-ha, that guy and his Spanish," Simmons replied. "We'll have to see. I might take you up on that offer. I'll let you know. And we didn't find anything. Same story as Montez. The cross looked the same. The wounds and the crown and everything were identical. However, there were no candles. I guess The Crucifier is environmentally enlightened and didn't want to cause a forest fire. At least the guy takes care of our trees."

"I see. Well keep in touch. Is there anything I need to know, or I can do for you?"

"No, not at the moment? Whitney? Is there anything Mr. Turner can do for us?"

There was a pause.

"No, I don't think so," Simmons followed up.

Ryan nodded. "Well, I'll talk to you again later. You two be safe."

Ryan ended the call and walked out of the office. The moment he entered the hallway, his phone rang again. He swore the majority of his days consisted of speaking on the phone. Really, phone calls made up the bulk of his job.

This time, it was Dr. Hill from the Ryker's Island prison.

"Hello?" Ryan answered.

"Mr. Turner, how are you?" Hill asked.

"I'm doing good," Ryan answered, "can't complain. You?"

"I am very well. I have some wonderful news for you. Cindy Caine just had her baby."

Ryan gasped. "Are you serious?"

"Serious as can be, Mr. Turner. The baby is healthy too. Nine pounds and two ounces."

Ryan grinned. "Oh, he's a chunky little guy! Awesome. Thank you for the news, Dr. Hill. What happens now?"

"That is a great question. If you are still set on taking the baby in as your own, Cindy has signed the paperwork to make it possible. I mean, everything is set for you to come get the baby by tomorrow at some point. At the 24-hour mark since birth, I should be able to release him to go home with you.

"Perfect," said Ryan.

"Out of curiosity," Hill said, "do you have a name for him?"

"Since we named our baby after the man who raised me, we plan on naming this one after Laura's father, who is named after Laura's favorite book in the Bible."

"Okay, okay, give me some clues. I've got a break for the first time today. I do like trivia."

"Do you read the Bible?" Ryan asked.

"Do I read the Bible?" Hill sounded appalled. "Of course. There are more of us doctors who do than people realize. I study every morning and night, Mr. Turner."

Ryan was impressed. He too tried to read and study his scriptures every chance he had.

"New Testament," Ryan said.

"Matthew, Mark, Luke, John, Roman, Timothy, James, Peter, Jude?" Hill listed in a hurry.

"No, sir."

"Hmm…"

"Laura loves the book because the first thing it talks about is eternal life and that before our lives on earth, it was promised to us by God. It also tells of living righteously, denying ungodliness, and seeking the Lord. Above all else though, I think she really likes the book because of the cool name and it being the name of her father."

"Let me think," Hill said. "Philemon?"

"Nope. That is one book too far."

"One book too far, huh…? Titus! Is it Titus?"

Ryan chuckled. "Yes, sir. You got it."

"Perfect! I like it. Little Titus. I will see you later, Mr. Turner. Have a safe trip over here!"

Ryan grinned. "Thank you so much for everything, Dr. Hill. See you soon."

Ryan quickly ended the call and hustled to find his wife to tell her the big news.

CHAPTER EIGHTEEN

Simmons and Lee arrived at the Fairmonton hotel at just after 8 p.m. They were physically and mentally drained. They had had enough for one day. They talked with the DC Chief of Police, and they looked through as much security footage as was available around the old bank. They also watched the security footage from a gas station just next to the run-down bank. After hours of studying it, Simmons and Lee could only conclude a few different things.

The day before Montez's death, three individuals unloaded a big cross to the building in a white van with Virginian license plates. The cross was obviously the cross Montez hung from. The plate numbers were tracked, and they belonged to Pablo Montez. Simmons and Lee should've been surprised, but they weren't. Actually, they had expected that to be the case. With the past victim, Tina Rington, the same sort of thing had proven true.

In the film, it was impossible to determine the identities of the people unloading the cross, or even attain much of a description of the individuals. Their faces were covered with half-ski-masks. They all wore overalls, long-sleeved shirts and boots. On their heads they wore construction hats with dark sunglasses covering their eyes.

Along with the cross, the individuals unloaded a rectangular box that looked almost like a coffin. The agents concluded that the box most likely contained Pablo Montez. It was fifteen to twenty minutes before the individuals returned to the van. Once they returned, they entered the vehicle and sped away. Two hours later, one single individual walked up to the run-down building and wandered inside. This individual was dressed completely in black, matching the pitch-black night. The person wore a white mask and carried a large duffel bag. It was The Crucifier. After some time, the individual exited the building and seemed to look directly at the camera. The Crucifier then waved and bowed before walking off into the darkness. The scene sent shivers down the two agents' spines.

When it was all said and done, the two FBI agents hadn't learned much new information. They each walked into their hotel rooms feeling exhausted, frustrated, and unsuccessful. The only accomplishment of the day was helping the distraught young woman named Viviana.

Lee's reservation was for room number 222. Simmons laid upon his bed in room 224. They each had beautiful suites and king-sized beds. Both agents were informed at the front desk that room service was readily available during all hours of the day and night. Before entering her room, Lee had told Simmons that she was going to bed as soon as she finished taking a shower.

Simmons on the other hand, although exhausted, was wide awake. The instant he walked into his room, he took a quick shower and brushed his teeth, then threw himself onto his bed. Once on his bed, he used his iPhone to facetime his girlfriend's cell phone. After eight rings there was an answer.

"Daddy!" Georgia exclaimed as her face filled the screen. Her hair was put up into two pigtails. She had bright-red lipstick all over her lips and cheeks. The lipstick was obviously self-applied.

Simmons smiled. The sound of Georgia's voice warmed his heart.

"Hey, you," he said. "How's my girl doing?"

"Good! Are you coming home yet?"

Simmons chuckled. "No, not yet."

"Why not? I miss you," Georgia whined.

"I miss you too, but don't worry, okay? I'll be back home in the next few days. It'll go by fast."

"Okay, daddy," Georgia replied. "I love you."

"Love you too, baby girl. Is your mom there?"

"Yes, here you go. Bye, daddy!"

Simmons smiled. "Talk to you later."

The screen temporarily portrayed the floor then Zaya's face filled the phone screen.

"Hey, Allen," she said.

Simmons looked at the beautiful diamond ring he now held in his hand. He kept it hidden from the view of the camera. He had retrieved it out of a pouch inside his wallet, which had been home to the ring for over a month now. It was an engagement ring. He stared it at now as he spoke to his girlfriend. He loved her. He loved her more than life itself, and he knew that he wanted to marry her. Not only did he wish to marry her, but he knew it was the right thing to do. For some reason though, something had been keeping him from posing the question to Zaya. He knew he wanted to spend the rest of his life with her. She loved him, even with his mood swings, cockiness, and quirkiness. She was always there for him.

However, he was scared. He didn't know why, but he was scared. It could've been because his parents went through a nasty divorce when he was young. Or it could have been due to how badly his previous relationship had ended. The day before his marriage, he found out that his fiancé had run off with another man, and he never heard from her again. Whatever the reason was, he remained hesitant to propose to Zaya.

"Hey, beautiful," Simmons answered.

"How's everything going, my love?"

Simmons smiled. "It's going. Slowly but surely."

"Have you gotten any leads yet? Found anything?"

Simmons shook his head and pursed his lips. "Nope, not yet, at least."

"I know you," Zaya said, "you'll start finding answers. Just keep searching for them."

"I will. Whitney doesn't know but I plan on heading out tonight. I don't know what I'll find, but hopefully something."

Zaya gave Simmons a sideways look. "Just stay inside. Get some rest. I don't know if I have the best feeling about you going out on your own."

"Zaya, you're my girl. It's your job to worry about me. I'll be okay, though. Trust me."

"Allen, please…"

"Zaya, I promise. I mean, this is my job. I'm absolutely exhausted, but I won't be able to sleep. When I get on a case, it becomes personal, and this is a big one for me."

Zaya looked down, avoiding eye contact. Simmons could see real concern in her eyes.

"I'm sorry," Simmons said, "I just…"

"No, no," Zaya interrupted, looking back up at Simmons. "I really do just worry…even though I shouldn't. I know you'll be okay, you always are. I want to be your wife someday…I just…I-I know-I know you don't like talking about that subject. It's okay too, I understand. The less you put yourself in danger, the better I feel, you know? I know I shouldn't think like that…but I don't want Georgia living her life without her father. I've seen it far too often. I don't know."

Zaya was tearing up now. Simmons looked down at the ring in the hand not holding the phone. He understood exactly what she was feeling. He stuffed the ring into his pocket.

"I know what you're saying. I'm sorry, Zaya. I'll stay in tonight. I'll have plenty of time tomorrow to try to find some answers. And listen, I don't mind you bringing up marriage. I really don't. And I…"

"Allen, no, it's okay. Like I said, I understand. I love you, and I'm always going to stand by you."

"I want to marry you, Zaya. I see it in my future. *Our* future. I want to spend the rest of my life with you. I promise you that, and someday it *will* happen."

Zaya kept her eyes low and smiled a slight smile. "I love you, Allen."

"I love you too. When I get back home, when all of this is over, we're going on a trip. Just you, me, and Georgia. Wherever you want to go, I'll make it happen. I promise."

Simmons and Zaya locked eyes.

"Sounds good to me," Zaya said. "Get some sleep. Call me in the morning!"

"I will," Simmons said with a smile.

Zaya blew Simmons a kiss. "Goodnight, babe."

"Goodnight, Zaya."

Zaya's face left the screen, and the call ended.

Simmons released a sigh. He missed her. He missed Georgia too. This was the part of his work he had never liked. He hated being away from them.

He began to research vacation spots. He searched for travel packages to the Galapagos Islands. For some reason, and Simmons never questioned why, Zaya had always talked about going to the islands. It was a dream of hers. She was an animal lover and loved to travel. She would go on about wanting to see the giant tortoises, the seals, the iguanas, and the thousands of birds.

Simmons found the most cost-efficient vacation package he could find. It ended up totaling just under three-thousand big ones. The package included a round-trip flight for him, Zaya, and Georgia, as well as a four-night stay at

Casa Playa Mann, which was a highly rated bed and breakfast. He didn't know when he would be able to return home, so he'd wait to book the package. Simmons was becoming giddy with excitement. He couldn't wait to tell Zaya. He stuck his hand into his pocket and fidgeted with the diamond ring. It was time. He knew it was. It felt right.

He decided the Galapagos Islands were where he was going to finally propose to Zaya. Simmons grinned as he shut down his cell phone. He walked over and plugged the phone into the wall next to the cushioned chair across from the foot of the bed. Simmons wandered back over to his bed and wrapped himself underneath the covers. He laid his head back, closed his eyes, and instantly fell asleep.

CHAPTER NINETEEN

Agent Whitney Lee stepped out of the shower and pulled a towel off the towel-rack above the commode. She quickly dried her body off and did her best to dry her extremely long hair too. She was never too successful drying her hair with a towel, so she immediately wrapped the damp towel around herself and instead did her best to dry her hair with the cheap blow-dryer the hotel provided. Once her hair was moderately dry, Lee tied it up into a long ponytail, which she then draped over her right shoulder. Using the back of her hand, she wiped the foggy mirror above the sink, so she could see her reflection. She groaned at the sight of the slight wrinkles that, over time, had begun to periodically appear on her face. She removed a facial product from her makeup bag and applied the cool cream, then yawned.

Lee was exhausted. She was mentally and physically drained. She had been through a lot during her FBI career. She had experienced so much and seen an immense variety of cases, but this Crucifier case was unlike anything she had ever seen before. It made her stomach churn, her heart ache. This serial killer, thus far, was so brutal, so twisted, and so very smart. This was one of the first times in her career that she felt a sense of worry and uncertainty. It was the first time she really worried for her life. Somehow, someway, The Crucifier had meticulously murdered four completely innocent people in the same, exact way, and had perfectly covered it all up. There were no leads. Nothing. In addition, every detective, agent, officer, and individual in law enforcement who investigated the deaths had all wound up dead themselves. That is what made her feel such trepidation. Lee shook her head and pushed the thought from her mind.

Lee exited the bathroom shivering as she entered the cool bedroom. She yawned again. Her eyes were heavy, her legs felt shaky. She needed sleep. Lee started to turn off the lights when she saw a piece of paper beneath the room's door. She slowly wandered to the door and picked it up from the floor. There was writing on it.

It read: *Your friend in the room next door asked to have this delivered to you. I knocked but you didn't answer. There's a tray outside your door in the hall. He said to tell you to sleep well and that tomorrow is going to be a big day. Have a great night.*

Room Service

B.B.

Lee cautiously cracked open the door and looked into the hallway. On the floor was a shiny platter holding a mug filled with tea and a plate holding a slice of cheesecake. Lee grinned. She absolutely loved cheesecake. She wasn't the biggest fan of tea, but she felt it would probably help her sleep well. Simmons frustrated her, yet he did have a sweet side. She bent over and retrieved the platter from the floor.

Lee froze, thinking she heard something. Someone. She shook the feeling, knowing that obviously it was normal to hear people in a crowded hotel. For some reason, though, she still felt like she was being watched. She couldn't shake it. Lee shivered and forced herself to ignore the feeling. She got those feelings far too often when she was in the field.

She thought about knocking on Simmons' door and thanking him. Instead, she decided against it and re-entered her own room, smelling the cheesecake while she strolled toward her bed. The dessert's aroma entered her nose and seemed to travel throughout her body. Placing the tea on the nightstand, she crawled onto the king-sized bed and lay on her side, propping her head up with her hand, posing rather like a beach model. She tore into the strawberry cheesecake. It was amazing. Once she had finished it, her mouth watered for more.

Lee placed the empty plate onto the floor next to the bed and reached for the cup of tea. She blew on the liquid inside the cup, causing small ripples to shimmer in the tea, then placed her face closer to the cup allowing the steam to fill her nostrils and warm her face. Lee sat up, dangling her legs over the bedside. She then grasped the warm mug with both hands and tenderly lifted it to her lips. The hot substance warmed her mouth, washing away the lingering taste of cheesecake. The tea traveled down her throat and into her stomach, seeming to warm her very soul. She downed half the cup, then pulled the mug away from her lips. As she went to place the cup back on the nightstand, she stopped short. Her arms suddenly felt tingly and weak. In fact, her entire body was tingling. She felt shaky. Her insides burned. She found that she couldn't breathe.

The mug fell from Lee's grasp, dropped onto her lap, and its contents splashed all over her legs. The hot tea burned her skin; however, she didn't notice. She grabbed at her throat. A burning pain seemed to surge from her throat down to her stomach. She still couldn't breathe. She simply couldn't catch a breath. Pressure built up in her head and chest as she felt the life being sucked out of her. Lee thrashed around, still tearing at her throat, trying to catch a breath, until her heart suddenly stopped. Her eyes went wide as her heart ceased from pumping and hands fell away from her throat. Her body slowly fell onto the floor, knocking the nightstand over. In the silence of a cold hotel room, next to an overturned nightstand and a shattered lamp, lay Agent Whitney Lee's lifeless body.

CHAPTER TWENTY

Allen Simmons startled awake at the sound of a ringing phone. It was the room's landline. He sat up and rubbed his eyes, then mid-yawn, he lifted the phone off its base.

"Hello," he said groggily into the beige colored phone.

"So sorry if I woke you," the voice said. "This is Lewis with the kitchen downstairs. A woman by the name of Whitney Lee? She placed an order for you and wanted it delivered to your room. She ordered our special cocktail of the day called 'Midnight Slumber', and said she hoped it would perhaps help you settle down and get some sleep. If you don't know who this woman is, or if it's too late at night and you just don't want it, we can cancel the order, of course."

"Whitney Lee ordered it for me?"

"Yes, sir, she said you were a friend of hers and that you'd had a long day today. What did she say…let me think? Something like-like that she was concerned about you."

Simmons yawned and smiled at the same time. He was already plenty tired and feeling fine, but Lee's gesture was kind. It really made him feel good. She seemed to be disappointed with him quite often, and sometimes he felt that she couldn't even stand him, but he knew deep,

deep…deep down she loved him. He decided to accept the thoughtful gesture.

"She's a good friend of mine. I'll take it. Do I need to come pick it up?"

"Oh, no, sir," Lewis said. "We will bring it up to your room. It's our pleasure and we'll rush the order to you."

"Sounds good. Thank you!"

Simmons extended his arms and stretched. He stood up from the bed and wandered blindly in his dark room, feeling around the walls for a light switch.

Eventually, he stumbled upon a lamp in the corner of the room and flipped the power switch to bring the lamp to life. Next to the lamp was a chair that Simmons plopped down into. On the arm of the chair sat his cell phone, which he had plugged into the wall earlier. His head was throbbing from waking up so suddenly.

Simmons turned on his device and began composing a text message to Agent Lee.

You're too kind, Whitney. Thank you. See you in the morning! God bless.

Simmons hit "send" then powered the cellular device off again. Within a few minutes, there was a knock at his door.

"Room service."

Simmons rose from the chair and opened the door, pulling it inward. In the hallway, stood a lean man with broad shoulders, wearing glasses and a full-blown tuxedo. There was something off about his face. Simmons couldn't quite place it. The man was holding a tray that held a glass of alcohol. He extended his arms to hand the tray over to Simmons.

"Is there anything else I can do for you?"

Simmons rubbed his eyes with the back of his free hand. He shook his head.

Man, the bellhops here sure dress nicely.

"No, thank you," he said, "have a good night." Simmons was a man of style and decided that the bellhop deserved a compliment. "And I love the outfit. Very classy look. I respect that."

The bellhop smiled. "Have a wonderful night."

Simmons shut the door then sat in the chair again where he had connected his phone to an outlet, tossed the tray to the side, and held the fancy glass in one hand. He then downed all its contents in a single tip of the glass. He guzzled it down and let out a loud, satified "AH!"

Simmons then stared into the empty glass. The red alcohol was gone; however, stuck at the bottom of the glass was a clumpy white substance. It looked like it used to be some sort of powder. It was a small amount, barely noticeable. Most people wouldn't have seen it. Simmons did. Just as he noticed it, he felt the inside of his throat begin to tighten.

His entire chest tightened as if in a vice. His head pounded. A burning sensation surged through his abdomen and up through his throat. Simmons couldn't breathe. With his chest heaving in and out, and his mouth hanging open, he grabbed at his throat and pounded his chest with both fists. Vomit streamed from his mouth, making it even harder to breathe. He frantically reached for his cell phone, fumbling it around in his grasp. Now, the pressure in his head was unbearable and his lungs felt as if they were going to explode. Simmons fell to his knees, but still managed to power on his phone. Though his hands and fingers could hardly function, he still willed them to. He had to. On the screen automatically appeared his recent messages to Lee. He tapped at the phone's keyboard with his now nearly useless fingers, until the device ultimately fell from his grasp. He grabbed his throat and attempted to yell, only to let out a horrific gargling noise.

Then his struggling suddenly ceased. His hands fell away from his throat. As he swayed from side to side, unable to keep himself upright, Simmons' last thought was of the last time he saw and would ever see Zaya and his beautiful little Georgia. He could almost see them in front of him now waving goodbye to him from the doorstep of their studio apartment. His head hung limp; his chin rested on his chest. Allen Simmons' lifeless body then fell facedown onto the carpeted floor.

CHAPTER TWENTY-ONE

*Phone calls...*phone calls...and more phone calls. It was Ryan's life now. How bad was it really, though? To earn six figures a year, while most of the "work" consisted of talking on the phone. Not so bad. Ryan enjoyed conversing with people, even when it was business related.

"How is Hawaii, my friend?" Ryan asked into the phone, not even bothering to answer with the usual "hello" or "This is Turner".

"Dude. How is Hawaii? It's freakin' amazing!"

Ryan laughed. "I'm glad you're enjoying it."

The man on the other end of the line was Zane Linton. Zane Linton the Serafina Pizza delivery man. The Zane Linton whom Ryan had promised $3,000. Ryan had far exceeded that promise, though. A few weeks back, after receiving his first paycheck as the Head of the Bureau, Ryan went to Serafina's Pizza and delivered a $3,000 check to Zane, along with an all-expense paid trip to Waikiki, Hawaii for a week.

When Ryan delivered the gifts to Zane, he was bombarded with uncomfortable hugs and slaps on the back. He was overjoyed. Ecstatic. He told Ryan he never expected a payment, but Ryan had indeed done that and more.

"Mr. Turner, I never could have imagined this. Thank you again, bro. Thank you. I've always dreamed of traveling to Hawaii, man, and it might have never been possible without you. For real, though, you might be the first bum to have ever given a guy a paid trip to Hawaii."

Ryan chuckled again. "It's no problem at all, glad you're enjoying it. I've been there, and it's an amazing place. Great people too."

"Yeah, bro. Too cool. *Way* too cool. I just wanted to tell you thanks again. I just finished snorkeling, bro, and I'm too hyped. Like I still can't believe I'm here."

"Well, again, it's no problem, Zane. Keep enjoying yourself! Talk to you later."

"Talk to you later, dude. Much love."

Ryan tucked the cell phone into his pocket.

"Who was that?" Laura asked, cradling little Ben against her chest.

"It was Zane Linton," Ryan said, pulling himself closer to Laura in bed.

She grinned.

"That was sweet of you to do that for him."

"It was the right thing to do. He's a good kid."

"And you're a great man," Laura said, kissing Ryan softly. "I can't believe we have all this. This miracle of a family we have. It's surreal to me. I mean, Ben already here, Titus will be with us soon, the girl Kayleen has become, now John even! I could've never imagined having all of this."

Ryan grinned. It truly was amazing. And to think that this family had been so close to being torn apart…Ryan tried not to think about it, yet the thought crept into his mind quite often. If Kuron and John hadn't saved the day at Gondleton Farms, Ryan knew he wouldn't be sitting in bed with his wife and baby boy right now. He knew they'd have all been killed. Or, knowing the man Caine was, Ryan might have been left to live to suffer alone and remain tortured for the remainder of his life.

Ryan shivered as the thoughts floated around his mind. He hated Caine. More than a man should ever hate someone. The thought of him sent an indescribable rage through Ryan's body. But Caine was gone now, nonexistent, and his plans and his empire had been all but destroyed. He was nothing but a really bad memory.

Ryan must have zoned out because Laura nudged him.

"Are you okay?" she asked. "I know you say that I'm hypnotizing, but I'm not a real hypnotist, Ryan. At least, I didn't think so?"

Ryan snapped back into reality and rolled his eyes. "Sorry, this mind of mine is always reeling."

"Well, you need to give it a rest sometimes."

Laura stood up and carefully took Ben to one of the two cradles beside the master bed. She slowly lowered Ben into it, covered him with a small white blanket and pulled his wool cap farther down his head. She then kissed him on the forehead before returning to bed.

"Now, close your eyes. Rest that crazy mind of yours. You better take advantage of the times Ben is asleep and *isn't* crying. He'll be awake in an hour, or so."

Ryan shook his head. "You think?"

"Pft. I know! I bet you within a few days, you'll be sleeping in the living room. Mark my words."

Ryan lowered himself into bed, nestling under the cool covers. He pulled Laura close to him.

"We'll see about that."

"Goodnight, Ryan," Laura said in the middle of a yawn.

"I love you, honey."

Ryan closed his eyes. He slept soundly for ten minutes before the sound of Ben's screaming erupted in the bedroom. Ryan rubbed his eyes with the arm that wasn't around Laura.

"Laura, your hypothesis about the whole hour deal was a little off."

Laura laughed quietly and ruffled Ryan's hair with her hand. "Welcome to parenthood, sweetheart."

CHAPTER TWENTY-TWO

It was six o'clock in the morning. Ryan sat, sunken into the living room couch with a hot cup of spearmint tea in his hand. He was currently running on little to no sleep. Laura's words popped back into his head.

"Welcome to parenthood, sweetheart."

Ryan shook his head. It had been a rude awakening for sure. Ryan was used to not getting much sleep anyway. Luckily, he didn't need very much rest at night to function the next day.

On the television, the Fox News channel played. In the recliner next to the couch sat John. He too held a mug filled with herbal tea, although his mug of tea contained enough sugar to kill a diabetic. Ryan often joked that John liked tea with his sugar, rather than sugar with tea.

It had become a morning ritual for Ryan and John. At six every morning, they had tea or coffee, watched the early morning news, and just talked. Then if Laura was home, she'd wake up around 6:30 and would make them all a heavenly breakfast.

Ryan took a sip of his tea. For reasons unknown to him, it didn't taste as good today. His stomach felt queasy. He had a sick feeling inside his gut. His sixth sense was kicking in. He tried to ignore the feeling and wanted to shake it off but couldn't.

He found that he simply couldn't stop thinking about Simmons and Lee. Ever since he left them at the airport, they hadn't left his mind. He was legitimately worried about them and wished he could be with them.

Ryan decided to call them to check up on how things were going.

He first called Lee's cell. It rang then went to voicemail.

He then called Simmons. Same result.

"Is everything good, bro?" John asked.

Ryan knew John could see the sense of worry written all over his face.

"Yeah, I think so…at least, I hope so."

"Any news yet on The Crucifier?"

Ryan looked at his brother who sat next to him on the living room sofa.

"Nope," Ryan answered. "Nothing at all."

"Man…the longer that psychopath is out there, the more infuriated I get. I'm serious. I can't deal with freaks like this. They have no business breathing."

Ryan shrugged. He certainly didn't disagree.

"I mean, you're not wrong, John," he said.

"Have you heard from Allen or Whitney?"

Ryan shook his head. "It's been a while."

John crossed his legs out in front of him, sipping his tea thoughtfully.

"They'll be fine, Ryan. You stress too much, man."

Ryan shrugged slightly. He did, honestly, which is one reason why he felt he was good at his job. He cared. He thought "too much." And he worried *a lot* about those he worked alongside.

"I'm serious, old man," John continued. "You'll have a full head of gray hair by next year if you don't settle down a bit."

CHAPTER TWENTY-THREE

It was three hours later when Ryan's cell phone rang. Three hours later when Ryan received a call that he wished he had never received. A call that made him numb.

He had fallen asleep on the couch. He couldn't even remember having fallen asleep. He fumbled his phone around. Anxiously, he lifted the phone up to his face. It was Felix.

"Mr. Felix, how are you?" Ryan answered groggily.

Mr. Felix's voice was solemn. He couldn't seem to get a coherent sentence out of his mouth. Ryan knew something was more than amiss.

"Sir, what's up?"

"Ryan. Ryan…we got…we got a call in from the DC police department. It-it was from one of my friends down at the department there. Long time investigator. He…" Felix's voice choked.

Ryan had a sick feeling in his gut. Mr. Felix didn't get choked up very often.

This isn't good.

Felix continued. "Agent Simmons and Agent Lee are dead."

The words hit Ryan hard. He felt like he had been shot in the chest. The room started to spin around him. He felt the rush of blood through his head and behind his ears.

His heartbeat pounded in his head. His hands were numb and tingly.

"Bro, you good?"

John said the words, but Ryan didn't hear them. John too had fallen asleep, but he now sat upright and fully alert in the recliner on the other side of the couch.

"I'm sorry," said Felix. "I don't even know what to say or do. This hurts. This hurts bad."

Ryan swallowed. He closed his eyes.

"How did they die?"

"They were found in their hotel rooms by a maid. So far, it's believed that they were both poisoned. Spilt drinks were found by each of their bodies."

Anger, despair, sorrow, and heartache filled Ryan's very soul. He had no words. The immediate pain in his chest was immense. His hands became shaky.

What am I going to do now?

Felix intuited the question that ran through Ryan's mind. "What are we going to do now?"

Ryan didn't know. So many thoughts and feelings ran through his head. Felix sounded desperate. There was despair in his voice. He had never really asked Ryan for help or advice before. Felix was a strong, independent man. He seemed to always be composed and have all the answers.

Ryan didn't say anything. He was completely tongue-tied and in shock.

"Listen, Ryan," Felix said, "take some time to think. I'm here at the annual WWW extravaganza. I have to give a toast and a speech here in a little bit. I have to let you go. Again, I'm so sorry. This is one of the worst phone calls I've ever made. Talk to you soon."

"Yeah, we'll talk again soon," Ryan replied emotionlessly.

The call ended. With robotic-like motions, Ryan shoved the cell phone into his pocket.

"Allen and Whitney are dead."

John gripped the armrests of his chair. "No! You're kidding me, right? How do we know for sure?"

"Felix got a call from some friends in the DC police department. They were both poisoned." Ryan stared down at the floor, his eyes empty.

John bolted out of his seat and began to pace the room. "There's no way, man...no..."

Ryan rested his face in his hands and blew out a breath.

This is out of control...how will I tell Zaya?

"Ryan, man, we have to do something. You've got to send me. Let me take down this guy, okay? Let me do it. Give me a chance."

Ryan shook his head. So many thoughts, feelings, and emotions raced through his entire being. He didn't know what to do.

"Ryan?" John was leaning over the chair he was in, his eyes locked on Ryan.

He stared at Ryan, looking somewhat irritated, and even hurt. Ryan could see it in his eyes. Especially in moments like these, Ryan truly appreciated John. He didn't just appreciate the great brother and uncle he was but the wonderful agent and man he was too. John took his job seriously. He loved his colleagues. He loved his job. He was passionate, emotional, and cared for everyone around him. He hadn't known Simmons and Lee for very long, but their deaths were hurting him. The Crucifier's relentless, seemingly unstoppable killing spree was hurting him. Ryan could see it.

Ryan lifted his head up. "John, please, listen. You need to take a deep breath, okay? You have to…"

"Don't give me that. Come on! I'm fine. Okay? I'm a little ticked off, but I'm fine." John threw himself into the leather chair he had occupied earlier. "We need to stop this guy. It's making me sick. People are going to keep dying. You realize that, right? People *close* to us are dying, Ryan. And it isn't going to stop. This guy is confident, and he's good at what he does. We're dealing with a professional, psychopathic killer."

Ryan bit the inside of his cheek. "I can't disagree with anything you just said. John, this hurts. This hurts me bad. Mr. Felix is hurting too. We will *all* be hurting for a while now. And I do realize this guy probably isn't going to stop. I realize that. But, I need time. *We all* need time. How can I just throw someone else at this guy, right now? I can't just casually assign one of our people onto this case again. We cannot afford that. There's no evidence as to who this guy is, we have no leads, no motive, no specific place where these people are being killed. Plus, I have to clean up this mess with Simmons and Lee first. I've got to figure out how to break the news to Zaya, and I just need a plan. A good, solid, *safe* plan. John, these agents we lost were some of our best. Whoever we are dealing with is dangerous. I mean, this is one of the most bizarre cases of my career. We have a lot to figure out."

John leaned forward in his seat and rubbed his forehead with the middle three fingers of his left hand. He inhaled a deep breath and held it for a while before exhaling.

John looked directly into Ryan's eyes. "Well, whatever it is we need to take care of, let's get to it. And promise me you'll send me when the time comes."

Ryan looked down at the floor and shook his head slightly.

"We'll see," he replied.

John leaned toward Ryan, "Bro, please. I *want* this."

Frustrated, Ryan threw his hands up. "Just give me time John. Please, just give me time." Ryan stood to his feet. "You can stick around for a while if you want. Laura will probably throw together some breakfast, or there's all sorts of delightful cereals next to the fridge. Kayleen would recommend the Choco Choco cereal."

Even in a time like this, the comment made John grin. "Kayleen does love her Choco Chocos."

"I'll see you in a bit," Ryan said, as he walked down the hall to his office.

CHAPTER TWENTY-FOUR

Escorted by secret service members, Felix exited a door leading out of the Pentagon. The meeting inside had gone well. It had included military leaders, CIA leaders, and the Secretary of Defense, who all joined together to discuss the issue of domestic terrorism, and the increasing number of school shootings that were spreading across the country at a rapid pace.

Felix threw on an overcoat that one of the secret service agents had been holding for him and pulled a pair of Oakley sunglasses over his eyes. He entered an awaiting black, bulletproof car, plopping himself into the back seat.

Felix closed the door behind him and sighed. If he were honest, there were days he wished he wasn't in the FBI at all. Today was one of those days. His work was often so dark, so depressing. It drained him.

As the car jerked away, Felix's mind wandered as he thought about the lack of trust the American people now had in the Bureau. It had been a topic of discussion in the Pentagon meeting. He thought about Lee and Simmons. He thought about their families and loved ones. Above all, he thought of the relentless serial killer that the media and the world had labelled as "The Crucifier". He thought of the fear that was currently running through the hearts and minds of people across the globe, particularly the U.S. He pictured The Crucifier's helpless, bloodied victims.

Felix shivered. Something had to be done and done fast. This case was one of the most bizarre of his career. The killer was precise and covered his tracks as well as anyone he had ever encountered. He had left no evidence, thus far, except for the dead religious figures across the country, and dead law enforcement members. The country was furious with the Bureau for the corruption that had existed and their inability to stop The Crucifier thus far.

Felix stared down at his phone screen. He knew he had one choice. Along with himself, there was one man in the agency that the country adored. One man they still respected. One man they trusted. There was one solution to this problem that Felix could not push out of his mind. One agent that he knew would have a shot at stopping this serial killer once and for all.

Ryan Turner.

CHAPTER TWENTY-FIVE

Ryan had to do it. He knew there was no way around it. He knew it had to be him. He had to deliver the news himself. It couldn't be through cable news or the newspaper. It couldn't be through a friend of Zaya's. It couldn't be through the NYPD. It had to be Ryan. And he knew that.

Ryan chose to drive his motorcycle. It wasn't the fastest means of transportation through New York City, but it gave him time to think, to compose himself. He knew it would be a while before the various news programs pounced onto the story of Simmons' and Lee's deaths. Once that happened, the news would spread through the country like wildfire.

Traffic was dense, to Ryan's frustration, but on the flipside, satisfied his need for reflection. He thought of Allen Simmons. So young. So talented. So much potential. So much life ahead of him. He really liked Simmons. He respected him greatly not only as an agent but as a man.

Death is hard. Not only because it ends the life of an individual, who especially in Simmons' case, had so much life left to live, but because of the way death affects their loved ones. Losing Simmons was a major blow to the strength of the Bureau. He was a young talent who was already impacting the Bureau in big ways. More importantly, Ryan's mind strayed to Zaya and Georgia. They were going to be devastated. Ryan was devastated for them. He couldn't even imagine their heartache. It made his stomach churn even thinking about it.

Ryan swerved to dodge a wiry man in the middle of the street who seemed to be under the influence of some sort of drug. The man screamed at Ryan, flailing his arms in the air.

Ryan thought of Agent Whitney Lee now too. She was an amazing soul. Ryan honestly looked up to her. He always did. She was an example of class, elegance and was a role model to all. She was loyal, respectable, trustworthy, hardworking, and blunt but loving. She put every ounce of her being into everything she did and never did anything half-heartedly.

Her death affected countless lives too. The Bureau lost an amazing human being and one of the best field agents the FBI had ever seen. Perhaps, worst of all, Lee's mother, who was ill, unhealthy and elderly had lost her daughter, her caretaker, her only family. Her young, vibrant daughter had passed from this world before she did. Ryan knew she would have to be permanently placed in a long-term care facility now, rather than temporarily during the times Whitney was away. Ryan knew the elderly woman's health would decline even faster now due to the stress of losing her daughter.

Bringing his bike to a halt, Ryan killed the ignition. For a few seconds he didn't move but remained seated on the motorcycle. He pulled off his helmet and held it on his lap. The vibrant sounds of the city filled his ears. Within a moment, his senses picked up on another sound. Laughter. It undeniably came from inside the home he was now parked in front of.

Though Ryan didn't think it was possible, his heart sunk even further. He stared through the long window at the front of the house, where he could very clearly see Georgia and Zaya inside. Giggling up a storm, Georgia was furiously running circles around the couch just inside the window. She was shirtless and seemed to be very proud of that fact. With a big smile plastered on her face, Zaya held a very tiny yellow shirt in her grasp and was playfully chasing Georgia around the couch.

In that moment, Ryan reached to turn the motorcycle's ignition back on. He couldn't do it. There was no way he could do this. No way. Pulling his hand away from the key, Ryan arched his neck and looked up into the sky. Yet, he had to. Somehow, someway he had to deliver the grave news that would destroy their world.

On unsteady legs, Ryan pulled himself away from the bike and made his way to the front door of the house. His heart and head were pounding. Time seemed to drag on. An eternity seemed to pass by from the time he stepped away from the bike to the time he stood in front of the door. The arm he raised up to the door felt extremely heavy. Ryan moved his wrist to knock on the door, but his hand stopped millimeters short of the white door. Taking a deep breath, he tried to block out the sound of laughter and utter happiness coming from the other side of the door. Ryan could feel himself shaking, a shaking that coursed through every layer of his body.

Finally, he went for it, giving the door three hard knocks.

"One second," came Zaya's reply from inside.

Ryan blinked hard, shook out his arms, and stood up even straighter. He had to be strong, or at least look like he was. Ryan could feel the young woman's eyes peering through the peephole, while he kept his own eyes locked on the top right-hand corner of the door. He heard the door being unlocked and it then flew open.

"Ryan, what's wrong?"

Instant concern was written all over Zaya's face. Ryan gulped. He sure hadn't done a good job hiding his pain and distress. It must have been written all over his face. He made eye contact with Zaya then immediately looked away.

"Zaya…" he managed, keeping his eyes on the ground.

"Ryan, you're scaring me. You don't look good? What happened?"

Ryan turned his focus back to the petite woman standing in the doorway and placed an arm on her shoulder then gazed into her eyes. Zaya's pleading eyes surveyed Ryan's face. He could only imagine the countless thoughts going through her head.

"Zaya, I…I don't even know how to-how to say this. I…you…Allen, he…he was…Director Felix called me this morning…"

Zaya was already shaking her head, her eyes remained locked on Ryan's face.

"Allen was found dead this morning. He passed away last night. I am so, so sorry, Zaya. I don't have the words to say how sorry I am."

"No...NO!" she screamed, shrugging Ryan's hand off her shoulder and taking two quick steps back.

Ryan stepped toward her. There was a crazed look in her eyes. She was trembling now as she stared at the floor. Out of the corner of his eye, Ryan could see Georgia slowly inching her way toward her mother and knew that the little girl could sense something was very, very wrong. Ryan's heart ached. It felt as though it were being torn in two.

"Mommy, what's wrong?"

Georgia trotted over and hugged her mother's leg. That is when Zaya really lost it. She began to sob uncontrollably. Pulling away from her mother, Georgia too began to cry.

"Liar!" Zaya cried. "You're lying!"

Ryan shook his head solemnly, keeping his eyes low.

The sobs grew louder and louder.

"NO! NO!" Zaya cried. "This...There is no way...Why...NO!"

Unsure what to do, not knowing what to say, Ryan stepped forward and attempted to pull Zaya into a hug.

I'm so sorr..." he began.

Before he could finish his sentence, Zaya relentlessly began to throw wild punches at Ryan' chest, landing a good number of them before he was able to put his arms tightly around her to stop her. Immediately she threw herself away from Ryan's embrace.

"Get out…" her voice was softer this time. "Please."

Ryan took a step toward Zaya. "Zaya, I am so sorry…"

That was a mistake.

"GET OUT! I said, LEAVE, Ryan! GO! Allen had so much life to live! YOU sent him out there! YOU KNEW it wasn't safe! YOU did this, Ryan! LEAVE!"

Ryan's heart shattered into a million pieces. He stood there dumbstruck, unable to speak, unable to move. He slowly shook his head from side to side. He knew he couldn't leave her like this.

I'm so sorry, Zaya.

"Please, just go, Ryan," Zaya said in a hushed, lifeless tone.

Ryan turned his back to the two girls. What more could he do or say? He stepped outside and placed his hand on the doorknob.

"We love you, Zaya. Please know that I and Laura are always here for you and for Georgia. *Always.*"

Ryan pulled the door closed and walked away. Once he returned to his bike, the sobs and screams from inside the house picked up again. Ryan wanted to crawl into a hole. He wished for nothing other than to get out of this mess he was in right now. He wished for nothing else but to have Allen and Whitney alive, and to mend Zaya and Georgia's broken hearts. Ryan stepped onto his bike. His day and its heartache were far from over. Now he had to figure out if there was any possible way to break the news in a better way to Whitney Lee's mother than he did to Zaya; however, deep down, he knew there simply wasn't a better way. No more than a half an hour later, Lee's mother would throw her frail arms around Ryan's waist and sob until she no longer had the energy left to cry.

CHAPTER TWENTY-SIX

Just like a scene from a movie, rain poured from the ominous black sky above. Not a single ray of sunlight escaped dark, heavy clouds that blanketed the sky. Moments before the funeral services began, the rain suddenly fell from the sky as if a giant bucket of water was being poured over all of New York City. There was no thunder, no lightning, just an onslaught of rain. People were instantly soaked; however, no one even cared or seemed to notice. They were all numb. Even those who weren't close to Whitney Lee and Allen Simmons were numb, standing in silence with the others, rain sticking their clothes to their bodies and rolling down their faces.

It was a depressing, solemn event, and the rain wasn't helping the cause. The ceremony was enormous. Not even half of the attendees were able to fit in the cathedral for the first half of the ceremony. Now, at the burial, the numbers really showed. People covered the Calvary cemetery grounds to pay their respects. The crowd included family and friends of Allen Simmons and Zaya, Whitney Lee's sweet mother, countless members of the FBI, local law enforcement, members of the armed forces who took part in the services, local New Yorkers, and various representatives and journalists from the different news outlets. The funeral was being streamed throughout the nation. Ryan didn't necessarily understand why, nor did he like it, but it was happening. He knew they could've fought it but what would it have mattered anyway? The media circus was a battle that was impossible to win.

On the positive side, viewers across the nation could see the devastation The Crucifier was causing, realize how dangerous this killer really was, and understand the true fear surrounding the things that were going on. Not only were good, innocent men and women being brutally murdered; the people who were supposed to keep the country safe were being killed too. It could make more people aware of the dire situation, and possibly open up more eyes to the severity of the issue, though Ryan didn't really buy into that narrative, though. Felix didn't either. This Crucifier character was performing these killings flawlessly. The country had been on the lookout and had already been aware, yet the murders continued. This wasn't going to change matters. If anything, based on Ryan's experience with serial killers, a televised event was exactly what the killer wanted. Publicity. Fame. Nation-wide fear.

As Ryan helped carry Lee's casket through the thick crowd of people, he squinted as a sudden gust of wind blew an onslaught of freezing drops of rain into his face. His black dress shirt was plastered to his skin and his pants were suctioned to his legs and felt incredibly heavy. Water sloshed around in his shoes with every step he took. In front of Ryan walked Kuron, also carrying the casket. Ryan's insides hurt. Pain had reached his inner spirit. Not just because *he* had lost two agents he cared about, but his heart and spirit ached for their families. His heart especially ached for Zaya, the sweet, young, and now single mother. Her life had been shattered all because of Ryan's choice to send Simmons after The Crucifier. All because a psychopath wanted Simmons dead. Though he knew he shouldn't, Ryan kept blaming himself, as his thoughts kept returning to Zaya.

She and Georgia had looked so distraught during the services in the big cathedral. Tears streamed tirelessly down their pale faces. Now realizing what was going on, Georgia's little heart was absolutely broken too. Throughout the memorial, her cries echoed off the walls of the old building.

Both caskets were simultaneously lowered into the ground while the traditional "taps" was played. The sound of the trumpet could only faintly be heard through the pouring rain. Ryan stood with his hands behind his back, his face down. On the other side of the open grave stood Zaya. She wasn't crying anymore but stood there emotionless. Lifeless. She looked like a dead woman walking. Her pale face stared on as her boyfriend's casket was slowly lowered into the cold, wet ground. A man dressed in military uniform held an umbrella over her head.

Georgia was nowhere to be found. Ryan guessed maybe Zaya's mother was keeping her out of the rain, and away from this depressing scene. The ceremony inside the cathedral had probably been more than enough for little Georgia.

Ryan avoided Zaya's eyes. He did everything he could to keep from making eye contact with her. He had tried comforting her inside the church, but she gave him the cold shoulder, not even letting Georgia talk to him. "Just give her space," Laura had told Ryan.

So, he had done just that. As the graves were finally covered with dirt, and the two fresh mounds of dirt were covered with mountains of flowers, the crowd began to disperse. Ryan, Kuron, and military members around him remained stationary as Zaya walked by, holding an umbrella over her head. Many patted her on the back or grasped her hand. Ryan glanced up as Zaya passed by. As Ryan had anticipated, she passed right by him without any sort of acknowledgement, completely avoiding Ryan's eyes. She gave Kuron a half hug, then started to continue down the line back toward the street where her car was awaiting. Then Zaya stopped abruptly and although her back was turned to him, Ryan could see that she was crying, as her shoulders heaved up and down. Zaya's arm then dropped to her side and the umbrella fell from her grasp.

Suddenly, and to Ryan's utter surprise, Zaya spun around and threw herself into Ryan, throwing her arms around him. In shock, Ryan tentatively embraced her, not exactly knowing what to do or say. Zaya's long, beautiful hair was drenched, and it clung to her back and shoulders. Her makeup had mixed with rain and tears, creating dark streaks that ran down her cheeks.

"I'm so sorry," she cried out with her head on Ryan's chest, "I'm so sorry, Ryan. I have been so…"

"Shh…stop. Stop, Zaya. It's okay. You have nothing to apologize for. It's okay."

Finally returning her embrace, Ryan didn't know what else to say, or how to comfort her. He wanted to apologize again, to tell her how heartbroken he was, how much he was hurting for her, how he blamed himself. He thought against it, though. Instead, they just stood there in the deafening rainstorm, next to Allen Simmons' grave while Zaya continued to sob. The crowd continued to disperse little by little. Soon, very few people remained. After what seemed like eternity, Zaya lifted her head slightly and kept one arm around Ryan.

"Can you walk me to the car?" she asked.

Ryan gave her a nod. "Of course."

With his arm around Zaya's shoulders, and Zaya's head on his chest, the two slowly made their way to the awaiting limo where Ryan also guessed they'd find Zaya's mother and little Georgia. Zaya's soft sobs continued. Her tears soaked Ryan's shirt, though he couldn't distinguish her tears from the rain that had already drenched him.

Once they reached the limo, Ryan opened up the car door and Zaya stepped inside. With her head low, she thanked Ryan. He nodded then pushed the door shut. He watched the car as it started down the crowded street. He felt a strong hand rest upon his shoulder and looked to his left to see Kuron, who gave him a solemn smile. Then, together the two watched the limo proceed on down the road until it was completely out of sight.

CHAPTER TWENTY-SEVEN

It was five o'clock in the morning when Ryan's cell phone rang. He knew the call was from one of three people. A toll-free call, John, or Director Felix. Picking up the phone from the right arm of the recliner he was sprawled out in, Ryan instantly saw who it was.

Felix.

With his other hand, Ryan used the television remote to pause the early morning news playing on the Fox News Network.

Phone in hand, Ryan stretched his arms over his head, and answered the call.

"Good morning, Mr. Felix."

"Ryan, good morning to you too. How are you this day?"

Ryan shrugged. "I'm doing okay, and you?"

"All things considered," Felix said, "I'm doing okay as well. Hanging in there."

Ryan didn't reply for a few moments, letting Felix have a chance to continue; however, he didn't.

"So," Ryan began, "what's going on? What's on your mind?"

"Oof, what's on my mind? That's quite the loaded question there, don't you think, Ryan?"

Ryan chuckled slightly. "You've got a good point. Sorry about that."

Felix laughed. "Well, there's most certainly a lot of my mind right now, as you can imagine. That said, it would take all day for me to tell you everything that is running through my mind right now. We don't have all day. So, to save you from that madness, I'll just give you the primary reason I called."

Ryan said nothing, allowing Director Felix to continue.

"We need you again. We need you in the field."

Ryan again said nothing.

"This may or may not be a surprise to you. You may have expected it even. Who knows? What I do know is that we need you. As soon as my meeting at the Pentagon wrapped up and my mind returned to reality, I knew I had to tell you. Ryan, I know we have to put you on this case. I honestly don't like the thought of it. I truly hate to do it, yet I know it's a must. It's what my gut feeling is telling me, and from what I've seen throughout my life, it's always in my best interest to follow that feeling."

Ryan bit the inside of his cheek, nodding as Felix spoke.

"Okay," he replied.

Part of him had known this would be coming. Part of him had been anticipating this very conversation ever since the deaths of Simmons and Lee. He knew he needed to do this.

"Are you okay with that? I know I'm *the* Director of the FBI and have a certain amount of power over you. I know I technically have the right to tell you to do this without caring too much about what you think…but I don't want that, because I do care what you think. Tell me what's going through your mind. Are you okay with getting thrown back into the field?"

Ryan thought about what Felix had just said. One thing he loved and respected about Felix was that he truly cared about those he led. Whether you were the Head of the Bureau, one of his top agents, or a custodian, he cared about you.

Ryan sunk into his chair and leaned back, staring up at the ceiling. He let himself think for a few moments. Felix waited patiently, giving Ryan as much time as he needed.

"You're right," he said finally. "I need to do this. I was actually anticipating this very conversation. This new position, this new lifestyle…it's been great. It really has been. I loved being a field agent, Mr. Felix. The adrenaline, the ability to truly make a direct difference on so many lives every single day, the ability to bring down serial killers like this, to crack cases. I lived for it. The satisfaction from succeeding in a case, bringing down such horrible people, is an incomparable thing. *Nothing* compares to it. There is nothing, nothing at all, that I would have rather been doing. I didn't care about what I was investigating, who I was chasing down, or how dangerous the situations I would put myself into. Not only did I personally enjoy the thrill of it all, but I was good. I've never been one to have a big head, but I was good at my job.

"Now, I say all this speaking in past-tense because it *was* the past. That was a different me. I don't say that from an ability or a skills standpoint, but from a personal-life standpoint. I was single, with absolutely no one tied to me. I think that is part of what made me so successful. I had nothing to lose. I sure do now. In a way, I have baggage. I don't mean that in a bad way at all, but there are people I love dearly. People in my life that mean more than anything to me. People I have already put in danger due to this sort of work. Even in the position I'm in now, there's that worry in the back of my mind. The worry that some past enemy will come back and exploit my most significant, maybe my only weakness. Those I love. Caine nearly broke me. For a while there, he had taken everything from me. *Everything.* I have so much to lose right now, and I don't know if that makes me a better or worse agent, but it's true.

"That's what's going through my mind. That's what's been going through my mind ever since we lost Allen and Whitney. This Crucifier is dangerous. He's a professional. In that sense, he reminds of Caine. It honestly scares me a little. But only just a little. Seeing how torn up Zaya is now, and even how torn up Whitney's mother is, is hard for me. I just don't want my family or myself to go through that. I know this is the small selfish side of me speaking, but again, this is what has been circulating through my mind."

Felix seemed to take a second to absorb everything Ryan had just said.

"Ryan, I understand…I understand completely. Now if you don't want…"

"Wait, before you go on. I *am* taking this case. You asked what was on my mind, so I gave it to you. Regardless, I *am* taking this case, and I will find this guy. One way or another, I'll find him. This is the other half of what I have been thinking. I *want* this. I acknowledge what I've been able to accomplish in the past. I've dealt with men and women just as psychotic and complicated as this Crucifier character. Just about as unpredictable. Just as dangerous. I can find him. I promise you that. I haven't been out of the field that long. I should be more than fine. I do want you to know that I'm all in."

"Hmm," Felix said thoughtfully.

Ryan could picture a pleased grin on Felix's face. The tone in his voice signaled it. Ryan had seen and heard it in person plenty of times. In the distance, through the wall behind him, came the sound of a crying baby. The cries were followed by the sound of a second baby crying. Ryan could hear Laura get up from their bed. He then heard the unique patter of Tripod's three little paws racing down the hallway.

Ryan smiled. Tripod still slept snuggly against Kayleen at night but was always very keenly attuned to Ben and Titus, and *very* protective of them. Every time either of them cried, little Tripod would come running to the rescue.

To get away from the chaos, Ryan rose from his seat and began to walk toward the front door.

"Just knowing you," Felix began as Ryan opened the front door, "I'm guessing that you've already, in one way or form, started to look even *more* in depth into this case. I would guess you've been doing some digging."

Ryan closed the door behind him and sat down on the top step of the steps leading up to the porch.

"You got me there," he said.

"I Figured. What have you found?"

"I meant to tell you earlier, but with everything going on it just slipped my mind, but I believe this Crucifier could be a copycat killer. There was the exact murder scene years ago in Berlin, Germany. Spitting image. I got in touch with a reporter from there named Godfrey Hackett. Good guy. He gave me a little bit of info and said he would get me in contact with the head detective who worked the case, a Detective Dobson. Hopefully I'll hear from him soon. Other than that, and what we already knew from before, that's all I've got."

"All you've got? Sounds pretty good to me. Let me know when you get in touch with Dobson and if you find out anything more from him."

"I will."

"Well, Ryan, sounds good. Are you going to need a partner on this case? I plan to pretty much stay out of your way on this one. I trust you, but I do recommend you have someone with you this time around."

Ryan pursed his lips. He knew the question was coming.

"John." Ryan simply stated. "I think I want to take John with me."

"Good choice. He called me last night practically begging me to convince his older brother to put him on this case."

Ryan couldn't hold back the smile creeping across his face.

John, John, John…

"Of course, he did," Ryan muttered.

"He's a great guy, Ryan. Even if he wasn't your brother, I'd be telling you the same thing. He's a talented kid."

"He's okay, I guess."

Felix chuckled. "Well, let me know the gameplan when you have it. Thank you for this."

"Of course," Ryan replied.

"Welcome back, Agent Turner."

CHAPTER TWENTY-EIGHT

The instant the call ended; Ryan's mind began to work at an uncontrollable speed. Thoughts, plans, and ideas poured into his mind like an unexpected hurricane. Now was a matter of reeling them all in, pulling them together.

Countless questions of what, why, when, where, how, who flooded his thoughts, racking his brain.

Just think. Pull it all in.

The sun still hadn't begun to rise in the East. The air was cool. Not cold, but cool. Ryan cupped his chin in his hands and gazed up at the few twinkling stars in the New York City sky. He breathed in the cool June air. It was his favorite time of the year. The treasured the early June mornings. The temperature was always *perfect.*

Every morning, Ryan loved to do exactly what he doing what he was doing in this very moment: just sitting on the steps in front of the house. Thinking. Pondering. Taking in the oddly peaceful feeling of the city, as compared to the cacophony that occurs throughout most of the day in the Big Apple. Very few cars would ever drive by. Very few people would ever stroll by. It was peaceful. It was calming. Therapeutic.

Ryan closed his eyes. Six…almost seven months. Almost seven months since the Crucifer's first hit on Tina Rington. Then for months on end he was quiet…aside from the deaths of investigators, officers, and agents that heavily pursued the case. Now chaos. Utter and complete chaos.

And still, after two more crucifixions and the funerals of two FBI agents, the Bureau had nothing. Simmons and Lee's deaths had been in vain. While their families mourned, the killer still roamed free, with no one able to track him down.

An old rusty pickup truck rattled on by, interrupting Ryan's thoughts. He turned his attention toward the loud vehicle and waved at the plump old man behind the wheel. Wearing a classy flat cap atop his head, the old man gave a nod and a wave in return, while smiling and showing a not-so-full set of teeth. Ryan sighed as he rose to his feet. Placing his hands on his hips, he arched his back to stretch. A few pops and crackles erupted down his spine.

Opening the front door, Ryan was immediately hit by the screams of his two newborn sons. He cringed slightly but smiled at the same time. Though already loud and difficult, he loved them. He decided he better offer Laura a helping hand to avoid spending time in the dog house in the near future. Although kicking back and watching Sportscenter sounded much more appealing at the moment, he knew being in Laura's good graces was far more important.

He strolled by the living room. As he did, he glanced over the back of the couch to see Kayleen curled up in a ball, with a little white blanket pulled over her head.

"Good morning, Sunshine," Ryan said, reaching over the couch and playfully shaking Kayleen.

Kayleen gave a long, drawn-out groan.

"And what's wrong with you?"

Head still covered by the blanket, Kayleen answered, "Sometimes I wish my ears were broken."

Ryan chuckled. "You what?"

"Sometimes. I wish. My ears. Were broken." Kayleen said in an annoyed, frustrated tone. "If they were broken, they wouldn't work. If they didn't work, I couldn't hear the babies crying. If I couldn't hear the babies crying, I could actually sleep."

Ryan shook his head, grinning. "You have really thought this out, haven't you?"

"Mhm," Kayleen replied in a dull tone.

"Well, try to get some sleep, Kay," Ryan said, continuing on his way toward his bedroom.

"Trust me, it isn't because I'm not trying," Kayleen chimed in under her breath, but just loud enough for Ryan to overhear her.

Ryan strolled into his bedroom to find Laura standing between the bed and the cradle, holding a baby in each arm.

"So, which of the two has distinguished himself as the loudest screamer?"

Laura looked at Ryan, frazzled and exhausted. "It's a *really* tight race right now."

Ryan approached his wife and gingerly took Titus from her right arm. Both babies were still crying and fussing, so there was no "good choice" when it came to that. He sat at the foot of the king-sized bed, rocking Titus side to side.

"Shhh," Ryan whispered softly. "Shhh."

As he comforted Titus, Laura pulled herself into bed and began to feed Benjamin, who immediately quieted down and seemed very pleased with the chance to nurse. Slowly, but surely, Titus too quieted down. After about ten minutes or so, Ryan and Laura exchanged babies, so Titus could get the chance to nurse. Ryan gently took Ben from Laura and cradled the sleeping boy in his arms. He was sound asleep and Ryan hoped to keep it that way. As incredibly loud as the two had been not too long before, Ben and Titus now looked as peaceful as can be. Ryan grinned as he looked down at Ben. Oh, how he loved being a dad.

"So, what's on Ryan Turner's agenda for the day?" Laura asked quietly.

"Honestly, I'm not sure. Here in a while, though, can you and I go out?"

"I mean, sure. If we can? Where are you wanting to go?"

"I just want some time for the two of us, where we can talk, spend some time together"

"Is this about work? Or what's going on?"

Laura didn't say a word, but by the look in her eyes and her body language, Ryan knew that she knew it was about work. She just wanted him to say it. So, he did.

"Yeah, it has to do with work."

"Okay, we'll see what we can do."

Ryan knew she wanted to say more. Looking into her eyes, he could see the wheels were turning in her head. He could tell she wanted to press him and ask more questions, but she never did. She left it at that. Instead, they sat, mostly in silence, until both Ben and Titus were sound asleep.

CHAPTER TWENTY-NINE

At the exact moment that Laura and Ryan exited their home to take a drive, Jack Grimes too stepped out of his home and into the New York City streets. It was precisely 8:30 a.m. He had just wrapped up his daily morning routine. Wake up at *exactly* 5:20 a.m. Eat breakfast at 5:30. Watch the news at 5:45. Take a shower from exactly 6:15 to 6:22. Write in his journal from 6:30 to 6:40. From 6:45 to 7:30, he would read either the newspaper or a book of his choosing. He'd then quickly put away his book or newspaper, rush down to his basement, and starting at *exactly* 7:33, he would sit on the floor in the middle of the dark basement. He sat in the same spot every day. It was marked with a smiley face that had been drawn with red spray paint. On that mark, *every* single morning, he would sit and meditate, until the clock hit exactly 8:15. It was his favorite time of the day. A time for just him and his thoughts. A time for him and his spirit. It was during that time that many of his ideas would come to him, whether it was what to do for the day, or a new idea for an art project.

Then, once the time was up, he would leave the basement, walk to the kitchen where he would feed his cat named Picasso, and then prepare to go out for the day. Once dressed for whatever the weather conditions were that day, Grimes would stand as close to the front door as possible, his nose just barely touching the wooden door, and wait until the clock in his head hit exactly 8:30, which would give him the "okay" to open the door and head out for the day.

As scripted and repetitive as his mornings were, this particular morning was a little different. It would be like no other morning that he had ever experienced before. For this very reason he was excited. Very excited. Thrilled even. His heart rate was always at 57 or 58 beats per minute. *Always.* He made sure it was. Grimes was never stressed. He never felt the sensation of fear. It didn't exist to him. Rarely did he feel excitement or anticipation. However, today he felt excited. Anxious. It was a feeling he wasn't very familiar with. It wasn't ordinary; thus, he usually tried to stay away from the feeling, but today was different. As he walked, he measured his heart rate.

70 beats per minute...too high.

It wasn't the usual; therefore, it wasn't good. As Grimes walked, he did everything he could, every breathing technique, every strategy he could think of to lower his heart rate. After fifteen minutes of walking, it was down to 60 beats. Not good enough for his liking, but it would work for today. He would work on controlling his heart rate later tonight when he returned to his basement to meditate. For now, 60 would have to do.

As he made his way to Battery Park, he took in the refreshing air. It was a beautiful day. Absolutely beautiful. This was his favorite time of the year. Step-by-step, he kept the same beat with every pace. Always the same. Never different. Each stride was three-quarters of a yard long. Twenty-seven inches. No more, no less. Sometimes it was hard to keep this pace with exactness, given that so many of the streets were so packed with people, but he almost always found a way. No one in New York City was courteous. It was every man for himself. He was no different. If he ran into people, that was fine. Keeping his paces the same length was more important than irritating a fellow New Yorker.

Jack Grimes's internal clock read 8:50 a.m.

Ten more minutes...

Eight more minutes until he reached his favorite bench at Battery Park. It sat right near the docks in front of two large trees and some little green bushes. In his opinion, it was the best view of the Statue of Liberty from Battery Park. Without actually going to see Lady Liberty by boat, this was the best view available. He loved Lady Liberty. Ever since he was a child, he had always been fascinated by her. His father took him to see the magnificent monument when he was only eight years old. It was a whole decade and a half back, yet it seemed like forever ago. His mind began to travel back in time. Memories of him and his father filled his thoughts. Some good but most of them bad. He shuddered at many of the thoughts.

Always replace the bad memories with good ones. Destroy the bad.

It was advice from his old therapist. The only advice of hers that he had ever truly appreciated. He hadn't seen her in four years, and he didn't miss her, but he did appreciate those two sentences of advice, and he now lived by those words. It took him one exhausting session of meditation a few months ago to realize the importance of her advice. It took him almost four years to fully grasp the idea and live by it. Way too much time for his liking. But better late than never.

He wished more people were like Lady Liberty. She was elegant. Beautiful. She stood for so much by doing so little. Most of all, she was unchanging. Always the same. She was predictable and he appreciated that.

He could see her now in the hazy distance. Tall. Strong. Elegant. He could see a ferry heading in her direction now. Almost to her. He had been on that very boat less than twenty-four hours earlier. Little black specks of people covered Liberty Island.

8:55 a.m.

On the dot. His mind never skipped a beat. He never wore a watch. Never carried a phone. Didn't have one. Didn't need one.

Grimes could see his bench now. An old woman sat upon it, but there was still room for him. She wore a big floppy hat to shade her face. She appeared to be throwing something on the ground. Maybe feeding the birds. He hated to have company. He wasn't one for conversation. He hoped she wouldn't bother him.

8:56 a.m...one minute until he reached the bench. Four minutes to go...

CHAPTER THIRTY

Ryan squeezed Laura's hand gently. They walked hand in hand, as they moved away from Ryan's parked Harley Davidson. It was 8:56 a.m.

They approached the nearest unoccupied bench in Battery Park. The closest bench to them was occupied by an elderly woman. She wore a floppy hat and looked to be feeding birds. Parallel to Laura and Ryan was a man walking with very odd, precise, almost robotic movements, who also looked to be making his way toward the bench where the old woman sat. Thirty yards farther down was an unoccupied bench. A rare sight in New York City. It was the one they were headed for.

"Gosh, it's a beautiful morning, Ryan."

"Isn't it?" Ryan replied.

"The air feels just so, I don't know, *fresh*. I cant describe it, but I love it."

Ryan smiled. "I know what you mean."

"We've always loved coming here," Laura said, as they arrived at the bench and sat down. "It's hectic around here, yet peaceful. Cluttered, yet beautiful."

"We sure have. Lots of deep conversations have taken place here."

Ryan immediately tried to swallow his words as they slipped out of his mouth, but he was unsuccessful. They had already escaped. He knew Laura had been talking just to talk. She wanted to avoid the inevitable conversation that was soon to come. She didn't know what Ryan was about to tell her exactly; however, she could always sense when something was awry. She had a sense for it. This time around was no different.

The moment the words left Ryan's mouth, Laura looked out into the distance and with a long sigh, blew out a long breath. She rested her elbows on her thighs and her head in her hands. For what felt like eternity, the two didn't say a word. Ryan didn't know how to bring it up. Countless times he had mentally rehearsed what to say. In the end, he knew there was no good way to say it, yet that didn't make it any easier.

They listened to the chattering all around them, and the constant sound of car horns blaring obnoxiously throughout the city streets. The lady with the floppy hat walked by. She was muttering incomprehensible nonsense. She appeared to be having a full-blown conversation with herself.

It was now 8:58 a.m.

"Why are we here, Ryan? Just let it out. I know it has to do with work…and it kills me to know that. Especially with the way you're acting. Just be straight up with me. Whatever it is, I can take it. Okay? It's okay. It's fine."

But it wasn't okay. It wasn't fine. Laura was rambling. She was speaking so quickly that her words sounded like they were all jumbled up into one big run-on sentence. Ryan could read her moods like a book. He almost always could. And it was obvious she was already upset.

He placed a hand on her thigh. "I'm going back into the field."

"Is it The Crucifier case?"

She knew. It was that extra sensory perception of hers.

Ryan nodded slowly, looking into his wife's deep blue eyes. "Yeah, The Crucifier case."

Laura was shaking her head. Not the blatant, hard, aggressive head shake, but the subtle kind where it was noticeable if you were up close and paying attention. And Ryan was.

"I'm so sorry," Ryan said. "I know we thought that the life of being out there, that the thrill, the danger, all of it was over. I was sure it was. But things just happen. It sucks, but things do happen. They need me. This whole deal is getting out of hand. Allen and Whitney lost their lives. The Bureau lost two wonderful agents. I lost two friends. It's just...I don't-I don't know. I talked to Director Felix. We agreed this was the best route to take. I *have* to find this guy, Laura. I *have* to."

Laura nodded her head slowly. The same subtle, hardly noticeable kind of movement.

"I understand," she said. There was very little emotion behind her voice. "Just tell me, Ryan," she said taking his right hand in both of hers, "why are you *really* doing this? Why are you *really* putting yourself on this case? I mean, gosh, there must be other options. There *are* other options. Plus, I know Director Felix wouldn't demand that you be on the case. He wouldn't give you a 'my way or the highway' ultimatum. I know him well enough to know that."

"I do, honestly, believe that this is a now or never situation. Two of our best agents were killed just because they were on the case. I can't afford to lose anyone else. I truly have to do…"

"And do you think *I* can afford to lose *you*? Because I can't. Everything is *finally* coming together for us, Ryan. Our lives are *finally* 'normal', whatever 'normal' means. We have two new baby boys. We have a family. You're a husband. You're a father. I'm not naïve. You talk to me here and there about particular cases and about work. I know the horrific things that have gone on surrounding The Crucifier case. I'm just…" Her voice cracked. She took a deep breath. "I'm just scared. Also, I know that isn't the only reason. One, you blame yourself for what happened. And two, I know you miss being out there too. I know it."

She wasn't wrong.

Tears were forming in her eyes. She was avoiding eye contact now, but Ryan had already seen the tears welling up in her eyes. He hated to see her cry. It was one of the absolute worst feelings. Seeing her cry tore at his chest. He wrapped an arm around her and pulled her close.

"I get it…I really do. And I really don't want to put myself back out there. I promise. Yet, I…"

Unknown to Ryan, Laura, and the majority of people in Battery Park, the clock hit 9 a.m. The moment the clock turned to nine, Ryan's sentence was cut short. His and

Laura's entire conversation was cut short. For a split second, Battery Park became silent.

Ryan saw it before he heard it. It was far enough away for the sight of what had happened and the sound not to occur in unison. Just below Lady Liberty, a ball of flame suddenly appeared. Sudden and intense. A dark, fierce cloud of smoke and debris leapt into the sky. A split second later came the resulting sound of the massive explosion. Ryan didn't know if it was in his head, but the ground seemed to shake beneath him. His eyes were locked on the burning scene near Liberty Island. Screams erupted all around him. Laura's hands fell from his.

Ryan stood to his feet.

This isn't good...

CHAPTER THIRTY-ONE

Chaos erupted all around him. People were screaming, pulling out their phones and cameras, running away from the park, shielding their eyes, running up as close to the water as possible and hanging over the rails to get a better look at the horrific scene. Horrific in many of their eyes, yet beautiful in those of Jack Grimes. He smiled. He watched on for as long as he could until a whole swarm of people flooded his view. He was fine with it. He saw what he needed to. He got the thrill. And through it all, his heart rate didn't exceed 60 BPM. It didn't go below it but didn't exceed it either. Not good enough. But good enough for today. Tomorrow would be better.

He stood to his feet. Slowly. Confidently. Smugly. A lingering smirk hung on his face. He couldn't help it. Emotion wasn't a common thing to him, so it was an odd feeling. He felt an almost overwhelming excitement. A satisfaction, even.

The people around him, mostly brainless tourists, fascinated him. The diversity of them all, particularly in the ways they reacted was fascinating. Many were scared yet awestruck. Enthralled even. Many were in absolute terror and didn't know what to do other than start running as far away from the scene as possible, which was amusing to Grimes given that the burning scene was clear far from them by Liberty Island. Many wanted to get the scene on camera, or on a livestream through whatever gosh-awful social media app was currently in vogue. Grimes never got into social media. He never liked it. Never liked the thought of it.

It was pointless to him. Grimes took one last good look at the inferno that was already slowly dying. There was little to nothing left of the ferry and the people that were on it.

Always replace the bad memories with good ones. Destroy the bad.

He had done just that. He was excited. Satisfied, even. Feelings he wasn't used to. He liked the feelings enough to let them linger for a bit, before pushing them out. Grimes looked up at the sky, closed his eyes, and rolled his neck from side to side. It popped a few times. He breathed in as deeply as he could, then let it all out in one big *WHOOSH*. He turned 90 degrees to his right and one step at a time, each pace being precisely twenty-seven inches long, he walked back home.

9:10 a.m.

His work was done.

CHAPTER THIRTY-TWO

Ryan's blood pumped fiercely through his veins. He could feel the blood pounding behind his ears. He had originally thought about waiting for local law enforcement to show up, but the moment Laura took a cab to leave, Ryan abandoned the thought. Just as the cab holding Laura sped away, a small Bowrider pulled up to the dock where previously excited people had been boarding a ferry to go visit Liberty Island. The people weren't as excited now. Many had run off the ferry, some stayed to stare awestricken at the scene. The little Bowrider pulled as close as it could next to the ferry and the dock, and two young men quickly tied their boat off a wooden beam that held up the dock. Then they swiftly climbed onto the deck.

Their eyes were wide with fear. They had come racing across the waters from the direction of the explosion. They must have been close to it. It was no wonder they looked so frightened.

The two men appeared to be Korean. When they started blabbering to each other and anyone around, Ryan was able to determine that they were in fact Korean. South or North, he didn't know, but he was able to recognize the dialect.

Ryan approached them.

"Excuse me, excuse me," he said, placing a hand on the shoulder of the shorter of the two.

The small man spun around. He stared at Ryan yet said nothing.

"My name is Ryan. I need to use your boat. I work for the FBI."

The man stared at Ryan with a blank expression on his face.

He doesn't understand me.

"Do you understand me?"

"No English," the man said, slowly shrugging Ryan's hand off of his shoulder.

Ryan pulled out his cell phone while putting a finger up, signaling the man to hold on. Thank goodness that was a universal signal. The man waited impatiently, his eyes darting back and forth from Ryan to what was left of the wreckage in the water.

Using the phone, Ryan looked up how to ask for the keys to the man's boat. The search ended up being way more complicated than he thought. Instead, he looked up how to say boat in Korean.

"Bo, hapsipsio," Ryan said, as he signified turning a key in the ignition.

The man seemed to maybe understand what Ryan was trying to say. Ryan then pointed to the boat, then to himself and pulled out his FBI badge. He carried it everywhere with him. It was habit. Often times, like now, it came in handy.

The man's eyes raised. He tapped his friend on the shoulder and told him something, then the two of them turned to face Ryan. The man who Ryan hadn't spoken with removed a key from his pocket and handed it to Ryan.

"Gamsa!" Ryan said, thanking the men.

He hoped the men didn't think they were in trouble. It was always hard speaking with people who didn't know English. Although impossible, he knew, he always wished he was able to speak every language there was. How amazing that would be...

Sirens could be heard now. They were getting closer and closer.

Ryan ignored them. They'd be here soon enough. As sick as he already felt, as much as his mind wandered about the things he might see at the scene, he knew he had to go to it. There could be survivors. He just had to see it. He had to be there up close.

He jumped into the Bowrider and unanchored it from the dock. He shoved the key into the ignition, spun the boat around, and as fast as he could, drove directly toward where ferry used to be.

CHAPTER THIRTY-THREE

The scene was every bit as bad as Ryan had imagined. He had encountered many situations like this before but being in the middle of a great body of water made it a little different. Boards, fabric, pieces of hats, shoes, clothing were floating all around him. The water was a nasty mix of red and black. The front end of the ferry was the only major part of the boat left. Triumphant flames danced on top of it. There was not a soul to be seen.

Ryan couldn't believe the destruction. There had to have been multiple explosives set on the boat. A single charge couldn't have taken down a ferry boat like this...unless it was of an extreme capacity and capability. Ryan doubted it, though.

No one had survived. Ryan felt sick to his stomach. Just as he started to imagine the bodies beneath him...what was left of them, he heard a voice. It was close. Faint, weak, but close.

"Is someone there?" Ryan called out.

He could hear the voice again. Ryan guided the boat quickly to the other side of the large piece of ferry that was still left, cursing himself for having not gone around earlier. He had come upon the scene and had been so awestricken by it all, that he honestly thought there was no way any one on that ferry had lived. As he approached the other side of the burning piece of ship, he craned his neck toward where he thought the voice was coming from. There, practically underneath the burning bow of the ship, was a young woman. She was very young: fifteen, maybe sixteen. Her innocent-looking face was horrifically burned. Her left arm was torn to shreds and hung limp in the water. Her right arm was holding tightly onto the side of the bow.

"Help," she was able to manage.

Her entire body shook uncontrollably. The water around her bobbing body was blood-red. The girl's eyes were fluttering open and closed. She was going into shock.

Ryan pulled the boat as close to her as he could, as fast as he could. He reached over into the water and took the girl into his arms. She was small and very petite. One-hundred pounds, *maybe*.

He lifted her out of the water, gingerly yet quickly. His heart stopped. Half of her right leg was missing. It had been blown off just below the knee. Sharp bone stuck out below the knee, along with dangling pieces of skin and meat.

CHAPTER THIRTY-FOUR

Ryan felt sick. If he was inexperienced with seeing this sort of thing, he would've most certainly vomited. It was a horrific scene.

With little help from the dying girl, Ryan pulled her out of the water and into the boat. His heart was racing. She was losing blood fast. It was nothing short of a miracle that she hadn't bled out yet. Her left leg was torn up pretty viciously as well. Her clothes from head to toe, were burnt and torn apart.

"It's going to be okay, alright?" Ryan told the girl. "Hang in there, kid. Hang in there!"

Her eyelids were no longer fluttering open and closed. She was still as a stone. Her drenched little body lay up against the side of the boat, her chin resting on her chest. She still had a pulse. For now. Ryan knew that wasn't going to be the case for much longer. She was fading fast.

Ryan pushed the boat as fast as he could over to the docks he had just left moments before. The boat was fast, and the distance wasn't much. Within a mere thirty seconds, Ryan had pulled up to the dock. Ambulances and police cars were already on the scene. Ryan was the one who called them. He assumed others had to have called in as well. They arrived fast. He was impressed.

Yelling for help, Ryan tied off the boat to the dock as fast as he could. Two paramedics were suddenly at

Ryan's side, carefully lifting the girl out of the boat. The remaining pedestrians who were sticking around all seemed to gasp at once at the sight of the girl.

Ryan followed the paramedics, who rushed her to the back of an ambulance.

"She was the only survivor I found," Ryan told the two older men who now had the girl in the back of the ambulance.

They both looked to be well over sixty. Their hair was as gray as could be without being white. One of the two was kind of plump and had big sunken eyes. He couldn't be more than an inch or two over five feet tall. The other man was tall and thin. He was a few inches taller than Ryan. He had a long face and wore round little glasses on the brim of his nose. The two were quite the pair.

"She has a pulse," Shorty said. "We need to get her to the hospital quick!"

Tall and lanky slammed the back doors shut on Shorty and the girl, then awkwardly ran to the driver's side of the ambulance.

"Thank you, sir!" he called back to Ryan as he jumped into the vehicle and sped off, sirens wailing.

Ryan turned around to find a young, plump woman in a police uniform next to his side. He stuck out a hand to greet her.

"Ryan Turner," he said. "FBI."

"Oh, I already know. Ryan Turner. The man, the myth, the legend. I'm Lieutenant Felicia Strodderbeck. What do you got for me?"

She was strong, commanding, had a good presence, and was straight to the point. Ryan liked her already.

"I was actually here with my wife. I was one of the people to call it in."

"Oof. What a way to ruin a date. Those aren't the sort of fireworks a couple wants to see while out on the town."

"Not at all. We had just arrived. Sat down on a bench. Started talking."

"About?" Strodderbeck asked.

Ryan tried to read her eyes. She wasn't serious.

"Not relevant."

"I know. Carry on."

"Mid-conversation, we see it just before we hear it. An incredible flash coming from Liberty Island, followed by a deafening *BOOM*. This was at exactly 9 a.m. On the dot."

"I see. Nine o'clock exactly. Evidence wise there obviously won't be much to find. Whatever sick mind is responsible for this, sure did the job thoroughly. The only possible real witness we have to anything that happened here is that poor girl that just got hauled off…you didn't see any signs of other survivors?"

Ryan shook his head solemnly. "Nope. Just the girl. The scene is exactly as you can imagine it. As you said, whoever did this was sure thorough. Other than a piece of the ship's bow, and random fabric and pieces of ship floating around, there's nothing left of anything or anyone."

"That girl is a survivor. It's by the grace of God she's alive."

"That's no lie. I just pray she makes it. Hopefully she has some way of leading us in the right direction so we can find out what happened here."

Strodderbeck turned and looked off toward the wreckage, folding her arms across her chest. Little police boats were speeding across the water toward the mess. They wouldn't find anything worthwhile.

"With what we have, which is close to nothing, my best bet is that this is an act of terrorism. Overseas, someone from our own soil, I don't know, nor do I really care. Terrorism is terrorism, murder is murder, and this is quite obviously a sickening example of both."

Ryan looked off at the wreckage too. He nodded, saying nothing.

"Well, Mr. Turner, there's not much else for either of us to see or do here, quite honestly. Not much else to talk about either. Thank you for going out and getting that girl. And thank you for all you do. I'm not just throwing that out there. I mean it."

Her words were sincere. Ryan could tell that she meant every word she spoke.

Ryan nodded. "Of course. And thank you. You all arrived here quick. It was very impressive."

"I'm almost positive that I'll be working closely with this case. To be quite frank, I'll make sure that I do. I already have a few of our detectives in mind that I may pull into this with me as well. That being said, I'm guessing the FBI will be involved too, or am I wrong?"

"No, you're correct. I was just thinking about putting together a team for this one. The more hands, the more departments on this, I think the better. From a leadership standpoint, Mr. Blackston has done a great job with your department. He's a pleasure to work with. I'll definitely get in touch with him."

"He's a good man," the lieutenant seconded. "A little weird but aren't we all? Well, I'm excited to work with whoever you get me. I guess the time is ticking now to put together this wacky puzzle we have here. I'll talk to you later, Mr. Turner."

Strodderbeck stuck out her hand and Ryan shook it. The blonde, stocky lieutenant then spun on her heels and walked away, leaving Ryan standing alone.

To Ryan's left, stood the two Korean men who had graciously turned over their keys. Ryan finally recognized that they were there, a mere ten yards away. Ryan jumped and swiftly walked over to them.

"Joesong haeyo!" Ryan said apologetically.

Both men put their hands up as to say, "It's okay."

Ryan tossed the keys to the one on the left. He thanked them, then walked away in the direction of his Harley. He looked over toward the wreckage one last time. Three police boats were gliding around through the wreck.

There was nothing left to see or do here.

CHAPTER THIRTY-FIVE

Late-night cartoons played on the living room television. Kayleen was asleep on Ryan's lap. Laura sat next to Ryan on the couch, her head resting lightly on his right shoulder.

"She's out cold," Laura said, running her fingers through Kayleen's hair.

Ryan smiled down at Kay. She really was. And she looked *very* comfortable too. She was a little angel on earth.

"She must've had a long day," Ryan said.

"She sure did. She found out her dad is leaving tomorrow, and she doesn't know when she'll see him again. I'd say that takes a lot out of a little girl."

Ryan couldn't argue that. She was right. Kayleen wasn't stupid. She always knew when something was going on.

Once Ryan returned home from Battery Park, he was on the phone, one call after the other. Now, finally, at nine o'clock at night, he had finally taken care of everything he needed to for the day. He and John were going to D.C. to try and learn what they could about The Crucifier and Simmons' and Lee's deaths. They planned to leave the ensuing morning. He had put Kuron in charge of working with NYPD on the bombing.

Just before dinner, right after 6:30, Ryan had pulled Laura aside and spoke to her in the backyard. Kayleen had found a way to listen in, and when Ryan returned back inside with Laura, Kayleen's door was closed, and muffled sobs could be heard from inside her room. It broke Ryan's heart to see her like that. It broke his heart being the sole reason for her sadness.

Ryan had talked to her and eventually calmed her down. They played soccer together outside after dinner, then sat down and watched late-night cartoons. It had all seemed to help. For now, at least.

"I can't argue that." Ryan replied. "It kills me seeing her so upset. She's too smart and too tender-hearted for her own good sometimes. I just pray that it all ends quickly and that I can be home soon."

"You're not the only one."

Her tone was sad and defeated. They had discussed everything in the backyard earlier. Ryan explained he was going and there was no way around it. He explained that he and John would leave in the morning.

With his left arm around Kayleen, Ryan wrapped his right around Laura.

"Like I told you earlier, I don't want to go. I wish I could avoid getting myself into this situation just as much as you do."

"I know. I understand"

Ryan knew that she really didn't, though. She didn't understand it at all. How could she? They had two newborns in the house now. Kayleen was in the middle of soccer season. Their lives had just seemed to be falling into place.

Everything was going perfectly and now Ryan *and* John were leaving, putting themselves into a very dangerous case, putting themselves into harm's way. Laura was understandably upset. She was not only angry with Ryan for leaving her alone at this time, but she was also full of uncertainty. She was scared.

Ryan kissed her on the forehead. "I love you so much. I promise everything will be okay. I promise I'll be home before you even realize I was gone."

Ryan would never tell her this, but he felt the same way she did. He too was full of uncertainty. He too, though he'd never admit it to himself either, was scared. He knew the next few days were going to be a great challenge. That being said, there was nothing that could prepare him for just how challenging they were about to be.

CHAPTER THIRTY-SIX

It was just after 9 a.m. when Ryan and John drove up to the Fairmonton Hotel in Washington DC. Just pulling into the parking garage next to the hotel made Ryan's stomach churn. Once inside the hotel lobby, the two were immediately met by a man who introduced himself as Detective Tyrique Fox.

"Good to meet you, Detective," Ryan said as he shook Fox's hand.

"I'm the head detective on this case. I'm so sorry for your loss, Mr. Turner. I truly am."

Fox was exactly the same height as Ryan. He was a slender black man with a receding headline, dark brown-almost black-eyes, and wore casual, though tasteful clothes. Fox carried a leather briefcase in his right hand. He was dressed in a white polo shirt, khaki shorts, along with red and black Jordan's on his feet. He was cordial and had a very warm smile. To Ryan, he seemed like a good guy. Ryan judged him to be in his mid-twenties. He assumed Fox must have been good at his job considering how young he was; especially to have been put on a case of such magnitude. Ryan was already impressed.

"Please, call me Ryan. Mr. Turner makes me feel old."

Fox grinned and nodded sheepishly.

"And how old are you, may I ask?" Ryan continued. "I'm not asking in a bad or condescending way. I'm just curious? You carry yourself really well."

Fox couldn't hold back a slightly self-satisfied grin and he seemed to straighten up at Ryan's comment. "Twenty-five, sir."

Ryan had guessed twenty-six.

"Okay, okay…that's about what I thought. How long have you been a detective?"

"Two years now. I'm still a greenie. The department has given me bigger and 'better' cases as time has gone by. With that being said, I've sure never been involved in one on a national scale, so this is foreign territory to me in a sense."

John put an arm around Fox's shoulders. "Well, man, welcome to the crew. Me and ole Ryan know how to get things done and I bet you'll fit right in. Now, I know this guy is Mr. Head of the Bureau and all that jazz, but if you ever want any sort of advice, feel free to come to me. I'm of course the smartest, best looking, just most well-rounded of the two of us. I'm the brother that got all the good genes, if you know what I mean, I'm just full of knowledge and wisdom."

Fox smirked and looked in Ryan's direction.

"Oh, I know he's definitely full of something," Ryan said, "but it sure isn't knowledge and wisdom."

The three laughed.

"Real talk, what have you found out so far, if anything?" John asked Fox. "What have you got for us?"

"I hate to say it, but not much. At the moment, the two of you probably know as much as I do. We believe Allen Simmons and Whitney Lee were killed at around the same time. Time of death was established around 8:15 p.m. It is believed that they were poisoned. Now, listen here, though, the one clue we *might* have is that we found something really bizarre in their systems"

"What do you mean?" asked Ryan.

"I mean no one, at least nobody I've spoken to, has seen anything like what we found in the two victims' bodies."

Fox already had Ryan's full attention. He knew they had been poisoned but he had assumed cyanide, arsenic powder, or even possibly strychnine had been used.

Ryan rose to his feet. "Let's walk. We have access to the rooms, right?"

"Yes, sir," Fox replied as he showed Ryan a hotel key.

"Perfect, lead the way, Detective Fox."

Fox turned around and walked straight for the elevators which were to the right of the front desk, positioned directly in the middle of a long hallway, and he pressed the button to go upward.

"So, what I was getting at, is that the two agents were poisoned. I'm sure the two of you heard that. However, after the medical examiner did the autopsies-I just spoke with her early this morning, actually-it was determined that, yes, they were in fact poisoned, but in a way she or myself had never seen before. Her findings go hand-in-hand with what our forensics team has reported thus far, as well."

The elevator doors closed, with the three now inside. Oncehe elevator began its ascent.

"The bizarre thing is that the toxin used is some sort of concoction that I've never heard of. I'm sure you have seen cases where arsenic powder was used. Of course, it is a deadly toxin in itself. It is pretty water soluble, can be easily added to drinks-which is exactly what we saw here-and is pretty deadly in itself."

There was a *ding* as the elevator doors slid open. The three men stepped out onto the second floor.

"So, traces of arsenic were found. Pretty common. However, the crazy thing is that another poison was found in both bodies and in the mug found in Whitney Lee's room and in the glass found in Allen Simmons' room. At first, our forensics crew had no idea what it was. They obviously hadn't seen anything like it used before. Come to find out, this poison wasn't a poison after all. It was, in fact, venom. Snake venom."

CHAPTER THIRTY-SEVEN

"A snake?" John cut in.

"Yeah. Bizarre, right? It gets crazier. So, the most common poisonous snake around this area is the copperhead and their venom certainly packs a punch. They can be deadly. We all know that. With that being said, it wasn't a copperhead's venom at all, but the venom was found to be from the Inland Taipan."

The group stopped in front of rooms 222 and 224.

Fox continued. "I did some research early this morning and found out this snake is native to the Australian continent. It is often referred to as the deadliest snake in the world. Its venom is said to be a witch's brew of toxins. It consists of toxins that I can't remember off the top of my head, but together a bite from this snake can paralyze muscles, inhibit breathing, cause hemorrhaging in blood vessels and tissues, and damage muscles. Now, I am no scientist or chemist of any sort, but I would guess that combining the effects of white arsenic along with this venom would be *extremely* fatal. We're not sure how the killer created this concoction, but it is highly effective. Looks like it works *very* fast too. I hate to add salt to the wound, nonetheless, to say it plainly, both agents died horrible deaths, though with that said, thankfully, they didn't suffer for long. From what we can see, the toxic cocktail did its work quickly."

This information infuriated Ryan and brought him real grief that Simmons and Lee had suffered such horrible deaths. Two amazing people. Two amazing lives simply lost. He was comforted, only in the slightest, that they had not suffered for long.

Venom from an Australian snake?

Ryan had immediately learned during his early years in the FBI that he would see many inexplicable things and knew right away that as his career progressed, he would see almost everything imaginable. This was just another example of The Crucifier's sick and unorthodox abilities.

"Well, it's certainly a very unique technique," Ryan said. "Just another calling card for this ghost we're trying to catch. Who knows? It may end up helping us in the end."

"'Ghost' is a perfect description of this killer." Fox replied. "It has blown my mind that we haven't had a solid lead yet. We've interviewed countless people, have questioned some we thought were solid witnesses, we've got video evidence of a mysterious van that we know is involved, yet in the end we've got nothing solid. It's absolutely inconceivable, really! Sorry, I ramble a lot."

Ryan chuckled, "You're perfectly fine."

It was true, though. It was one thing Ryan had already noticed about Fox. He was a good kid, though he did have the tendency to ramble. Ryan couldn't figure out if it was nervousness, trying to fit in working with FBI agents, or just generally wanting to sound intelligent and passionate. None of the possibilities were bad; in fact, they all had a positive side to them.

Fox opened the door leading into room 222

As Ryan walked into the room, his body went cold, but the cooling system in the room had nothing to do with it. This was the room where Whitney Lee had died.

Ryan wandered around, John at his side. Everyone remained quiet. Ryan could tell Fox wanted to say something, anything, but refrained from doing so.

After Ryan made his rounds, he sat down on the floor straight across from the side of the bed where Lee had drunk a cup of tea and breathed her last breaths as a result. He sat with his back against the wall, the bathroom door on the same wall directly to his left. John and Fox lingered around the foot of the bed, standing in an almost awkward, uncomfortable way.

"Alright, Detective Fox," Ryan said. "What happened here? What do you have for us?"

Fox straightened up. "Oh, yes, sir. Um, like I said, as you know they were poisoned. Moments before Lee died, she ate a slice of cheesecake and drank a cup of chamomile tea. Both came on a platter from the little restaurant downstairs. Room service is popular here. She had just showered. As I explained a little earlier, the venom from the snake causes terrible effects on the body. Her face and her entire body were tight, clenched. Her throat was severely swollen. She…"

"With all due respect, Detective," John interrupted, his arms crossed, "I don't think we need to know those details. I don't know if I can speak for Ryan here too; however, I kind of want to know if there's anything you can tell us that can maybe spark something in our minds. Things that we maybe don't know yet. For me, the more I hear about how they looked when they died, the more ticked off I get. I just…don't really care to hear that. Again, all due respect, but you know what I mean?"

Ryan lifted a brow and nodded his head approvingly. Fox placed a hand on John's shoulder.

"Yes, of course," Fox said quickly, "Again, my apologies. I do tend to ramble and expand on unnecessary things at times. Forgive me."

John kindly waved off the apology with a slight smile as to say, "Don't worry about it."

"Important details…" Fox pondered. "There are no cameras in the hallways. I know, it's frustrating. Why in the world wouldn't they have cameras in their hallways? Come to find out, there are many hotels that don't. However, after intensive examinations into the security feed from the lobby, restaurant, and outside the hotel, there were a few suspicious-looking people. We believe that our guy is a man that walked in through the front doors a mere thirty minutes prior to the agents' deaths. This man is average height. Fairly muscular. Looks to be very fit. We got a really good shot of his face from the camera in the lobby. I would say this is the best piece of evidence we've had since the first murder months ago, but we've already seen this face before. And *still*, we haven't been able to catch him."

CHAPTER THIRTY-EIGHT

Fox retrieved a manila envelope from inside the brief case he had set on the bed., and pulled out a plastic, see-through folder that held a stack of photographs. He slipped the photos out of the plastic, flipped through them, then handed one of the many to John.

John took the photograph from Fox's grasp and brought the picture up close to his eyes. While he gazed intently at the picture, he slowly strolled over to where Ryan was sitting.

"Looks like a normal dude to me," he said as he handed Ryan the photo.

Ryan peered down at the photograph that he now held in his hands. The man was white, fit, looked to maybe have dirty blonde hair. It was hard to determine eye color. He was dressed in very high-dollar clothing. He wore a full-on tuxedo. Ryan stared at the man's face. The guy seemed to be staring directly into the camera.

"Same guy we've seen a few times now," Ryan said, handing the photo back to John. "So, I mean, not necessarily a new lead there. This face has been plastered all over the media for months. All three of us have seen it, everyone and their mother has seen it. He's in good shape, not young but not old either. Definitely older than myself. This guy is arrogant, cocky, isn't afraid to be seen. Obviously, he isn't in the system. Detective, correct me if

I'm wrong, but we haven't had a single helpful tip on who he may be. There have been calls from around the country saying this guy looked familiar, yet none of the tips have gotten any traction whatsoever, right?"

Fox shrugged. "It's true."

"His arrogance is what gets me. I saw the tapes from the old bank, warehouse-type place, whatever it is, here in DC where Montez was killed. Your Chief of Police, Portman, isn't it? He sent me the footage. On the video, one of the men, who I assume is this same suspicious character that was at this hotel, looked directly into the security camera that caught him. He even tauntingly waved and bowed. For someone this cocky, I'm surprised we still have nothing on him. He obviously isn't in the system. He doesn't have a social security number. From what I have seen, or I guess *haven't* seen, we can pretty much guarantee that. He is, quite seriously, a living ghost."

Fox rummaged through the stack of photographs in his hands and then handed a few to John, who looked them over before giving them to Ryan.

"These are all the still-frames we got from the scene outside the bank where Montez's body was found," Fox said.

Ryan looked through them. Many of them were of the van at different times and close ups of the people that came out of the van. There was a blurry close-up of the plates. Ryan assumed the license plate had already been run. Whoever this guy was, he wasn't dumb enough to be careless when it came to license plates. Ryan looked more intently at some photos of the van that were taken at different locations in the city.

"Yes, I have seen these photos. This isn't the first time, although seeing them again does reaffirm some thoughts I wanted to share with both of you."

Both Fox and John seemed to stand up a little straighter.

"One, and it doesn't really have to do with these pictures a whole lot, but the guy in the tuxedo who we believed to have killed our two agents? He isn't alone. There's a good chance he might not even be the puppet master in this case. There could be someone over him even. We can't know for sure. There's zero chance that he's a lone wolf in all of this. It's a scary thought, but it's also a good thing for us. The more people involved in this madness, the more likely it is for there to be a slip-up from someone at some point. Although they've been flawless thus far in carrying out these killings, everyone involved *is* human. Mistakes are bound to happen.

"Along with the idea that there are multiple persons of interest involved, I believe the other two people who unloaded the cross at that bank are women. I've gone over the reports a thousand times, and I know we had eye-witnesses state that they saw these three people unload the cross. A few stated that they believed two of the masked individuals were female. I'm not certain, but if you watch the way they hold themselves and the way they move in the security footage, it would be easy to assume they are female. Whatever that's worth. I just think a lot of times, I know I do it, we assume these kinds of people are male. There are bad women out there who do some terrible things too. Most cases, it's men who are responsible for murders like this, but not always. So, that's one thing the three of us need to keep in mind through this process. There may be many people, specifically a group of women helping this guy.

"The second thing is there's footage showing the van leaving the city by means of Interstate 395, I believe? Both times the van was at that bank: first when the cross was dropped off and then when Mon`tez was taken inside via the large chest we see in film, it left afterwards by means of I-395. After some time, the interstate leaves urban areas and makes its way southwest-ish. At that point, of course, we lose the ability to get film from buildings and businesses.

"Anyway, the point I am making is that this is significant, and I have a plan to go from here. I want us three to find a way to put all kinds of manpower into this. We know that the van is from somewhere southeast of DC. I am guessing a maximum of a three-hour one-way trip. Montez lived in DC. These people came to him and killed him here. I don't know the significance of that, but it is what it is. To me, I think it's a public display. There are plenty of rural areas where they could have done something like this and then kept it hidden from the world. That said, we have ourselves a radius of, let's say, 200 miles, give or take. We know these people don't reside east of DC, or northward either. We need to physically draw out all the possibilities as to where we may find this van, and in turn, find these people. They could come to DC again. In fact, it's very likely."

Ryan stood to his feet. "So, Detective Fox. I want you to get a crew together. I want officers strung out along I-395 until we find this van. Spread them out. There needs to be people at each spot 24/7. I don't care how you set up their shifts. That's up to you. Not only are we going to plaster this guys' face everywhere, but this van as well.

They may have ditched it by now; however, we can't eliminate the possibility that they still have it."

John was nodding his head. "Along with everything you're saying, all three victims so far were killed around the DC area, correct? I guess that's one constant that we have here."

"You're right. DC seems to be their feeding grounds. Mrs. Tina Rington was from North Carolina. Come to find out her husband reported her missing one week prior to when she was pronounced dead. Somehow, for some reason, she was brought to this area. She was held somewhere unkown for a week before they took her life."

CHAPTER THIRTY-NINE

Now Fox decided to chip in. "It's our best bet that these people held her in a rural place, somewhere out of the way. That said, we can narrow our search with the knowledge that there is most likely a particular diameter in which these people live. My, this is good stuff, Mr. Turner."

"Good," Ryan said. "I like the direction your mind is headed. I don't think we've hit this case hard enough. We've lost good, good people. I can't stand the thought of losing anyone else. I think we need to start sending people into any little town, any little community in our area that we map out. John and I will stick around the city and closely investigate the scenes and try to uncover any little pieces of evidence that there may be. Depending on what time entails, we may work our way into the surrounding areas as well. I hate to let the thought even cross my mind, yet it has to…this guy, these people, whoever they may be, aren't finished. The guy we saw in the picture taken here at the hotel and the picture taken at the site of Montez's death is confident. He is very sure of himself. So far, for good reason. It is more than likely there will be more crucifixions coming.

"I like being on the scene and talking while on the scene about these sorts of things, these hypotheses and plans. It's how I've always worked. I think we're finished here, though. There's not much else to see or do, really. Detective, I take it your guys here at the department have swept the room thoroughly, gotten prints off the plates, the mug and the cup? Things such as that?"

"Yes, sir…I mean, Ryan, we're on top of it," Fox replied.

Ryan nodded approvingly, heading toward the door now. "Good, good. Then I don't see any reason for us to stay here any longer. We have a game plan now. Another thing…" Ryan stopped as he went to open the door. "Detective, please be careful," he said in a more hushed and serious tone. "I mean it. Like I already said, I don't want to lose anyone else. Trust no one. Period. Always be aware and alert. The three of us can never be too careful, got it?"

John and Fox nodded in unison.

Ryan opened the door. "I would say let's check out 224 as well, but I just don't see any point at this time. Detective, let's go to the station. I want to see every shred of evidence we may have gathered thus far, including all the test results, pictures, surveillance footage, both agents' cell phones, the whole nine yards. That'll be our first step on this crazy journey that I'm anticipating. I need to see it all for myself to see if we're missing anything."

The three men made their way down to the lobby by means of the elevator before splitting ways in the parking garage. Fox wandered over to his car, which was parked at the back of the garage. Ryan and John's car was much closer.

"I'll have to say, man," John said as he got inside the vehicle and closed the door behind him. "I'm already impressed. Nice to see you in action."

Ryan shook his head. "It hasn't even been a year and I feel like I've been out of the field for decades."

"I saw you take control in there and saw your gears turning. Even if you had been out of the game for decades, you'd never lose that side of you. It's a part of you."

Ryan threw the car into gear and backed out of the compact parking spot.

"You may be right, John. I would never openly confess it to Laura, but I can honestly say I missed this. We just got here, and I hate the circumstances that brought us here, but I can say it feels so good to be back in it."

"Ha-ha. Oh, I'm loving this! Welcome back, old man."

CHAPTER FORTY

With the absolute madness that was DC traffic, Ryan and John arrived at the police headquarters in just under thirty, though it was merely a few miles away. It was nowhere near what it was like trying to drive through the middle of New York City, nevertheless it was still a mess.

There wasn't much to see evidence-wise. It frustrated Ryan, yet he hadn't expected much in the first place. There were a few gems, though, things he felt that he maybe could end up getting something from, or that could possibly spark a thought or realization. The first of these things was the handwritten note found in Whitney Lee's room, which read as follows:

"Your friend in the room next to you said to deliver this to you. I knocked but you didn't answer. It is outside your door in the hallway. He said to tell you to sleep well and that tomorrow is going to be a big day. Have a great night.

Room Service

B.B."

The first thought Ryan had when he saw the note was, *Why hadn't Lee been suspicious?* But again, why would she be? Yes, it was a cheesy, random note, with a random cup of tea and a slice of cheesecake. It was honestly something Allen Simmons probably would have done. It was plausible.

Then Ryan was immediately drawn to the last part of the note.

B.B...?

He couldn't figure out if it was significant or not. His gut feeling was that it was, in fact, significant. It could have simply ended with: "Room Service." However, it didn't. The question Ryan had was why? He guessed the B.B. was someone's initials. But again, why would they put them? Carelessness? Habit? Arrogance, again? Ryan didn't know. It *was* something, though. Something he'd keep in mind.

There had been no significant, note-worthy, fingerprints or DNA extracted from the kitchenware or from the hotel room doors. Nothing, and no one out of the ordinary. Ryan had gone into the headquarters assuming as much. The pictures there weren't helpful. The photos of Simmons' and Lee's lifeless bodies made him sick, but other than that, they told him nothing. The second piece of evidence that intrigued Ryan was Simmons' cell phone. Lee's was boring, to say the least. There wasn't much to find in hers. She very rarely used it, as looking at the call and text history proved. There was nothing of interest in her notes, her call history, texts, maps, or in any of her apps. Simmons on the other hand, being the young and in love man he was, used his phone quite a bit. He had liked a number of posts on Facebook, posted a picture of Georgia the morning of his death, texted Zaya a number of times throughout the day, and then had a facetime call with her just before his recorded time of death. He had read the Bible on his phone just after the facetime call. Early the next morning, the morning following his death, there was a missed call from "Ryan Turner". Ryan's stomach dropped when he saw that. He remembered the sick feeling he had inside when he couldn't get ahold of Simmons *or* Lee that morning.

Of all that, none of it seemed of much importance. None of it seemed like it would help progress the case forward. But there was one last thing...Ryan thought about it now as he stared down at Allen Simmons' cell phone. He and John were back in the car. DC's Chief of Police, Edgar Portman, had agreed to let Ryan take the phone.

The two sat in the car now, the engine idly running. Ryan stared down at the bright phone screen, his mind working furiously.

"I see those gears turning again," John said, "What do you got?"

Ryan shut off the phone and placed it on the seat between his legs. He nodded slowly, looking at the steering wheel.

"I'm not sure yet," he said. "But there's something about this text..."

Ryan put his fingers on the bridge of his nose, forming a tent with them. "I think Simmons was trying to tell Lee something, and in turn is trying to tell us something. I don't know what it is yet. You saw the text-or what was going to be a text. It looked like he was trying to say the woman *something*…and after that I can't even begin to decipher anything else since it's just a bunch of gibberish. The first part must be 'The woman we'? It's so intriguing to me. What was he trying to tell her in his last moments? I mean, that had to have been when this text was being put together. Fox said that when they opened the phone up, the first thing that popped up was the text conversation between the two agents. The phone was found on the floor near Simmons' body. I don't think any of that is coincidence. Most likely, he was intentionally typing 'the woman we' and from there lost all control. Based on what Detective Fox said about the toxin that was found in the two bodies, Simmons had to have been dying a terrible death. I'm surprised he had the wherewithal to pick up his phone and begin composing a text."

"Can I check out that phone again?" John asked.

Ryan picked the phone up from between his legs and handed it to his brother. John unlocked the phone using the password that a team in the MPD was able to crack. Immediately the text message conversation between Lee and Simmons appeared on the screen. The text that was never sent read:

The womnasn we eawse fghtyhj.

"It's odd to me that he didn't begin the text with some sort of warning to Whitney," John said. "Like an obvious, to the point kind of warning, you know? Looking at the conversation that came before, they hadn't exchanged texts since before they arrived in DC. It could be that Allen had started to send this at some other point during the trip and then just never sent it. But the team they have here said it was the first thing that appeared when they unlocked the phone. So, based on this knowledge and this unintelligible text, I feel like we can be almost a hundred percent sure that the message was being composed in his final moments. This second word sure does look a lot like woman. And like you said, it looks very likely 'the woman we' is what he was shooting for."

"Well, we're going to roll with it. It's as good of a lead as any other in this case. Even if it takes us nowhere, it's well worth a shot to look into it."

John nodded. "So, there are a few words that can come after we. That is if he intentionally typed 'we'. It has got to be a verb of some sort. Saw? Talked to? Heard about? Met? It's likely the next word would have inferred some sort of interaction between the two of them and a woman. But dude, I really have no clue, this is all just speculation with no supporting evidence whatsoever."

Ryan was nodding but didn't reply for a bit. The car's ignition remained on and it remained stationary in front of the police station.

"No, I like where this is all going already," Ryan eventually said as he threw the car into reverse. "I also like the point you made about him not giving Whitney a more direct text of warning. I think I already have a couple answers to that thought." Ryan turned to face John more directly. "What he wanted to say was obviously of the utmost importance in that moment. These are quite literally his last words. This was the *one* thing he was going to tell Whitney. To me it sounds like he had a sudden realization as he felt the life being sucked out of him. Something clicked inside his brain. Along with that, and I may be reaching a little, I think he really was trying to tell *us* something. He knew in that moment that it was too late for him. He may have realized that it was highly likely that Whitney was in the same boat as he was. On that note, he couldn't have actually known that for sure, so there was still a chance she was alive. The text would have been a warning to her in some way. She would have been confused and then concerned, and if she never did see the text, someone else eventually would have. I honestly think Simmons knew that. Now we just need to figure out what he was trying to tell us."

CHAPTER FORTY-ONE

Jack Grimes set his paint brush down into the bucket at his feet and took a step back. He gazed at the painting in front of him. The light in his basement was dim. It added to the peaceful environment that he so loved. He was more than satisfied with the work that sat on the easel in front of him.

It was one of seven paintings that sat on easels against the back wall of the basement. It was now one of two that were fully completed. The other five were all but complete and only needed a few finishing touches. So much time and energy had been put into these paintings. It had taken years of work to get to this point, to get to this very week. One painting would be finished per day now. He had originally planned to finalize one project every two days, spreading it out over two weeks. However, after yesterday's exhilarating experience at Battery Park, Grimes wanted more. He wanted to speed up the process. After all, what was the point of waiting any longer?

The painting, some parts of it still wet, looked as good as he could have ever imagined. The final touches were perfect, exactly what was needed to finish the project. The finishing touch he had been anxiously waiting to add. His morning routine was complete. His painting was now complete. Now it was time to carry out his work. It was time for step two.

Always replace the bad memories with good ones. Destroy the bad.

Grimes gazed at the painting. It was the exact depiction of the hotel room that had so long haunted his mind. It matched the image in his mind with precision. It was a room on the twelfth floor of the Ritz Carlton. The room was magnificent. The view was stunning. A telescope sat at the window which gave a great view of the Statue of Liberty. The sky outside the window was a beautiful blue just as he remembered. The king-sized bed had white and gold sheets and pillows. The walls were covered in gorgeous paintings. Everything was in place just as he remembered.

However, the finishing touches were new. They were not yet a part of his memory. Homemade explosives could be seen planted under the bed, behind two paintings and behind the bed's headboard. Outside the window he had drawn a giant mirror covering parts of the building below and part of the blue sky. The mirror showed the flip image of the room...or what was once the room. The mirror showed great flames, smoke, and debris. It showed a big burning hole in the side of the Ritz Carlton.

This afternoon, step two would commence.

CHAPTER FORTY-TWO

"We're on it," Ryan said just before ending the call with Director Felix. John's eyes stared intently and not very patiently at Ryan, like a dog waiting for a treat.

"So?" he urged.

Ryan shoved his cell phone into his pocket. "Packer Hackings. He's an inspirational speaker. Speaks about our spiritual well beings and speaks in testimony of God. He has little 'shows' all around the country. I've actually heard of him. Pretty big-name guy."

"Yeah, yeah, so have I. So, what's the deal?"

"He's missing. At the moment, it's impossible to know whether or not this has to do with our case and the same wacko we have been dealing with, but it's highly possible. It fits the bill, at least. He is from Cleveland, Ohio, and was last seen at his home. His wife went out to get groceries, came back home and Mr. Hackings was gone. She called, texted, but heard nothing from her husband. Then she found his phone had slid under a couch in their living room. The living room was a mess. Looked like some sort of scuffle had occurred. Things were knocked over, stuff everywhere. She called the police, and the situation was immediately put on our radar, for good reason. This Crucifier has everyone on the lookout and has everyone up tight. Long story short, we all need to stay locked in and on the lookout. I'm going to call Detective Fox right away. All the murders have been around or in this city. If this is The Crucifier at work, I don't see why Mr. Hackings' place of death would be any different."

John was looking down at his feet, nodding. "Call him. I've also got a good feeling about this."

Ryan whipped out his phone again and scrolled through his contacts until he came across Detective Tyrique Fox's name and number.

"Mr. Fox, I have some information for you."

"Awesome! Let me hear it."

Ryan cleared his throat, as he paced the dark basement where Pablo Montez had been killed. "I just got a call from Director Trey Felix. A man has been reported missing. He's been gone since yesterday, and it's believed that he was abducted. His name is Packer Hackings. Good man, inspirational speaker, religious, down-to-earth. He's certainly on our radar. The Crucifier and his people may have something to do with this. We need everyone to keep their heads up, staying locked in. Make sure your guys are staked out. I want every town in the area we mapped out to have at least one set of officers in it. I want our guys strung out across Interstate 395. We can't be sure if Hackings' disappearance fits into our case, but if it does, we'll be ready. All the crucifixions have been around the DC area. I wouldn't expect anything different."

"Woo," Fox blew out, "yes, sir. We're on it. Thanks!"

"Stay in touch, Detective."

With that, Ryan ended the call

"Let's get out of here," John said, slapping Ryan's back. "This place gives me the creeps. And it isn't looking like we're going to find anything of use here."

Ryan stood with his hands on his hips, taking in the entire basement. He pictured Montez on the cross and transferred the images he had seen in the pictures to the basement he now stood in. He shivered. He didn't like this place either. He turned and followed John out of the building and into the streets of Washington DC.

CHAPTER FORTY-THREE

Now sitting in the passenger seat, a spot unfamiliar to Ryan, his phone began to ring. He allowed it to obnoxiously ring a few times before answering it. The number looked completely unfamiliar to him. He didn't think that he had ever even seen the area code before. Then it clicked. It was a German phone number. Ryan pulled the phone up next to his ear and turned down the radio in the car. Behind the wheel, John's eyebrows scrunched, and he gave Ryan a sort of upward nod as if to ask, "Who's that?"

Ryan put a finger up. "Hello?"

"Is this Ryan Turner?"

"This is him. And who's this?"

"My name is Danley Dobson, from Berlin. I was told by a Mr. Godfrey Hackett that you needed to speak with me?"

Dobson had a raspy, weak-sounding voice. Evidently, he was an older gentleman. He sounded a little frail, yet there was still an apparent strength behind his voice.

"Yes, sir. As you already know, my name is Ryan Turner. I'm currently the Head of the Bureau out of New York City. I wanted to speak to you about an old case you had many years ago. The Aldrik Bach murder case."

"Mr. Hackett explained as much to me. Before we get started, would you mind humoring me a bit? What do you know about me?"

The car stopped abruptly, causing Ryan to jerk forward and drop his phone from his ear. Ryan looked up to see a taxi had cut them off badly, and he then scrambled to pick his phone up off the floor. John already had his head hanging out the window, screaming every explicit word and phrase known to man. As Ryan lifted the phone back up to his ear, he could see the cab driver in front of him throw a middle finger out his driver-side window.

Ryan shook his head.

Cab drivers are ruthless.

"Sorry about that, what was that you said?"

Dobson cleared his throat. "I asked you to tell me what you know about me. If you don't mind, that is."

Slightly confused, Ryan tilted his head to the side like a dog that had been struck by a sudden curiosity or confusion.

"Well," Ryan began, "I know that you were a detective out of Berlin for many years. You retired about a year and a half ago. Although the case was short-lived, you were the head detective on the case surrounding Bach's murder."

"Oh, come on, Mr. Turner. Don't hold back. What do you *really* know about me?"

Ryan thought for a second or two. "Danley Dobson. Born September 15, 1949. You're a Brit, but have lived in Germany most of your life. Your father was a police officer. Your mother stayed at home and took care of the children. You are the youngest of eight. You have two older sisters and five older brothers. Of your siblings, they have all passed away except for one sister and one brother. Your sister, Yvonne, currently lives in the United States. She is married to a military man, and they live in Atlanta, Georgia. She and her husband are both retired. You became a policeman at the tender age of seventeen. You worked in law enforcement for over fifty years. You were recently inducted into the Polizei Berlin hall of fame.

"You're married to Cicely Davis, now Cicely Dobson, who was born and raised in the United States. The two of you met while she was studying abroad at Humboldt University in Berlin during her senior year of college. The two of you married the month after she graduated. You have five children.

"Now, if you want personal traits and characteristics. You are just under six feet tall. You have dark green eyes, once had jet black hair, which has become more of a hazy white color. You have always been in great shape, not too scrawny, not too fat. You have never really had any sort of major medical complications, probably due to your active lifestyle and your healthy living. There was a cancer scare when you were in your forties, but it was caught early, and you haven't had any complications since. You've never drank, smoked, none of that good stuff. You seem like a great guy, Mr. Dobson.

"As for your police work, I'm genuinely impressed with your history, and I'm honestly honored to be speaking with you. If you ever wanted to come to the States and had the desire to get back into field work, I would hire you here at the Bureau in a heartbeat. That's for sure."

Next to Ryan, John rolled his eyes.

"Show off," he muttered.

"Ha-ha," Dobson chuckled. "That's more like it. I worked with a young man from the Bureau many, many years ago. It had to have been in the late seventies. And then I worked with a pair of FBI agents a few years back too. I've always been impressed by you all. I heard you were the best of the best, so as a retired old man that misses your kind of line of work, I just wanted you to humor me a bit."

Ryan chuckled too. "I assumed that you were looking for something like that."

"Anyway," Dobson said, "what is it you want to know from me? Any specifics?"

"There are a few. But really it would just be nice to first hear you give me an overview of the Aldrik Bach case, and maybe add any insights that could be helpful to me and my team."

Dobson didn't answer immediately. "Obviously, it was a very odd case, as you should now know better than anyone. You work all these years tracking down killers and solving case after case, some more bizarre than others. Then you get hit with something like this that shows you just how sick our world can be, and how unpredictable this line of work really is. I could never have imagined up a case as gruesome as this. I could never have imagined that someone would be so sick and twisted that they would go about killing someone as Aldrik Bach was killed."

CHAPTER FORTY-FOUR

Dobson cleared his throat. "Anyhow, I was immediately called to the scene. Anytime something crazy like this happened, I was always the first detective to be notified. Bach, of course, was already dead when I found him. I must confess that I quite literally vomited on the scene. My sudden rush of nausea was then closely followed by pure rage. With this particular case, I take very little, I guess you would call it pride, or credit? This is due to the fact that I had very little to do with finding the killer. A few hours after I first saw the body, our headquarters got a call saying that another body was found in a downtown apartment building and that it could be linked to Bach's death.

"I'm sure you've done your research. Come to find out, the body belonged to a man by the name of Ferdinand Schneider. It was like a confession. The blade found in his room contained both he and Bach's blood, and contained numerous traces of Schneider's fingerprints. No other prints or DNA were found on the blade, which matched the wound in Bach's side. It was an open and closed case. In and out. Then the next day, I got sucked into another big case and every ounce of my attention was focused on it."

"I see, I see."

"I realize that probably wasn't helpful in any way. I'm sorry."

"No, no. I asked for a run down and that's exactly what you gave me. May I ask, was Bach's thumb removed by his killer, or had he always been missing it? I wasn't able to uncover any close ups that told me much."

"Oh, yes. It was cut off that day. Oddly, the thumb was never found, either. That was the one hole in the case; however, we did not read too much into it."

"I take it you searched the killer's car, home, belongings?"

"Yes, we did. I immediately surmised that taking the thumb was a trophy. So, I did assume we would eventually find it in a bag, a jar, somewhere. Yet, we never did."

"That's very interesting...did you ever have doubts that the man you found beside that suicide note wasn't actually the killer?"

"Yes, I certainly did. To be honest with you, Mr. Turner, I still do at times."

Ryan more than understood why Dobson would still have his doubts. He sat up straighter in his seat. "And how so?"

"You probably understand this as well as anyone would...somehow it just seemed too, what's the word, easy? I understand that things happen like this all the time. Killer murders person or persons. Killer then kills himself. Somehow, this did feel different to me for whatever reasons. The biggest piece that led to me questioning it all *was* the thumb. Why do that? It had to have been a trophy. I mean why else, would a man's thumb be removed? Or it could have somehow been cut off when Bach was abducted. Cut off during a struggle, maybe? But that seemed unlikely The cut was clean. The thumb had been perfectly cut off."

Exactly.

Dobson was echoing and legitimizing the thoughts that had gone through Ryan's head ever since he first heard about the German case.

"And now these cases are appearing in the United States," Dobson continued. "Bach's murder was very well-known in Germany. He was an outstanding man who was loved by people all over our country. But, from what I know, it didn't really receive *that* much publicity outside of Germany. The killings you're dealing with right now are *exactly* like what we saw with Bach. The crosses appear to be identical to the cross that we found Bach nailed to. All the wounds are identical to what we saw. I probably overthink, and there are truly many cases from my past that I still ponder and go over in my head to this day, but after hearing about these murders in the United States my doubts about that case have been brought to light."

"We are paid to analyze, overthink, and question everything," Ryan commented. "It isn't a bad thing. But it can just be frustrating. I know how it goes."

"This is true," Dobson replied.

"I've been having these same thoughts. I assumed the thumb had been cut off the day Bach was killed but I had to be certain. I also have to be certain that you're saying exactly what I have been thinking these last few days, ever since I heard about your case in Germany. Please be one-hundred percent honest with me, do you believe that Ferdinand Schneider really did kill Aldrik Bach?"

There was no quick reply. Ryan patiently waited. He understood the internal frustration and battle Dobson was going through now to say the words he was about to say. Bach's murder had been his case. He had closed the case by declaring that Schneider was Aldrik Bach's killer. All these years, Ryan knew that Dobson had done everything he could to convince himself that this was the truth, that Ferdinand Schneider had killed Aldrik Bach. Now, his longtime internal struggle had been brought back out and put under a spotlight. Now he had someone else, maybe the only other person in the world, aside from the true killer, who knew the truth. Up until this point, Dobson was the only person who had ever questioned the findings.

Dobson sighed deeply. "No, I have to conclude that he did not kill Aldrik Bach. I believe Bach's killer is still out there."

CHAPTER FORTY-FIVE

"I just needed the reassurance," Ryan said. "The second opinion. Someone else to say it. I'm sure you needed that as well."

"I did. Up until I spoke to Hackett, I had convinced myself that Schneider was Bach's killer. Ever since my conversation with Hackett, my doubts returned, and oh, were they stronger than ever. It makes me sick to say those words. My skin crawls having said them, but I do believe it is the truth, although I still hope it is not."

"Like I said, I know how it is...there are still cases I've solved, people I've put behind bars, people who were put on death row because of me that still haunt me to this day. I still question myself about cases from when I first got into the Bureau. Even some that were clearly solved without a shadow of a doubt. It's how we work, as frustrating as it can be for us sometimes.

"We will get to the bottom of this. I promise you that. And I do hope for your sake that this is not the same killer who took Aldrik Bach's life. But if it is, justice will finally be served. You have my word, detective."

"Thank you. God bless you, Mr. Turner."

Ryan cleared his throat, "And Detective Dobson?"

"Oh, come on, call me Dan."

"I know what case you immersed yourself into immediately after Aldrik Bach's death."

Dobson said nothing.

"You went to Spain," Ryan continued. "Madrid, to be exact. Your son, Wilhelm, was helping to lead a political revolution. He and the leader, Mariano Botin, had put together a large rally in Central Madrid. Although Wilhelm was from Germany, he left his home country for love. Married a woman from Spain. As most of the Spanish people at the time, he was angry with Spanish leadership and policies. Mariano Botin was a coworker of his and they started the 'Resistance Party'. I know this is all information which you already know far better than myself, but I'm just putting it out there.

"The day after Schneider was found dead with the suicide note, Wilhelm and Mariano were shot dead at the rally in Madrid. You flew to Madrid immediately after you heard the news. Although you technically had no business there, you immersed yourself in the case. You even took a leave of absence from the Berlin Department. You went off the grid to hunt down your son's killer. Understandable. I would have done the exact same thing. At some point you finally gave up, though I imagine the pain never left you. You never really stopped looking for the killer. Everyone knew who had done it. It was the work of the Invisible Man. As usual, in the long run it was easy to tell it was him. His signature bullets were found. The Invisible Man never cared that people knew it was him. He was so good that it didn't matter. No one knew what he looked like because no one ever saw him. That didn't stop you, though. And I imagine you have been trying to find him ever since that day. You and our Bureau were one in the same when it came to that.

"I just wanted you to know that he's been stopped. He was killed this past year. His name was Braxton Kyler Reddick. For the last few years of his life, he went by the alias Kyle Harrison. He was killed this past year. Dan, you don't have to hunt him any longer."

There was a pause before Dobson answered. "I know. And I am very thankful to you, Mr. Turner. I have been wanting to thank you for quite some time now. A big part of me just wishes I had been the one to end him. But, thank you. I know it was you, and I thank you."

"Of course," Ryan said. "Thank you for speaking with me. If you think of anything that may help us in this investigation, feel free to give me a call."

"Definitely. Good day, Mr. Turner."

Ryan ended the call then set the phone between his legs.

"Quite the conversation you had there," John asked as they pulled up to the Metropolitan Police Department Headquarters.

"How much of it did you hear?"

"Not too much. Caught pieces here and there."

"I'll catch you up inside," Ryan said opening the car door. "Long story short, looks like we don't have a copycat killer after all. The person we are after may very well be the same person who murdered Aldrik Bach in Germany those many years ago."

CHAPTER FORTY-SIX

Five to two. Three-point game. Ten minutes of game time left. It was as intense of a little league soccer game as six-year-olds could put forth. Kayleen's Lil Lions were losing, and the time was running out. Kayleen hadn't been her usual, dominant self thus far in the contest. Many tears had been shed by her prior to the start of the game. It was going to be the All-Metro Semi-Finals game against one of the best teams in New York City, and Ryan would not be there. She was understandably distraught. It was showing in her game too. She didn't have the usual high energy, the hustle, the competitive spirit. She hadn't scored a single goal yet, and her team was losing to a team they had already beaten earlier in the season. That said, it didn't seem to faze her. Competitive, intense, dominant Kayleen was nowhere to be found today.

Laura sat in her usual fold-up chair, her chin resting in her hands. She hadn't yelled at Kayleen once, cheered crazily, or given any fist pumps. That was always Ryan's job and he wasn't there to rile her up either. It wasn't very often she would get super excited and intense like the usual parent, but when she did it was usually Ryan's energy rubbing off on her.

She was alone. The babies were at home with Zaya, who had more than willingly offered to watch them. Laura promised she wouldn't be long and that they would get home as soon as possible. She hoped that everything would be alright while she was away.

At mid-field there was a pile of girls kicking wildly at the ball. They looked like a huddle of crazed Antarctic penguins. Suddenly the ball popped out of the confusion and rolled toward the Lil Lion's goal where their goalie was paying little to no attention to what was happening. A girl from the opposing team, The New York Select, broke free from the pack, dribbled the ball a few times then casually kicked the ball into the back of the net with her left foot. Six to two. Select. Nine minutes remaining.

The game appeared to be all but over. Laura kept her eyes locked intently on her daughter. Her body-language said it all. She looked defeated. Laura's heart ached for Kayleen.

If only she knew the real reason behind why her father isn't here.

"GO LIONS!"

The yell made Laura jump and turn around in her seat.

"Let's go Lil Lions! Let's go!"

Laura smiled and shook her head slightly. It was Kuron with Malaya close behind, her face as red as Laura's now felt.

With a sheepish smirk on her face, she mouthed the words, "I'm so sorry."

The couple marched right towards Laura, who rose from her chair.

"Hey, thank you both for coming. She's going to love seeing you."

"Come on, Momma," Kuron said putting a hand on Laura's shoulder, "You're lacking some excitement. What's going on?"

Laura rolled her eyes and before she could answer Kuron yelled out again.

"GO LIONS!"

All the spectators looked in Kuron's direction again. Some people's faces showed obvious looks of annoyance but others laughed or smiled.

Laura hugged Malaya. "Good to see you, Mal."

Malaya rubbed Laura's back. "Always good to see you too, girl. How are you doing?"

"I'm good. A little exhausted and overwhelmed but hanging in there."

"Well sit on down, Laura. Let's enjoy the rest of this game. What's the score anyway? How's our girl doing?"

Laura plopped back down in her chair. "Well," she began, "it's been a rough one to say the least. At least she gets to play and have fun, and that's what really matters."

Kuron folded his arms across his chest. "Oh, come on, I know that isn't how Kay rolls. She's here to win...KAY! KAYLEEN!"

Standing back on defense, about ten yards in front of the Lil Lion goalie, Kayleen perked up and looked in

Kuron's direction. Kuron threw his arms up as if to say, "What the heck?" and pointed at the scoreboard

Kayleen sheepishly smiled while giving a slight shrug.

"Come on!" Kuron said, clapping his hands loudly. "Pick it up! We've got eight minutes left, okay? How about let's see what we can do with it, yeah?"

Kayleen's smile grew, and she flashed Kuron a double thumbs up. Her demeanor instantly changed. She was locked in. Kayleen was back in business.

CHAPTER FORTY-SEVEN

Crucifixion was a brutal method of capital punishment that began during ancient times. This method of public execution originated with the Assyrians and Babylonians. It was used in a systematical way by the Persians in the 6th century BC. In the 4th century BC, Alexander the Great brought the method of crucifixion to the countries in the east Mediterranean and the Phoenicians later introduced it in Rome. Crucifixion is the process by which an individual is tied or nailed to a large wooden beam and left to die. In ancient times, before death occurred, the suffering usually lasted as few as six hours, or up to as many as four days.

Right now, Packer Hackings was that individual. He knew a lot about the process of a crucifixion and knew this was exactly his fate. Hackings just hoped that his suffering would end closer to the six-hour mark than the four-day mark. He had lost track of time but guessed he had been in this same spot for a few hours now. His throat was dry and burned badly. He had yelled and screamed for hours before his voice became nothing more than a whisper. His entire body ached with so many different forms of pain that his mind found it hard to pinpoint the origins of it all.

He was in an old, run-down building. It was evidently an old barn of some sort. He was able to conclude that when there was still daylight left. There was maybe an hour or so left of it. He could hear the sound of crickets chirping and a strong wind disrupting nearby trees. A breeze struck his skin every so often and it felt as if even the wind on his skin was causing him pain.

Suddenly there was another noise. It was the sound of a creaking door opening. It sounded old, rugged. It scraped across the floor as it opened. Then there were footsteps.

Lifting his head, Hackings could see the opened door and a dark figure approaching him.

"Please, let me go," Hackings hoarsely said. "Please."

There was no reply. The figure came closer and closer.

"Please…"

The masked individual stopped a yard or two in front of Hackings. The individual was dressed in all black aside from a white mask accompanied with a gold cross hanging from a silver necklace.

"I am deeply sorry that this isn't as ceremonial as it should be. My deepest apologies. The wind and our unfamiliar venue have thrown some wrinkles in my plan."

The voice was deep and muffled. Hackings could easily tell that the person before him was using a voice modifier. From what he could tell, there looked to be a bulge under the mask where the individual's mouth would be.

"I know who you are," Hackings said. From deep inside, he conjured a sort of newfound energy. However, he grimaced as he spoke, as the nails tore at his hands and the gash in his forehead throbbed.

"Oh, do you, my dear friend?"

"They call you The Crucifier," Hackings managed. "I'm not your first victim. I know what my fate is."

"Yes, it is the name they have given me. And rest assured, Mr. Hackings, you will not be my last victim either. The work is in perfect motion, but we are far from the end of it."

Hackings said nothing. He wanted to beg for his life. He wanted to ask the killer's true identity. He wanted to say *something*, though he decided not to. He was helpless, and more than anything, he just wanted his suffering to end.

There was a long, jagged blade in The Crucifier's right hand. The Crucifier stepped forward as close to Hackings as possible and then looked upward at him. The killer's eyes were parallel with Hackings' waist.

"Your suffering shall end, Mr. Hackings. You have humbly accepted your fate."

The Crucifier lifted the blade high up and shoved it deep into Hackings' side, slicing through skin, tissue and the dying man's ribcage.

Holding the blade in place, The Crucifier said, "I am The Crucifier. You are not the first, Packer Hackings. You are part of something bigger. Something greater. And now, you will be able to truly be judged for the things you have or have not done in this life. For me on this earth, and for you beyond this life, this is only the beginning."

The knife was then jerked violently out of Hackings' side. Blood instantly gushed from the freshly opened wound. Hackings began to choke, and blood streamed from his mouth. The Crucifier stepped back a few steps. Once Hackings had breathed his last breath, The Crucifier then stepped forward and kissed Hackings' bare feet. Then using Hackings' personal cell phone, the killer dialed 911, to report the location of the body and then threw the phone across the floor.

Pointing a finger into the air, The Crucifier then turned to leave.

"It was a pleasure, Mr. Hackings," the killer called out, just before walking out into the dark night.

CHAPTER FORTY-EIGHT

Six to four. Kayleen was her normal self again. She had taken over the game, and with only two minutes left, she had single-handedly cut the deficit down to only two. Laura was out of her seat. She was getting excited. Kuron had brought it out of her. He had brought the energy out of Kayleen as well. She was all business. Laura loved the look she now saw in her daughter's eye.

"Keep it up Lil Lions! Keep it up!" Kuron exclaimed.

He was no longer getting weird looks from people. Either they were already used to it, or their attention was locked in on the game. Or, most likely, it was a combination of the two.

The ball soared through the air and the Lil Lions' goalie caught it just before it entered the net. The Lil Lions crowd gasped, which was followed by a roar of excitement. Kayleen waved her arms in the air and the goalie threw the ball to her. Now dribbling the ball, she raced down the left sideline, blowing past defenders and teammates. No one came close to stopping her. Everyone on the field seemed almost in a daze at her aggressiveness. In a matter of no time, it was just her and the Select goalie. It looked like Kayleen was going to try to shoot with her left leg, but mid-kick she stopped and softly knocked the ball into the net with the inside of her right foot.

"GOAL!" Kuron yelled. "Atta girl, Kay! Let's go, defense. Get that ball back!"

As if on cue, Kayleen pretended that she was nonchalantly running back down the field to set up on defense when she spun around and stole the ball from an unsuspecting girl attempting to dribble down the right sideline.

Only a minute left.

Kayleen then passed the ball to a teammate trotting toward the goal. The girl struggled to smoothly receive the pass and tried to kick it toward the goal. The ball came off her foot slowly and was going far right. The goalie didn't even move, assuming the ball would fly out of bounds. However, it didn't. The ball was moving so slowly, it gave Kayleen time to react. She met the ball just before it rolled out of bounds, and with her right foot she drilled it and it sailed into the back of the net.

The crowd really erupted this time.

Six to six. All tied up.

"Wow!" Kuron exclaimed. He dropped to his haunches with his eyes glued on the game in front of him. Laura looked cool and confident, yet it was easy to tell she was filled with excitement. Her right foot tapped repetitively on the ground.

Thirty seconds to go.

Select's best player now had the ball and was sprinting down the field. She was a great player, almost as skilled and competitive as Kayleen. Select's coach was now screaming at her to hurry and score. The girl was locked in. Although only six, she was a competitor.

Twenty seconds.

Two girls on the Lil Lions' team were nowhere near the action but were "cherry-picking" down by Select's goal. One of the girls was Maddy. With a sour look on his face, her father, Bob, was sitting on the bleachers with his arms folded across his chest. The girl with the ball then made an unexpected mistake. She tripped on herself and the ball sailed forward, directly into Kayleen.

Fifteen seconds.

The two girls at the other end of the field were wide open. Realizing that their team now had the ball, they began to wave their arms wildly. Kayleen didn't acknowledge them, though. She acted as if she didn't even see them there.

With five seconds to go, she barreled past Maddy and sent the ball flying toward the goal. The ball flew right at the goalie. The little, red-headed goalie threw her arms out in front of her and looked like she was going to easily stop the ball. Everyone in attendance held their collective breath. At the very last moment, the goalie ducked, and threw a hand over her head to half-heartedly attempt to stop the ball. It wasn't enough, though. The ball sailed through the air, grazed the girl's fingertips and kissed the back of the net. Two seconds later, the horn went off.

Ball game. Seven to six.

Kuron wasn't able to contain his excitement. He jumped around, squealing like a 6'6", 250 pound little girl. He swept Malaya into his arms and spun her around once before dropping her back down to her feet.

"That was incredible!" Kuron exclaimed. "Best soccer game I've ever seen...and these little things are only six!"

Even Laura couldn't contain her excitement. Her beautiful smile was as wide and genuine as could be. She was still clapping her hands vigorously.

Kayleen was being hugged and high-fived by a number of her teammates. Others didn't really care and were there just because their parents wanted them to be soccer players, and some girls looked annoyed that Kayleen had single-handedly won the game, particularly Maddy and the other "cherry-picking" girl.

After shaking hands with the opposing team and more hugs, Kayleen came sprinting out of the pack. She reached Laura and instead of embracing her mother, she jumped into Kuron's arms and threw her arms around his neck.

"Thank you so much for coming. Thank you, thank you, thank you."

Laura couldn't help feeling one of those proud Mom moments taking over. She became emotional and had to fight back tears. She had been feeling as stressed as could be. Actually, feeling stressed was an understatement. The babies, Allen and Whitney's deaths, Ryan taking over the case with John, Kayleen being upset and not being able to completely understand where her dad was. It was all a lot for Laura. Right here, as she watched Kayleen hug and thank the Taylors, she felt happy, she felt at peace. None of the worries, the stresses, the heartache were there anymore.

Kayleen ran over and hugged Laura's legs. "I'm so glad they came, Mom. Thank you for telling them. And thank you for cheering me on too."

Laura grinned and one measly tear slid down her cheek. "You're so welcome, Kay."

CHAPTER FORTY-NINE

"I take it that you're Kayleen's fan club?"

Laura, Kuron and Malaya all turned to find the origin of the deep voice. It was Bob. Maddy's father.

Already, Kayleen was cowering behind Laura's leg, trying to avoid looking at the man.

"I would avoid looking at me too," Bob said. "I have a little girl over there in the car, who is bawling her eyes out because someone doesn't know how to play well with her teammates. I have held my tongue long enough, Mrs. Turner. He was now looking directly at Laura, pointing his chubby finger at her. I take it that you're Mrs. Turner, right? My girl did not touch the ball ONCE the whole second half. Not once! My wife and I got Maddy into this league for her to learn to love the game, improve, learn to play with others, so on and so forth. Your little girl is taking away opportunities not just from my girl but from others as well. Other parents just don't have the guts to talk to you about it. You need to…"

"I'm going to stop your fat, jolly self right there," Kuron chimed in, stepping between Bob and Laura. "I don't know your name, nor will I ever care to know your name. First things first, this woman right here is an absolute saint. So is this little girl. Hearts of gold like you have never seen before. You have *nothing* to say to either one of them. Nothing. You got me?"

"No, I need to…"

"No, first, you need to keep your mouth shut." Kuron was staring down at the blonde-headed, overweight man, now jabbing a finger in his face. "And if you can't figure out how to do that, I'll gladly help make it happen. Second, it's a six-year-old soccer league. Let me repeat that, a *six-year-old soccer league*. So, chill out. This isn't the World Cup. You got me? Kayleen can't help it that she's head and shoulders above everyone else. She has always been mature for her age in many more ways than one. She just got your little team to the championship…you can thank her later. Last of all, she and her mother here have gone through more than you can even wrap your head around. More than your puny mind can comprehend.

"This is a release, a get-away, an outlet. That's partially why this girl here is so good. She uses this sport as an outlet and puts so much time into this sport already. On her *own*. You don't know the half of who she is, what she's been through, the half of who we all are. Keep your asinine comments to yourself and enjoy watching this team play. If you don't like what's going on, keep your mouth shut, or find another team for your girl to play on, or find another sport. It's simple. It's not rocket science."

Bob said nothing. He looked pathetically inferior standing in front of Kuron's gigantic frame. He looked up at Kuron with an angry, hostile look in his eye. With his arms held at his sides, he balled up a fist.

Kuron chuckled. "You even touch me, buddy, and I will put you to sleep. Get out of here. We'll see you next week."

Without saying a single word, Bob turned his back to Kuron and stormed off.

CHAPTER FIFTY

Ryan knew it was bad news before he even answered the phone. Sadly, the majority of his conversations with Director Felix weren't the most happy and upbeat. They almost always involved work. And most things involved with work were dark and depressing.

"Hello," Ryan answered.

"Packer Hackings is dead. They've found the body."

Ryan swallowed. His gut feeling had been correct. This conversation wasn't going to involve any good news.

"Where?"

Felix cleared his throat, started to speak, and then cleared his throat again. "Ugh. My apologies. He has been found in the middle of nowhere. Just outside of Cleveland, Ohio in an old barn. Same exact scene as we have found with our other victims."

Ryan rose from his bed. It was nine o'clock. The sun had been down for a little while now. Outside the streets of DC still had life to them. Ryan walked over to the window and threw open the curtains. He and John had gotten a room at the downtown Comfort Inn and Suites. It was a very nice and not too pricey hotel. They had decided on one room with two queen-sized beds. John had thought having their own separate rooms would be fine, but Ryan took the initiative and just got one. After what happened to

Simmons and Lee, Ryan knew he and John would be better off sticking together at all times.

"So, this gives us the first victim outside the DC area. It throws a wrinkle into our investigation for sure."

"The detective out of Ohio I spoke to? I told him to hold off and wait for us to arrive at the scene. I figured you'd want that."

Ryan could hear John rustling around behind him. He had crashed out almost as soon as they'd gotten settled into their room. It had been a long day, even by their standards. A long day with very little luck or success.

After visiting the basement that Pablo Montez had been murdered in, the two spent almost the entirety of their day at the DC police headquarters. Using some incredible software that G-Man had created, they worked with a tech at headquarters to hack into security cameras all across the city. By doing so, they did their best to track Simmons' and Lee's whereabouts the day leading up to their deaths. They hadn't found much. Nothing suspicious. Nothing too out of the ordinary.

The two agents had spent a majority of their time at MPD Headquarters. They had lunch at a local Mexican restaurant, went to a coffee shop midday, spent time at the site of Montez's death, had random encounters with people at crosswalks, in the streets, in the hotel lobby. They even stopped and helped a distraught woman with her broke-down car. They never came across the man from the hotel footage. The hours in front of screens watching film ended up giving the two agents little to no success, doing nothing but draining them.

"Yes, sir," Ryan said. "Thank you. You think we could get out there by sunup?"

"When there's a will, there's a way. I'll see what strings I can pull. I'll call you soon."

"And I want to find a way to get G-Man and some more of our guys to meet us there."

"I'll see what we can do."

With that, the call ended as suddenly as it had begun. Felix had sounded lifeless, defeated. Ryan couldn't help but accept that he himself may have sounded the same way as well. The same day that Hackings was pronounced missing, he was found dead. The Crucifier's other victims were missing for far longer before the 911 call was made tipping off the location of their bodies. This murder was different in that sense. But why? And this time around, it happened in a completely different part of the country.

"Alright, what do we have now, Captain? You've been on that phone a lot, and lately it hasn't been a good thing."

Ryan turned away from the window to see John sitting up in his bed. John flipped on the bedside lamp which sat between the two beds.

"That was Director Felix," Ryan said. "Hackings was found dead just outside of Cleveland."

John shook his head slowly, staring down at the floor. "And I'm going to guess he was found hanging from a cross."

"You got it."

John cursed under his breath. "We going tonight?"

Ryan nodded. "I'm hoping so."

"Let's drive."

"If Felix can't figure out how to fly us out soon then we will."

"Well, it's about a five-hour drive, give or take," John said, scratching his lower back. "We can leave now and get to the area by three."

"I know. We'll give Felix an hour and then we'll decide from there."

John stood up and stretched, patted Ryan on the back, and made his way to the bathroom.

"Don't worry, we're going to find this guy, Ryan," he said.

"I know. I know we will."

CHAPTER FIFTY-ONE

At Five minutes till ten, Felix called Ryan back. This call involved good news, given the recent circumstances. Felix had located a private plane and pilot to take Ryan and John to Cleveland then back to DC. He also found a plane for G-Man and a team to fly to Cleveland from New York City. They were set to arrive from New York at 5 a.m. With that in mind, Ryan and John would leave just before 3:30 in the morning, given that the duration of their flight would be around an hour and twenty minutes. It was a better alternative than driving, not that Ryan minded driving. He honestly enjoyed road trips, but this time around, flying was more than preferable.

At five minutes after ten, there was a knock at the door, causing Ryan and John both to freeze. There were two solid knocks then nothing more. With his head, Ryan motioned toward the nightstand between the two beds where John's gun lay. John carefully slid off the bed and opening the drawer in the nightstand, he came out with his trusty Glock.

Ryan stood to his feet and motioned towards the door. The two stealthily crept over to it. Behind them, Ryan's cell began to ring on the nightstand, buzzing and vibrating obnoxiously. Ryan paid it no mind, neither did John. The two knocks were still all there had been. Nothing more. About a minute had now passed. Ryan reached the door first and peered through the peep hole toward the top of the door.

Nothing.

Ryan motioned John over to do the same. He looked through the hole.

Same result.

Ryan placed one hand on the door handle as he held the other up in the air. John stood up against the wall, opposite the direction the door would swing. Ryan put one finger up in the air...then two...then three. The moment his right ring finger came up, he pulled open the door, and in one hard step John was out in the hallway. There was a loud *THUD* and John suddenly had a man pinned to the ground.

"John! John! John! It's me! It's only me!" the man whimpered.

John growled and jumped to his feet. "What is wrong with you?"

Ryan couldn't help but smirk a little. Pulling himself off the floor, Detective Tyrique Fox dusted himself off and stood up straight, wearing a sheepish grin on his face.

"But seriously? What's wrong with you, man?" John repeated.

"I am so, so very sorry," Fox said, his eyes shifting between the two agents and the ground.

"Well, come on inside," Ryan said, with his foot in the door.

The three walked into the room. Ryan sat at the foot of his bed, John at the foot of the other, and Fox stood up against the wall in front of the two.

"What's going on, Detective?" Ryan queried.

Now that the embarrassment and shame had begun to leave Fox. He looked almost giddy with excitement.

"Guys, I found the van," Fox said, excitedly. "I mean, *we* found the van. I gave two of our officers, Barbara and Celeste, instructions to search the city for the van. It is literally all they've been doing. They've been very diligent about it."

"Where is it?" Ryan asked sharply.

"They found it at Cash for Cars, at the intersection of 12th Street Northwest and G Street Northwest. They questioned the owner about it. And he said a hooded woman dropped it off. He told them that they didn't get the woman's name. She pulled up, got out of the van, then just walked away. The owner told them it was the first time he had ever had someone just drop off a vehicle without getting paid for it. He called after her and tried following her but never got a response."

"Weird…" John pondered.

"So, although it isn't much, it is something. We have the van back at headquarters. It'll be inspected thoroughly. We really do have a good team here."

"I believe it," Ryan said. "And this definitely is something. Thank you. Detective. If anything, it gives us a bit of hope. I just don't think we can get our hopes too high. This killer has been perfect thus far."

"Certainly, sir…I mean Mr. Turner-I mean Ryan. Have you heard anything more about Packer Hackings and his whereabouts?"

In a measured voice, John delivered the unhappy news. "He's dead. They found him just outside of Cleveland. It was clearly The Crucifier's work again."

Fox's positive energy seemed to leave him all at once. "That's horrible. Wow."

"We just spoke to Director Felix," said Ryan. "We're going to head to the scene early in the morning. We were planning on giving you the heads up, but you just so happened to show up here anyway."

"About that, I am so sorry! My apartment is really close to here and I was out getting a bite to eat. I was heading home when Celeste called to tell me about their day. I have no idea what took them so long to reach me. I guess it was a long process for them to speak to the owner, since the business was closed when they discovered the van. My cell phone had died-I really need to get a new battery-so I just decided to come see you in person. However, after I knocked, I was worried you were both either asleep or that you were not around. Then my phone miraculously came back to life inside my pocket, buzzing a few times, so I called you, but you didn't pick up."

"Yeah, because we were approaching the door, getting ready to put a beat down on whoever was out there," John said.

"Gosh, I know. Bad move. I'm really sorry."

Ryan put a hand up. "No need to apologize, Detective. All is well now. I just don't recommend doing something like that again. We're all on pins and needles right now with everything that's going on."

"Won't happen again," said Fox. "Well, I'll get going. Sorry that my news isn't as exciting as it sounded earlier in my head. While you're away, I'll do my best to try to ID the woman."

"What did she look like?" John said. He was leaning forward, focusing very intently on what Fox's next words would be.

"Well, umm, it's hard to really say. I have to say, the camera that captured her was not all that great, plus the hood covered any sort of apparent physical features. She kept her head low throughout the film we watched. All I can say is she looked to be short. She kind of walked with a weird limp, maybe? Or I might have been imagining it."

"*The woman we…*" Ryan said to himself under his breath.

"Your wheels are turning, Ryan, what's up?" John asked.

Ryan and John locked eyes.

"*The woman we…* " Ryan repeated.

John's face and demeanor completely changed. "Do you think?"

"A petite woman, with a limp was one of the last people we saw with Allen and Whitney," Ryan replied.

"I know…this may just be us reaching, though."

"But there's a chance that's her. We can't be *too* thorough."

John nodded. "True. I did have a weird feeling about that whole exchange."

"I have a good feeling about this."

"Me too."

"Guys?" Fox looked as confused as a college student on the first day of Calculus Three.

"Sorry, Detective," Ryan apologized. "It's the brother-brother dynamic kicking into gear. But it looks like your officers' discovery wasn't so insignificant after all."

John rose to his feet. "In fact, we may have just cracked this case wide open."

CHAPTER FIFTY-TWO

Ryan arrived in Cleveland at 4:48 in the morning. It was still dark. The air was cool for a summer night. He was alone for now. John had hung back in DC to help Fox with their new lead. After speaking with Fox, John couldn't sleep. He was excited. More than excited. After some deliberation they agreed that John would stay behind and get a jump start on discovering the ID of the mystery woman. John had promised to not isolate himself. They couldn't afford to take any chances this time around. They agreed that they had to be overcautious.

Ryan waited inside the rental car that Felix had gotten them. It was a red Honda Civic. The thirty minutes he waited seemed like thirty hours. He was anxious to examine the scene, to see what they could find. It would be the first aftermath of the crucifixions that Ryan would see firsthand. He had a good feeling about this, which added to his anxiety. Although he felt good about being there in Cleveland, he also felt very uneasy about leaving John in DC. John did have Fox and the rest of the department there; however, he still felt a sense of dread and uncertainty upon leaving, but he couldn't figure out why. John was smart, tough, talented, and could handle himself well. He was good at what he did. Maybe it was the fact that he was family, which caused Ryan's instinctive concern. Or maybe there really was reason to worry…

Sitting there, his mind also wandered back to his family at home.

Man, I miss them.

He and John hadn't even been gone for very long, and it was already the hardest part of being away. Not the fact that they were chasing a serial killer with no leads, or any helpful evidence, let alone witnesses of any sort, but that he hated to be away from his loved ones. His job, which was once the most important thing in his life and what he lived for, now played second fiddle to his family life. The most important part of himself, which he valued most of all, was his role as a husband and a father. He sent a text to Laura telling her he loved her and that he would call in a few hours. He really did miss them dearly. He missed them so much, but to a certain extent, he was still happy to be where he was now; to be immersed in the case, making a direct difference…hopefully making a difference, that is.

He hadn't been honest with himself, and he hadn't been completely honest with Laura either when they spoke in Battery Park. He really had missed his former job. The thrill. The chase. Perhaps taking on the case himself was due to some type of selfishness. Working as a field agent had been a part of him for so long. It was nice to be back.

At 5:20, the plane holding G-Man along with two FBI forensic interns touched down on the tarmac. G-Man was dressed in white Khaki shorts, a short-sleeved collared-shirt, white Converse, and a cap that sat backwards on his head. It may have been the most casual Ryan had ever seen G-Man look. He had upgraded his usual look from "nerd" to "nerdy-tourist".

Ryan stuck an arm out the window and waved the three men down. With an oddly shaped bag slung over his shoulder, G-Man quickly shuffled over to the car in an awkward fashion that brought the image of Quasimodo to Ryan's mind. The other two men followed closely behind. Ryan popped the trunk, G-Man threw the bag inside, then plopped himself into the passenger seat.

"Ryan Turner," G-Man said as he slammed the door shut. "How's it going, my good lad?""

"Always better when you're here, Gary."

"Aw-w-w," G-Man said, slapping Ryan on the shoulder. "Aren't you just so sweet. You like the new outfit?"

Ryan raised his brows with a smile on his face. "Very cute, Gary."

G-man did the best theatrical bow he could manage. "Put it together myself. I don't get out of New York City much, you know. I've got to treat this little trip like a vacation. Got to look the part too, my friend."

"Hey," Ryan said with a small chuckle, "whatever floats your boat."

G-Man put his feet on the dash and placed his hands behind his head. "Alright, fellas, let's get this show on the road. Now where's this body at?"

CHAPTER FIFTY-THREE

He arose from his bed at precisely 5:20 a.m. just as he did every morning. Jack Grimes didn't wake up happy, though. The previous day, he had been anticipating that this very morning would be a joyous one. He expected to wake up this morning feeling a sense of accomplishment. That was not the case. The hotel room in the Ritz Carlton still looked like it did the first time he had been there so many years before. There had been no destruction. No change. Somehow, his plan had completely fallen through.

Once inside the hotel, he had prowled around just outside the room, room 1205, hoping to get an opportunity to get himself inside. However, one never came. Finally, he put his maid disguise to the test. He knocked on the door twice.

"Housekeeping."

There was no reply. He repeated the same knocks and spoke the same single word. No reply. He then knocked louder and spoke louder. No answer.

Maybe no one is here.

It was early in the afternoon, so it was likely that no one was in the room at the moment. Using a key he had gotten from one of the real maids on the first floor, he opened the door. As he entered the room, there was a scream and a pillow was chucked in Grimes's direction.

The woman sitting on the king-sized bed yelled, "Get out, you creep! My room is clearly clean! Go stick your nose somewhere else."

She appeared to be the only one in the room. Grimes knew he could easily kill her. It wouldn't take much. His blood boiled. She had just ruined his plan and was now disrespecting him. He had wanted to kill her right then and there but thought better than to do so. He had to stick to the plan and her death was not part of the day's plan. He decided in that moment that this next step could wait, and he retreated out of the room.

At 5:30 a.m., Grimes sat down at his dining room table and scarfed down a bowl of cereal. In between bites, he cursed under his breath as he thought about the previous day.

That awful woman ruined everything.

This morning's meditation session was going to be much needed. The anger from the previous day was still lingering in his heart. He needed to banish it. He wished that he could start his session now and skip watching the news, taking a shower, writing in his journal, and reading. But he knew he couldn't. He *had* to stick to his daily routine. It's who he was.

Grimes knew he would return to the Ritz Carlton today. He would follow the same routine. He hoped today would be the day.

"Why dwell on yesterday, when you have a brand-new start today? Yesterday does not define the possibilities of today."

The words echoed in Grimes's mind. It was another quote from his old therapist, which sometimes brought him much needed wisdom and peace of mind. Today was one of those days. And today would be the day that he would yet again enter the Ritz Carlton, work his way into room 1205, and this time around, ultimately remove that room from existence.

CHAPTER FIFTY-FOUR

Just as Ryan opened the barn door and stepped inside the old building, the smell of death hit him like a slamming door. He recognized the smell immediately. It wasn't a vile enough smell to make him gag, but it was enough to cause his stomach to feel queasy. With Ryan was G-Man, G-Man's two travel partners, a local detective by the name of Kody Willis, a local CSI photographer, and then a whole slew of police officers who were waiting outside of the barn.

"That's a rank smell," one of G-Man's counterparts said, holding a hand over his nose.

"Oh, you'll get used to it, Leonard," G-Man said reassuringly, while he fiddled with the small baggies in his hands.

"How does it already smell?" the second man asked. "Like, didn't this guy die less than a day ago?"

"Let me tell you, Marquez," G-Man began.

Before continuing, he finished placing the small baggies into a secure pouch inside the bulky bag he carried. The small bags contained the lifting tape he had just used on the doorknob prior to their entry.

"So," G-Man continued, "the human body begins decomposing a mere three to four-ish minutes after death. This guy has been dead for at least twelve hours. So, I would say that the body has only been going through step one of decomposition, which is called autolysis. It's six thirty now, so I would say twelve hours is the bare minimum since his last breath. He had probably been bleeding, dying and suffering for heaven knows how long." The group stopped in front of the body that hung from the cross at the back end of the barn, and G-Man stepped in close, gesturing at the gaping wound in Hackings' side. "A lot of what we're smelling are the bodily fluids which have already escaped due to the severity of his wounds. That's probably the main factor attributing to our stench issue. I mean, the big wound in the side right here was caused by a blade of some sort which looks to have gone through ribs, badly punctured a lung, and due to the large amount of blood from this single wound, I'm guessing the lateral thoracic artery was ruptured as well. Lots of different fluids, tissue, bone, etcetera from this single wound. Now, as I already stated, once death occurs, the body immediately begins decomposition. The body *needs* oxygen. Of course, when we die, we no longer consume oxygen."

The two young men in training, who came with G-Man, looked very engaged. Ryan, on the other hand, did his best to ignore G-man's sudden urge to show how much he knew. He was somewhat curious why G-Man had decided on bringing two greenies. Whatever his motives may have been, Ryan trusted G-Man with his life. If he wanted to bring two greenies, there must have been a valid reason why. Besides, G-Man was the very best there was when it came to forensics and sweeping a crime scene. He could have brought a couple of monkeys with him for all Ryan cared. Instead of involving himself with G-Man's conversation, Ryan conversed with Willis.

He hadn't learned too much, thus far. The recording of the 911 call was the same as all the rest. It showed the same, deep, eerie, modified voice.

"Packer Hackings is dead. His judgement on this earth is complete. His judgement in the afterlife will soon follow."

Then the voice went on to give the exact address where the body was. Hackings had been dead when they found him. The only difference at this site, which Ryan recognized right away, was that the crime scene was missing an important element. The "extra touch", the pizazz, was completely missing. There were no melted down candle sticks or gold candle plates. Also, Ryan had the feeling that Hackings hadn't been left to suffer as long as the previous victims. His face didn't look as drawn up. It was just an assumption more than an accurate finding, for the moment.

"Without oxygen," G-Man continued, accompanying his words with various hand motions, "cellular respiration is impossible. It can't happen. Therefore, a dead body ends up with excess carbon dioxide inside, due to its inability to go through cellular respiration, circulate blood and remove wastes. Also, though this is beside the point, as we can see, the body has stiffened. This is called *Rigor mortis.* If it wasn't something involving death, I would say it's a pretty cool thing, but instead I'll choose the word *fascinating.*

"So, Rigor mortis occurs two to six hours after death. With the heat, I would say closer to six. Now, although the heat slows down the Rigor mortis process, we know an increase in temperature almost always leads to chemical reactions overcoming their activation energy much faster. You guys know this. During this hot time of the year, and inside this hot, muggy barn, I'm sure the decomposition process is in overdrive. If Packer Hackings, bless his soul, was crucified in Antarctica, well, he'd sure be stiff, but decomposition would never have the ability to take its course. The activation energy required, could never be overcome."

"So, part of the stench is due to the heat causing the chemical reactions inside the dead body to accelerate, and then a big part of it is due to the blood and bodily fluids from the gaping wounds?" Marquez asked.

"Exactly," G-man confirmed. "Excess carbon dioxide causes an acidic environment, which in turn, causes membranes inside the cells to rupture. Boom! The membranes release enzymes that begin eating the cells from the inside out, and the smell comes from the various gases being released during decomposition. If not for the gaping wounds, the smell that has overtaken this entire barn would be much more tolerable. Now if the body had been decomposing for, say, two or three days in this hot, muggy place, then, because of your unfamiliarity with a scene like this, you two would have already lost your airport breakfast all over the floor."

"I hate to interrupt your lecture, Professor Richards," Ryan said, placing a hand on G-Man's back, "but can you guys give us a hand? We need to pull this cross down."

CHAPTER FIFTY-FIVE

Using the pocketknife that he carried with him at all times, Ryan cut the ropes that held the cross upward. The ones that were easy to untie, he simply untied. The cross was driven through the wooden barn floor, which kept the cross stable, in itself. However, the thick ropes simply added to its stability. There were four of them all attached to the middle of the cross, stretching out in four different directions, attaching to livestock stalls and some large wooden pillars.

The photographer had already snapped pictures of the cross as it held Hackings and was now wandering around taking pictures of every other little thing he could. The other men held the cross in place, then gingerly laid it down on its backside once Ryan finished releasing the ropes.

The moment the cross hit the floor, Ryan asked nobody in particular, "How many people do you think it would take to bring in that thing and set it up the way it was?"

"I'm not sure," Willis answered. "A couple, probably."

Ryan walked over and helped the men cut Hackings' body free from the cross. Carefully, respectfully, he assisted the men in carrying the body to the side and gingerly setting it on a medical, forensics tarp that was spread out on the floor.

"Now let's see how many of us it takes to carry this cross and set it in the ground where it was," Ryan said, bending over. "G-Man, Willis, you two help me first."

The three all positioned themselves around the large piece of wood and lifted it up. They did so fairly easy.

"Three, or maybe even two somewhat strong people can move this and position the cross as needed," Ryan said, "Go ahead and set it down."

Ryan continued. "On film, from the area one of the previous victims was found, we saw three individuals carry a cross from a van. I imagine the same happened here. Most likely three, but possibly two people. I would say most likely three because a 200-pound man definitely adds to the weight of the cross. I do believe whoever we are dealing with is from around the DC area. For whatever reason, they decided to kill Hackings fast and decided to do it here. I don't understand why, just yet, but knowing that there were three people *is* significant. The more people here, the more likely for there to be a mistake. The more likely it is for us to ID one of these people. For one thing, they needed a large vehicle to haul his cross.

"Willis, I want you to be relentless about searching security footage all across the Cleveland area and anywhere that's close to where we are right now. Thoroughly seek out security footage and possible eyewitnesses near the Hackings' home. We need to search for a suspicious vehicle that could transport a cross of this size and/or three suspicious people in a group. I am going to make an educated guess and say that these people were in the area for at least twenty-four hours. I would say no more than forty-eight hours, but no less than twenty-four. They had to stalk Hackings and find the right time to take him. Next, they had to unload the cross at some point and set it all up. Then they had to place Hackings on the cross, and I'm guessing they let him suffer for a bit. Based on autopsies, the other victims suffered for quite a while before they finally died. This time around, thankfully, I don't think our victim suffered as long as the others did. This feels rushed. Bottomline, we have a time frame, Detective Willis. And I want you to be my secret weapon on this while I'm back in DC."

"We'll do everything we can," he replied.

"Like I said, the more people who were involved, the more likely for there to have been a slip-up, and statistically, the more likely for one of them to have been or to be seen at some point. Another thought…this could very well be the first time that multiple people were in the room when the victim was stabbed in the side and ultimately killed. I know with Pablo Montez, there was only a single person that came out of the building around the time of his death preceding the 911 call. I assume the same occurred with the others around the DC area."

"So, that would reaffirm these guys are centralized somewhere around the DC area," G-Man chipped in.

"Right," Ryan said. "They're out of their comfort zone here, they rushed this crucifixion, and there were multiple people here multiple times. All in all, this Crucifier character may have made one of his very first mistakes here."

G-Man was rubbing his hands together. "Ooh, I like the sound of this. We do like ourselves some mistakes."

As if the universe also loved Ryan's comments and wanted to help bring them to light as well, the photographer perked up. He was down on his knees at the front of the barn; near the door and had been snapping away, locked in on something on the floor. He stood upright suddenly.

"Guys," he said, still staring at the ground. "I think I might have something here. You may want to come take a look at this."

CHAPTER FIFTY-SIX

It was a hair. One single, long strand of dark-brown hair. Since it was such a small thing that blended in with the dark brown barn floor, it was impossible to see from a standing point of view. Kneeling down, though, Ryan saw it clearly.

"What could you do with this?" Ryan asked, looking up at G-Man.

"Oh, I could do plenty."

"We could identify who it belongs to, right?" Willis asked.

"I'm thinking so," Ryan said, glancing over at G-Man for his approval.

Digging around in his bag, G-Man put up a finger. He then came out of it wearing gloves and holding yet another small baggie.

"Okay, how do I dumb this down…" G-Man said, winking at Ryan. "Proteins are extremely abundant in hair, and they are much more stable than DNA. Plus, you learn to work with and denature proteins in general chemistry; first year of college…shout out to professor Williamson. Anyways, they're easy to work with if you know what you're doing and it's easy to retrieve specific information from proteins. So, finding a hair is a pretty good thing. It just isn't *DNA* analysis that we'll do. As hair grows longer and longer, the cells that make up the hair shaft die off because they get stretched, which moves them further away from their supply of nutrients. That's why you can't get sufficient DNA from a hair. However, mutations in DNA translate to proteins and, at times, even change the protein structure by swapping out one amino acid for another. Sorry, I'm probably getting too geeky on you now. Long story short, we have learned to identify individuals based on the benign variations in the proteins found in hair. Our protein analysis has proven accurate about ninety-eight percent of the time. By my standards, that isn't too bad at all."

G-Man retrieved the hair from the floor, pulled it close to his eyes and gazed at it for a moment, then placed it in the small plastic bag.

"As of right now, the only downside to this, is that protein analyses taken from hairs don't hold up in a court of law."

"How does it not…?" Willis began.

G-Man put up a finger. "Let me finish. As I said, DNA translates to proteins and changes structures at times. This occurs in hair. That change in structure is what we look for. It's the unique thing that helps to separate individuals. We've actually found a way to trace the protein structure changes back to one's specific DNA. So, whoever's hair this is? There is *maybe* one other person out of 100,000 people who share the same, *exact* protein structure change. Yes, the human body is a miraculous thing. This whole idea is a fairly new concept to forensic science, but it has proven to be quite effective, just not effective enough for our judicial system. But with new improvements and technology, which my team and I have put together over the years, not to pat myself on the back or anything, I can almost one hundred percent trust our findings. Or I have ninety-eight percent trust in them, to be precise."

"How do we know this isn't a horse's hair, or some other animal?" asked Leonard.

"*Great* question, Leonard," G-Man said, almost sarcastically. "The very end of the strand shows that it's bleached. It's usually hard to see with just one strand of hair, but I noticed it right away. Very few animals can bleach their hair or have the means to pay for a hairdresser. All joking aside, we really can't know for sure if it's human until we get into a lab. However, from my years of experience, I can tell you that, yes, it's a human hair. We also can't know for sure if this hair fell out or was pulled out by force. The reason that this is relevant is because if it just fell out, then most likely there isn't a root attached. From what I can see and based on the fact that there's just one lonely hair here, I believe it probably just fell out like many of our hairs do every day."

Ryan folded his arms across his chest. "And if there is a root, that means you'd be able to retrieve DNA, right?"

"Bingo! Which would give us even more accuracy and hope. BUT I'm planning worst-case scenario, and worst-case scenario isn't half bad, right? So, either way, we'll take it. Like I said, I've sure been a fan of our recent strides with protein analysis."

"You got that right," Ryan said. "We'll take it, for sure. This is potentially the first bit of helpful evidence that anyone has uncovered so far."

"Knock on wood," Willis said. "Don't speak too soon, Mr. Turner."

"I'm not." Ryan turned to look back at Packer Hackings' body. "I've got a feeling that the tide may finally be turning in our favor."

CHAPTER FIFTY-SEVEN

By six-thirty in the morning, John had already met up with Tyrique Fox. He gave Fox the same run down he and Ryan had already given him the night before. The two had casually looked over the van that now sat in a cubicle in the Metropolitan Police Department headquarters, and now were looking over the security tape that had been retrieved from Cash for Cars.

"Yup," John said coolly. "That's her, the same woman."

"Are you sure?" Fox asked, with his hand on the computer mouse.

"Positive. Same build, holds herself the same, moves the same, same limp. It's got to be her. It isn't a coincidence that our two agents had an encounter with her and hours later they were found dead. Agent Simmons tried to send Lee a message as he was dying. It read, 'The woman we'. This individual could be that 'woman'. Man, she could even be the key to finding The Crucifier."

"Well, your friend's last mission, and last action on this earth, may not have been in vain after all."

John nodded. "Maybe not. Good ole Allen Simmons, bless his rested soul. The one officer that attributed to finding the van...what's here name...? Celeste, right? Has she seen the films of this woman?"

"No, not yet, but she should be here any minute now."

"Perfect. I want us three to look at this one, and also look at the footage of Simmons and Lee helping the woman with her car. Celeste found the van, so it's only fair that she should get to help us out with this too. That's why I wanted you to bring her in."

"Sounds like a plan. I certainly agree with you."

"Your CSI guys, have you heard anything from them?"

Fox shook his head. "No, not yet. Like I told you, they swept the entire van. They're being super thorough. We should hear from them any minute, as well. They're in there working hard."

"Sweet, sweet."

"Do you expect them to find anything of significance?"

"I mean, you never know. Any little thing could be of help us."

Fox shrugged. "I'm a very optimistic person. I want to believe that they'll find something, but this killer has been *extremely* careful throughout the entire case."

John nodded his head. "I doubt they'll find anything useful. I think finding this woman is our key."

Fox gave a slight nod of agreement. "But at the same time, why would she allow herself to be caught by a security camera, and then drop off the van in a public place for no apparent reason?"

John gave the question some thought. As careful as these people had been so far, it seemed awfully peculiar that they would let down their guard like this.

"I honestly don't know how to answer that one. It does seem odd, man. Tell me once again what the Cash for Cars manager told you."

Fox cleared his throat. "The officers reported that he was at the front desk when he heard a car pull up. He said that business had been slow not only that day, but for the past week or so. He got up immediately and went outside to greet the person. He said that the person, who was already walking away from the van, looked to be a woman. She wore tight, blue jeans and a white hoodie, had her back turned to him, walked with a slight limp, never turned around, never responded to him calling out to her, walked away, and was simply gone. Vanished."

It was the third time Fox had told John the story. He just wanted to hear it again. He wanted to create a very vivid picture in his mind of the scene.

"What kind of shoes did she have on?" John asked.

Fox couldn't help chuckling before responding. "My apologies, sir. That just came across as a strange-sounding question in my mind. To be completely honest with you, I highly doubt that was asked."

"Well, let's give that manager a call and ask him."

CHAPTER FIFTY-EIGHT

John whipped out his phone and searched "DC Cash for Cars" in his internet search engine. After a few scrolls and clicks, he found the business's phone number. The phone began to ring.

"Lucky for us, they open at six-thirty," John said to Fox.

John put the call on speaker and set the device on the table.

"Good morning, Cash for Cars, this is Yvette. How may I help you?"

"Hi, Yvette, my name is John Drexel, how are you?"

"Oh, I'm-I'm good, yourself, Mr. Drexel?"

"Doing just fine, thanks for asking. You sound young? Sixteen? Seventeen, possibly? Don't freak out, okay? You've probably never had a conversation like this before."

"He-he," Yvette laughed nervously. "Are you an assistant to the President? Or are you about to abduct me and hold me for ransom? Because neither experience will be new to me."

John swallowed. "Wow! Hold up, you've been abducted before?"

"No, I haven't, Mr. Drexel. Got you. I have spoken to people from the White House, though. Pretty cool, I'll have to say. What's your reason for calling, Mr. Drexel?"

John was somewhat taken aback.

Witty little girl.

"You remind me of my niece. I like it. I work for the FBI. I'm on a case here in the DC area and need to speak to your manager as soon as possible."

"You're right, this is a new experience. I've never spoken to an FBI agent before. I'm here to tell you that Mr. Patel is clean. He wouldn't hurt a fly. Trust me, it shows, because this office is filled with those nasty things."

John laughed. "He's got nothing to worry about. He came across one of our persons of interest, so I just need to get a few more details from him."

"He isn't at work today, but I can give you his cell. Does that work? Or do you want his social security number too?"

"That's perfect. The social security number only if you want."

Fox pulled out his phone, putting in the number that Yvette provided.

"Thank you so much."

"Of course. Good luck with that case. If there's any sort of bounty for who you're after, you better not forget I was the one to get you the infamous Mr. Patel's number for you."

John smirked. "Thanks again, young lady," he said before ending the call.

Fox immediately dialed Aditya Patel's phone number, placed it on speaker, and set it down on the tabletop in front of them. After four rings, there was an answer.

"Hello?" Patel's groggy voice said.

"Mr. Patel," John said cheerfully. "Good morning, sir."

"Huh? Who is this?"

"I'm Agent John Drexel. FBI. I'm on a case here in the DC area and need to ask a few questions of you, if that's okay? I'm sitting here with Detective Fox, who is out of the MPD. He'll be listening in on the conversation."

There was a rustling around on Patel's end of the line for a good ten seconds before he spoke again.

"Yes," Patel said, in his strong Indian accent. "Yes, whatever you need."

"You spoke with two officers yesterday about a woman who dropped off a van at your business. Is that right?"

"Yes, I did. That is correct."

"I have a question about the same woman. Can you confirm what that mystery woman was wearing?"

"I can do that, sir. Tight-fitting, blue jeans. And a thin, white hoodie."

"Can you also recall what kind of shoes she wore?"

"Hm," Patel pondered. "Let me think about this."

"Picture the exact scenario. Put yourself back in time to when you stepped out of your office to find this woman walking away from the van. What do you hear, feel, see?"

"Hm…" Patel continued to ponder.

John waited for the man to respond.

"Ooh, yes, she wore white shoes. They were high-tops. Nikes. All white."

"Perfect. And you're positive about that description."

"Yes, sir. Positive."

"Can you confirm she walked with a limp?"

"Yes, sir. A slight limp. Not an obvious limp, but only enough for me to notice it."

John gave Fox a thumbs up.

"Thank you so much," John said. "That is all we have for you. You can go back to sleep now, Mr. Patel, unless you have anything else to tell us that may be helpful in finding this woman."

"Ha-ha. No, sir. I do not have anything else. Good day to you."

"Have a good one, Mr. Patel."

CHAPTER FIFTY-NINE

John nodded to Fox, who in turn ended the call.

"So, what did you get from that?" Fox asked

"Those are the same shoes that were worn by the woman we saw with Simmons and Lee hours before they died," John answered. "Coincidence? I really don't think so."

"Wow, this is great! Absolutely great, John! I mean, Agent Drexel."

John smirked, shaking his head slightly. "Dude, 'John' works just fine. You're good."

"Sorry, sorry, sorry. John, this is great, though. Do you think we can ID this woman just from the tapes?"

"I think so. There were some decent shots of her face when she encountered our two agents. She was convinced she wouldn't be suspected of anything. She thought she was home free and was cool and confident in that moment. She certainly wasn't expecting us to be sitting right here looking at her face on our screen. That was never a possibility in her mind. That said, we have great guys up in NYC, and an incredible database that can identify her."

Behind the two men, the door to the room opened.

"Excuse me, sir, I'm sorry I'm late."

It was Celeste. John stood and turned to greet the woman. Suddenly it felt as if his heart stopped beating. His hands became clammy. A warm sensation shot up his spine. He couldn't find words. He couldn't speak. He was paralyzed.

"Officer Ventana," Fox said, "this is Special Agent John Drexel. John, this is Officer Celeste Ventana."

John simply stared at Celeste. He couldn't break his stare. She gave him a questioning, confused smile while tilting her head slightly to the side.

"Is everything okay, Agent Drexel?" she asked, sticking her hand out.

John lifted his hand up and shook hers in an almost robotic-like fashion. No, everything wasn't okay. John knew Celeste Ventana's face. She was the spitting image of his ex-girlfriend, Delia. The same Delia who had now been dead for five years.

CHAPTER SIXTY

"I'm-I-I'm great," John stammered. "Everything is A-OK. Sorry, I just, I just zoned out. I-I don't know what got into me."

Celeste lifted her eyebrows. "Apology accepted. You look like you've seen a ghost. Maybe you should sit down, Agent Drexel?"

I feel like I'm looking at one.

John sat. He felt light-headed. Celeste couldn't possibly look any more like Delia. She had the same long, blonde hair, button nose, deep blue eyes, round little chin, athletic build, and was pretty much the same height, even. Her voice was obviously different, but the physical features the women shared were astonishingly similar. Even though it had been over five years since Delia's death, John still thought about her every day. Every. Single. Day. Since her death, he hadn't even gone on a single date. Her death had messed him up. It messed him up bad.

She wasn't only an "ex", she had been his fiancé, and before that, his high school and college sweetheart. The only girlfriend he had ever had. She was the sweetest person he had ever met. There was never any drama between them, never even an argument. She died in John's arms a mere two days after he had proposed to her.

"You can call this guy *John*," Fox said to Celeste. "He doesn't like any of that *Agent* or *sir* stuff."

John snapped out of his trance and chuckled uncomfortably.

"Yeah, I'm not superior to either of you. John works just fine. Pull up a seat, Celeste."

"Don't mind if I do," Celeste said, pulling up a chair to John's left.

"Want to show her the film now?" Fox asked.

"Yeah, let's do it," John said.

As John used the mouse to navigate the cursor on the computer screen, Fox spoke to Celeste.

"I think we're onto something here, Celeste," Fox said.

Celeste seemed very interested in everything going on. Her eyes were locked on the computer screen,

"What have you guys found?" she asked.

"The woman that dropped off the van?" Fox said. "John found her in another piece of film we've taken. We may be able to identify her."

"Shut up. Are you serious?"

"Here we go," John said.

The screen in front of him now showed three people in the street. Two women, one man. One woman was Asian-American. The other was a fair-skinned, Caucasian woman with blonde, almost white hair that hung down past her shoulders. She looked distressed. John started the film. Celeste sat to John's left, Fox to his right.

"So, this is the other security footage where we find the mystery woman," John said. "She's the blonde one."

On the screen, the three people were conversing. Mid-conversation, with an exasperated look on her face, the blonde woman threw her head up toward the security camera's gaze. John quickly paused the tape, and then carefully zoomed in on the mystery woman's distressed face.

Celeste leaned in close to the screen, almost pushing John out of the way. Her mouth fell open. Now *she* looked like the one who was seeing a ghost.

"Celeste, are you okay?" Fox asked.

Celeste fell back into her chair and put her hands atop of her head.

"I know her, Tyrique," she said. "I know that woman."

CHAPTER SIXTY-ONE

The instant Ryan reached the rental car to leave the scene of the murder, Detective Willis was suddenly calling out to him. As they came out of the barn, Willis had received a phone call. Now, just a little way behind him, Ryan could hear Willis frantically calling out his name.

"Ryan, come here," Willis called out, panting. "Quickly, please."

Ryan turned and in a couple of strides he was back at Willis' side.

Willis handed him the cell phone. "It's for you. It's *him*."

Willis looked pale as a ghost. Ryan took the phone confidently.

"Hello," he said.

"Ryan Turner," the caller said. "The man, the myth, the legend. Is it really you?"

It was a man's voice. It wasn't real deep but not squeaky either, was raspy, and accompanied with a slight accent of some sort that Ryan noted but couldn't place.

"Who am I speaking to?"

"Well, I spoke to Detective Willis already and I told him who I am. Just take a quick look at his face, and I'm quite sure you can figure out who exactly it is you're speaking to."

"You're him. You're The Crucifier."

"Umm, sure? Something like that."

"How do I know it's you? And what do you want?"

"I know you're at that rickety barn right this very moment. I know you found Packer Hackings inside. I assume that you noticed early on that the candles were not used this time. Simply budgetary reasons. I know there are six cars parked outside, including your adorable Civic. I know you arrived at the barn around six-thirty this fine morning."

"You're here," Ryan said, spinning around, searching his surroundings.

"No, you foolish man. But I do have eyes there. You are blind to those around you. For such an honored name as yours, you are too quick to trust those close to you. You of all people should know better. For example, you remember Kyler Reddick. Doesn't his name just strike a nerve? He was there right under your nose the entire time. Just as I am now. Your brother John better keep this in mind too, and he better do so hastily. He too puts instant trust in those around him. And that will be the reason for his death, Turner. Psalms tells of David and his ventures and tribulations. It tells of how he was betrayed so many times by those closest to him. Do you recall? He did eventually learn from it, however. Psalms one-eighteen, verses eight through nine say: *It is better to take refuge in the Lord than to trust in man.* That's what I have done. It is the very reason why why you cannot stop me."

"Enough of your B.S.," Ryan interrupted. "I don't have the time for it and neither do you. I know you didn't call out of the blue just to give me a scriptural lesson. Where are you and what do you want? Cut to the chase."

"Well, originally, I hoped to call and give you the chance to back out now, to take yourself out of this mess. You are a good person, Ryan. There is a good aura surrounding you. However, I know it isn't like you to quit something, and I also know *exactly* what you're going through. We are very much alike, Turner. More than you know. And my goodness, would it be a pleasure to meet you in person. You and I? We believe in justice, and we stop at nothing to do what we believe is right. To bring justice where justice must be served. To finish what we start. Just know, through all this, that I am not some monster, Turner. If only you understood."

"Help me understand then."

"Not now. Maybe another time. I do like you, Ryan. I know this call is being traced. I know I don't have much time left with you, although this has been fun. I am going to give you the chance to save a life today. Pretty grand, right? I'll give you one name. And I'll give you one clue. Nothing less, nothing more. Are you ready?"

Ryan said nothing.

"Garrett Jepson. Remember that name. Got it? *Garrett. Jepson.* Ten hours ago, he went missing, though he hasn't been labelled as missing quite yet. In due time he will be. His mother doesn't even know that he's gone. You'll find your clue soon enough because I do assume you all will trace my call, my location and eventually you will find yourself in the very place that I sit now, only to find that I am long gone. If you choose to be ignorant, and don't come here, then you will not have access to the one clue that I am willing to give you. And in that case, young Garrett Jepson *will* die. I would love to talk more, but I really ought to go. Garrett arrived where he is now not too long ago. It's just past seven now. You have three hours, Turner. It was a pleasure. We'll have to do this again sometime."

CHAPTER SIXTY-TWO

"Do you think it's a trap?" G-Man asked the moment Ryan handed Willis his phone back.

"It's very possible," Ryan replied.

"Crazy, right?" said Willis. "Just out of the blue. And just exactly how is that freak show watching us?"

Ryan shook his head. "Crazy is an understatement."

"This is weird," Willis said, staring at the ground. "That whole exchange was weird. I don't like it. I don't like any of this. I don't…."

"Detective, you're going to have to settle down, alright? Question, he had to have called the department, then the call was transferred to you, right?"

Willis nodded. "Yeah. The call was from the station. First Waylon told me someone called the department and said he had to speak with me and that it sounded like the person knew me well. Then I was suddenly speaking to that freak."

"We'll discuss this more later. Right now, we need to figure out where that call came from. Hopefully, this Waylon guy, or whoever transferred that call to you, has already done the tracing."

"Waylon's always on top of things, so I would bet money that he did just that," Willis replied.

"Ryan, I don't know about this," G-Man stated. "All the people who have gone after this guy have wound up dead. He's smart. He's ruthless. Remember, we can't trust a single thing he says."

"I don't know either, but first things first, we need to trace that call and we need to determine if this Garrett Jepson is really missing, or not. If we can save a life, we will. I don't care what The Crucifier's motives are."

Turning to Willis, Ryan continued, "Detective, I need you and your department to take care of both those issues as soon as possible."

Willis nodded. "On it…oh, this could be Waylon now…"

Willis placed his phone up to his ear.

Ryan set a hand on G-Man's shoulder. "I need you to go to Detective Willis' building. I think there's a decent CSI unit out of there. *3895, West 100th Street.* You'll see it. It's a pretty building. Go ahead and take the car. I'll ride with Detective Willis. Just see if you can get your protein analysis done on that hair."

"Will do," G-Man said. "I just hope they've got what I need. If not, is it okay if we make our way back to New York?"

"Yeah, that'll be fine."

"Mr. Turner," Willis said, "Waylon traced the call."

Ryan moved to hand G-Man the keys to the Civic and started to reply to Willis but abruptly stopped short of both. He saw something. It glimmered in the sunlight. It was lying in some wild grass about twenty to thirty yards away.

Ryan walked toward the shining object. "One second, fellas."

Ryan reached down and picked up the object. It was a sterling silver, locket on a silver chain. Ryan opened the locket. Inside was a photo of three little boys, who were holding gifts underneath a Christmas tree. The oldest looked to be no older than eight or nine. The youngest was maybe three.

On the ground where the locket had been found, Ryan then noticed a whole slew of other things. A decent-sized area of the grass had been smashed. Some of it had even been uprooted. He then noticed a small chunk of hair in that very spot.

Human hair.

"Detective, G-Man, come take a look at this."

The two trotted over quickly.

"Looks like there was some sort of scuffle here. The grass and plant life in this spot are disrupted and smashed down. This locket is broken, and it looks like the chain was broken by force."

Ryan handed the necklace to G-Man.

"And here," Ryan continued, "is a chunk of hair, obviously torn out by force. The roots are still attached to the base of the strands. And here…look here!" Ryan pointed at footprints leading away from the spot. "There are two different sets of footprints. Let's take a look and see where they lead us."

CHAPTER SIXTY-THREE

"Her name is Viviana," Celeste said. "Viviana Newport."

John couldn't believe it. He looked at the screen, back at Celeste, then back at the screen again.

"Are you serious?" he asked.

"She's my neighbor. There's no doubt in my mind that's her…this is exciting, but-but I don't know, shocking? Depressing? I feel sick."

"It's okay to feel like this. It's completely understandable." John blew out a breath. "But wow…just wow. Do you know her well? Are you close?"

Celeste nodded solemnly. "Yes, actually. She is such a kind woman with such a positive light about her. There is no way she's involved in this! There's no way…I need to get some air. Excuse me."

Celeste rose from her chair and walked out of the cubicle with her head hung low, leaving John and Fox stunned.

"I sure wasn't expecting that," Fox muttered.

"What are the chances?" John asked. "This is unbelievable. Well, I was right when I said we would be able to identify the woman from the tape. I just would've never guessed the way it ended up happening!"

"You were right about bringing in Celeste too. This is a miracle. I feel bad for the girl, but golly, this is a miracle for sure."

"With the lack of luck anyone has had with this case, we were bound to get some good luck sooner rather than later. And it looks like we just hit the luck jackpot."

Fox stood up. "I think I'll go talk to Celeste."

John stood up quickly. "Let me do it. I'll check on her."

Fox stopped and sat back down. "Oh, of course. Go ahead! Sorry, I should have asked you if you wanted to, or if you wanted to go with me, or…"

John placed a hand on Fox's shoulder. "Tyrique. Chill. You're good."

Fox smiled nervously and nodded his head.

"I'll be right back," John said.

CHAPTER SIXTY-FOUR

"I'm really sorry," John said.

Celeste was sitting on a curb at the front of a parking spot. Her back was to him. She didn't turn to respond.

"It's okay," she said. "It's just-just…WOW! I don't know. I can't explain the way I feel. I really can't."

John sat down next to her. "I totally understand," he said. "I've personally never experienced or felt what you must be feeling right now. Yes, I've had the occasional betrayals from friends I thought were loyal, but never anything like this. However, my brother, Ryan, went through something very similar to what you're going through right now."

Celeste turned her body slightly and was attentively taking in each and every word John spoke. John locked eyes with her mid-sentence. She was *beautiful*. Stunning. John's heart began to pound inside his chest, trying to break free from its captivity. She looked so much like Delia. He felt as if he was with Delia now. He hadn't felt this feeling in a *long* time.

"It was this past year when it all happened," John continued. "He's an agent in the FBI as well. He was framed for murder and ended up on the run. By the end of all the madness, come to find out, one of Ryan's best friends was the man who orchestrated it all. Not only that, but he was also previously and infamously known as the Invisible Man."

"Kyler Reddick?" Celeste interrupted. "Kyler Reddick was your brother's best friend?"

"As astonishing as it seems, yes. He had been disguised as an FBI agent for years, working closely with Ryan. He had even gotten plastic surgery, which changed his face completely. Crazy, crazy dude. On top of it all, he was working for Cybris Caine. In the end, Ryan had to put a knife through Kyler's heart. Ryan took the man's life, and talk about heartache? It messed Ryan up and he was hurting for quite some time. I'm sure it still shakes him up to this day.

"The point I'm trying to make is this: there are times we don't know the half of who our closest friends are. Sometimes those closest to us are as much of strangers as someone you would meet on the street. It's a scary thought, but it's true. Even those closest to us, we can't afford to put our entire trust into. Gosh, especially in this business, we learn to stay on our toes! We learn to trust no one. It's kind of unfortunate that we have to live and think that way, but unless human beings drastically change anytime soon, it's simply reality that we have to be that way."

"Thanks for that," Celeste said. "That helps. I just can't believe that is really her."

"We still don't know the whole story, though. We still can't know how or why she is involved in all this."

"True, but somehow she is, and no matter how or why she's involved, it's still heartbreaking."

"Celeste, you found that van when no one else had been able to. You were out late into the day, past your shift looking for it. *You* are the reason we have already identified this person of interest. And *you* are going to go with me to talk with her. You may have just saved the lives of a lot of people, Celeste. And I already am thankful to you for that. At the FBI, we lost two agents to this Crucifier. Your police department here has also lost good people at the hands of this killer."

Celeste was looking down at the ground now. She looked lost in deep contemplation.

"Those two agents," she said, "what were they like? Can you tell me about them?"

John cocked his head to the side at the question and nodded slowly. "Of course. Up front, honestly, I didn't know them super, super well, but I did know them well enough. They were both nearly saints. Whitney Lee was an older woman. She was a very blunt, no nonsense kind of woman, yet at the same time she had a wonderful heart. She had no family other than her mother, whom she cared for. So, her mother had to have her daughter pass from this life before herself and is left with nothing. The poor old woman had to be moved to an assisted living home.

"Allen Simmons was the other agent. He was a young, new, vibrant agent in the Bureau. He had a girlfriend and a little girl named Georgia. *The* cutest little girl you will ever see; actually, let me take that back, *second* cutest behind my little niece, but I'm pretty biased. He was witty, could be a jerk sometimes, but was such a good partner and a loving father. I don't know. Those are just some short rundowns for you. All I know, is that this world isn't as good now as it was before their deaths. We lost two really good people that day."

Keeping her eyes on the ground, Celeste gently placed a hand on John's forearm. Then she lifted her head up to look into John's eyes. Tears were welling up in her eyes.

"Thank you," she said. "For all of that. *All* of it was exactly what I needed to hear. So, thank you."

A shockwave of chills shot up John's arm. Why was he feeling like this? He didn't even know the girl. But if he was being honest with himself, he did know the answer as to why he was feeling this way. It was obvious. She looked *just like* Delia. She was also kind-hearted, seemed genuine, and was dedicated and insightful too. If Delia had a clone, it would be Celeste.

"You're welcome," John said. "Now are you finished with this crying nonsense and ready to get back to business? We've got a neighbor to confront and a killer to catch."

Celeste smiled a big, genuine smile. "Let's make it happen."

CHAPTER SIXTY-FIVE

The footprints led deep into the brush and trees. After about two-hundred yards, Ryan stopped.

Here we go.

At the spot where they now stood, Ryan bent down and pointed out another chunk of hair. This chunk was bigger and looked to be the same color.

Must be from the same person.

There was also blood painting the grass before them. There weren't puddles or large splotches of blood, but instead merely small spots and trickles here and there.

"Another scuffle occured," Ryan pointed out.

"Uh…ummm…Ryan?" G-Man said nervously.

Ryan turned. "Yeah, what's up?"

"You might want to take a look at this."

Leading from the bloodied spot, there were drag marks through the dirt and weeds leading into thick brush.

Ryan followed the marks. He climbed through the brush then stopped abruptly.

"Wow…" he said.

"What have we got?" Willis asked.

Ryan shook his head. "A body. We have another body."

The brush went down a slight incline and there in the middle of it, just out of sight from where they previously stood, was a corpse.

From Ryan's view, all he could make out was a lower leg and an arm. He reached into the prickly bushes and pulled some away to get a better view.

It was a woman. She was thin, lengthy, brunette, middle-aged.

"Help me move some of this brush out of the way," Ryan said. "Just keep from touching the body, if you can."

Ryan, G-Man, Willis, Leonard and Marquez all tore at brush and branches to better uncover the body.

"That'll work," Ryan said.

The body lay face-up. The woman wore leggings, a skin-tight t-shirt, running shoes, and a fanny pack around her waist.

"She must have been out on a run," Ryan said quietly to himself.

With a better view, it became easy to see the cause of death. There were dark, purple rings around the woman's neck. Her eyes were bulging, and her pupils were dilated.

Strangulation.

"Poor, poor woman," G-Man said shaking his head, and pushing his glasses higher up on his nose.

Ryan reached down and grasped the woman's right wrist. The body was stiff, but he did his best to lift the arm slightly. Her fingernails were covered in blood.

"She was a fighter," Ryan said.

"And that's a good thing for us," G-Man chimed in. "By the looks of things, we'll be able to retrieve DNA from under her fingernails. In comparison with this, that measly little hair we found earlier may not be such a big deal after all."

"Exactly," Ryan confirmed. "G-Man, you and your guys stick around here for as long as needed. Be as thorough as possible. Work your magic. I'll leave the car with you; the keys will be inside. Detective Willis, we need to go. We're on the clock and time is running out."

CHAPTER SIXTY-SIX

After a night that included only two hours of sleep, Laura drug herself into the kitchen at 7:30a.m. The two newborns didn't ever help make her nightly sleep schedule any smoother, but through the previous night it was even more than that. The babies had actually slept fairly consistently, but Laura just couldn't shut her mind down, even as emotionally, physically and mentally drained as she felt. Sleep just never came.

No part of her had wanted Ryan to leave. She knew the stress and worry it would bring; however, she didn't realize it would be *this* bad. She hadn't heard anything from him since he departed until just a couple hours ago, at around five in the morning. He had sent her a simple text:

So sorry. It has already been crazy. We're doing good, no need to worry. I got a new lead and just arrived in Cleveland. Will call you as soon as I can. Love you

It was reassuring to hear from him, but still she worried greatly. She wanted to hear his voice, *needed* to hear his voice. She understood that he couldn't speak to her every single minute, but still...

She grabbed a pot from the cupboard to begin preparing some peppermint tea. It was her favorite morning drink. As she poured a few cups of water into the pot, Zaya walked into the kitchen. After Kayleen's big soccer game, Zaya asked if it would be okay if she stayed with Laura while Ryan was away. Laura, of course, loved the idea, not only for Zaya's sake but for her own as well. Zaya was an *amazing* help around the house, but was most importantly a great comforter, and right now, *both* women needed comfort. It was good for them both. Plus, the house had a guest bedroom anyway, so it worked out perfectly.

"Good morning," Laura said. "Tea?"

Zaya smiled groggily and sat at the dining room table. "Yes, please, I'd love some."

"How'd you sleep?" Laura asked, turning the burner on the stovetop too high.

"If I'm being honest with you, I didn't sleep good at all. An hour? Two, maybe? I guess it's just a normal thing now."

"Zaya," Laura said as she sat down. "I completely understand, but you have to take care of yourself."

"Well, and just how did *you* sleep?" Zaya asked with her eyebrows raised questioningly.

Laura smiled sheepishly. "I have no room to talk. Slept about the same as you."

"And not because of the babies, huh?"

"No."

"Have you heard anything from him? How they're doing?"

"Just a text," Laura replied, with a small sigh. "But it sounds like they're doing alright. Ryan's in Cleveland. He said he got a new lead."

"Well that sounds promising."

"I guess so."

"Laura?"

"Yeah?"

Zaya's eyes welled up. "Thank you…thank-thank you for everything. I know I already told you, but just thank you. For Ryan---for Ryan too. I mean for being okay with him doing this. I know he's going to find Allen's killer. I feel it in my bones. I just know it."

Zaya's voice cracked with her last words. She took several deep breaths trying to compose herself.

"Honestly, I wasn't okay with Ryan's choice to leave. I still don't think I am. I know it's what brought us together, I know we may have never met if it wasn't for it, but I hate his line of work."

"But you support him. And you always will. And that gives him strength, Laura. That is why he's going to find the Crucifier. And he *will* come home. For both of us."

Laura looked up at Zaya. She hoped the young woman in front of her was right. Laura was surprised at how strong Zaya was being through all of this. She had lost the love of her life, she was now a single, jobless mother, soon her home would be taken from her, and so much more she was going through. Her life had turned into one big, seemingly endless tragedy.

"Thank you. I know he will too."

"I hated Allen's line of work. I hated it so, *so* much. I hate it even more now. But, in the end, it was who he was. And I fell in love with the man he was. You and I knew what we were getting into when we chose to spend our lives with these men. Allen brought me…" Zaya choked up and it took her a second to continue. "He brought me happiness no one else ever could or ever will. He showed me what it was like to be loved. He gave me Georgia. And for that I will forever be grateful to him. What I'm trying to say, and I'm saying it for both of us to hear really, is that the world needs people like Ryan and Allen. It *needs* them badly. If we didn't have people like them doing what they do, can you just imagine what this world would be like?"

Even all the time she and Ryan had been together, that particular thought had never really crossed Laura's mind. She did know how important Ryan's line of work was. She also knew how good he was at his job, and knew how much he loved it. She would've never guessed in this moment that Zaya would be bringing so much needed comfort to her instead of the other way around.

Silent tears streamed down Laura's cheeks.

"You're right," she said. "You're exactly right."

"It's funny, but sad in a way," Zaya continued. "I guess it took Allen's death for me to really accept all this, but his line of work was what he was born for. He was put on this earth to do exactly what he did. Of course, I tried convincing him to find another job every chance I got. I would even proactively search for good jobs in the area that he could go into. Yet, still, deep down I always knew that no number of words or convincing could've ever changed his mind. They do what they do because they genuinely care about and love *everyone* around them. Putting themselves in danger doesn't mean they love us any less.

"Allen dying…Allen…him dying on a dangerous case didn't mean he loved me any less. And, Laura, the same is true with Ryan. He loves you so much. The way he looks at you, Laura, the way you two click, that love is undeniable. His work will always bring stress to you, it will always bring you heartache and pain. But you knew what you were getting yourself into. We both knew what we were getting into when we chose to spend our lives with them.

"You need to accept that he may be in this line of work for the rest of his life, in one way another. He may never be able to leave it behind. You have to learn to always trust and support him, and most importantly just accept your lives. I wish it…I wish it hadn't taken Allen's death for me to finally realize that. I just don't want you to go through what I have in the way that I regret not fully supporting Allen. Not fully appreciating what it took for him to put himself out there to help and save countless lives. I know I'm rambling on, and oh my goodness, I'm pouring out my heart and thoughts and emotions at seven-thirty in the morning, but it all hit me this morning. It's all just coming out at once. Thank you again for letting us stay here. Thank you for yours and Ryan's love and support and thank you for hearing out all the gibberish I throw out there. Ah, I'm emotional, and a little over the edge right now. I'm sorry."

Behind Laura, the water on the stovetop was boiling down at a rapid pace. She paid no mind to it, though. Silent tears continued to stream down her face, and she rose to her feet.

Zaya quickly shot out of her chair, sniffling back tears of her own. She pulled herself around to Laura's side of the table.

"I'm so sorry. Goodness, I'm terrible. I'm sorry, Laura. I never meant to upset you."

Laura threw her arms around the young girl.

"No," Laura said. "Thank you. Thank you so, so much, Zaya."

Never in a million years would she have imagined that it would be the words of a twenty-three-year-old girl that would bring her the much-needed peace she so desperately needed. Ryan's life was in danger. That worried her to death. She wasn't sleeping because of it. But she knew now that she simply had to accept it. She had to *fully* accept who her husband was. He was a hero. A selfless, loving hero who would not only put his life on the line for his family but for a complete stranger. It was who he was. And Laura knew it was who he would always be.

CHAPTER SIXTY-SEVEN

That was exactly what Ryan was doing now: putting his life on the line for an utter stranger. Ryan and Willis arrived at the scene just before eight-thirty. Ryan hadn't had high hopes that the killer would be around, so he didn't even consider that a possibility in his mind. All he cared about now was saving Garrett Jepson. Waylon, Willis' intel guy, had tracked the phone call to a dry cleaning business called Sunshine Dry Cleaners. The place didn't look to be busy. There was one lone car in front of the building.

On the way to the scene, Willis made a few calls and was able to verify that Jepson was, in fact, missing. According to his mother, he was supposed to be staying overnight at a friend's house. Come to find out, he never made it to his friend's house and never returned home either. He wasn't answering calls. No one had seen him.

"Are you sure about this?" Willis asked, putting the car in park.

"Honestly, no," Ryan replied. "But we need to stay on our toes. We need to be ready for anything."

"There is no way the Crucifier guy is just turning a kid over to us with no repercussions, no side-game," Willis said.

Beads of sweat perspired on the man's forehead, underneath his black head of hair. Willis was a tall man, who stood just under six-three. He had what many would call a "dad-body", but it was easy to see that he was a strong guy under all the fluff. His face was twisted up in a permanent scowl, but Ryan was able to read right through it the very first time they met. He was a softy. In this moment, Ryan could see the fear radiating off of him.

"There's certainly a side-game," said Ryan. "He's playing with us in some way."

"Then that's what I'm saying. He's setting us up."

"We'll be okay."

"We're taking a big risk here, Turner. Just look at this place. There's no one here. I have a family at home..."

Ryan quickly cut him off at that comment. "And you think I don't? C'mon, Detective. Seriously. I have two newborns at home, a little girl, and a beautiful wife. Do you really think I *want* to be here? Answer me that, Detective."

"I'm just saying..."

"No, Detective, *I'm just saying* there's lives at risk and I *know* I can make a difference. As for right now? There's a kid's life hanging in the balance and you and I are the only ones who can save him. No one else. I don't care if we're being set up, I don't care what this psychopath's ulterior motive is. Am I clear?"

"Yes," Willis answered. "I'm sorry. I'm just scared, to be honest with you. I've never been in on a case of this magnitude, and I've heard the horror stories that've gone along with this whole Crucifier case."

"We're going to be okay, Detective. You got that? Just follow my lead. Expect the unexpected. We have an hour and a half."

CHAPTER SIXTY-EIGHT

They walked into Sunshine Dry Cleaners with their guns locked and loaded at their sides. There wasn't a soul inside, except for a short, elderly woman standing behind the front desk.

"Welcome," she said, her beady little eyes peering over the top of the desk.

Ryan took in his surroundings the moment they walked in. The place had a strong lavender scent that was almost overwhelming. Behind the woman were lines and lines of bagged clothes strung up. On the walls hung three photographs. On the East wall hung a photo of Bobby Knight wearing an Indiana Hoosiers shirt. On the West wall was a photo of the inside of the Grand Ole Opry, and directly underneath that photograph was a beautiful photo of the Graceland Mansion.

The woman had to have been in her late seventies, or possibly early eighties. She had a full head of long, permed, white hair that looked almost like a wig. She was tiny and far from intimidating.

"Good morning, ma'am," Ryan said stepping up to the desk.

"How may I help you guys…" a sudden look of realization crept over her feature. "Oh! I've been expecting you."

Ryan and Willis exchanged glances, somewhat puzzled.

"Excuse me, but you were expecting us?" Ryan asked.

"Yes," she said, turning her back to the two men and walking between the rows of freshly cleaned clothes. "Well, don't get me wrong, I have no idea who you two fine gentlemen are. I hardly remember my own name sometimes, much less know two absolute strangers. I mean, maybe I've seen you here before, but maybe not. My old brain wouldn't remember, regardless."

The woman opened a door at the back end of the shop and went inside. Confused, Ryan and Willis waited in silence. The woman didn't take long before reemerging out of the back room. In one hand, she held a t-shirt that read "I love Cleveland" with a big heart beneath the lettering. In the other, she clutched a small box, holding it against her waist.

"He sure was an odd fellow," she said, "but I won't judge him, given that you gentlemen are friends of his. He dropped this stuff off with me and hung up these new framed photos that you see in here. He told me he was with a religious group and they were going around doing good deeds for the day."

"Interesting," Ryan said. "Didn't you think hanging up random paintings in random places was a bit of a peculiar service project?"

"Well, I reckon this place did need some sprucing up. He seemed like a really nice fellow. Yes, he was odd, but he had good, bubbly feel to him."

"What did he say about us?" Willis asked.

"Well, let me tell you. He acted almost giddy about it. It was sort of cute in a way. He said two of his uptight, law enforcement friends would be dropping off some clothes this morning and he instructed me to give them a gift. So, I saw you two fine, and yes, I suppose, slightly uptight, gentlemen walk in with guns on your hips and I knew at first glance that it was you."

Ryan was shaking his head. "This man you're talking about is wanted for murder. He's a certified psychopath. He's toying with us. We're currently on his trail. He abducted a teenage boy and now we are trying to save him."

It was blunt, to the point. The woman's response was no surprise. She gasped and caught herself on the desk with both hands, the t-shirt and box falling from her grasp. She pulled herself down into the chair behind the desk.

"Oh, dear," she exclaimed. "I am so sorry."

"None of this is your fault. You're a sweet woman and you had no way of knowing any of that," Ryan reassured her. "But right now, we need your help. In this moment, you are very important to our efforts in saving this boy. We need you."

CHAPTER SIXTY-NINE

The old woman handed Ryan the box and the shirt.

"What's your name?" Ryan asked. "I apologize for not asking. That was rude of me."

"It's Dorothy Ann," she replied.

"I'm Ryan Turner with the FBI. This is Detective Kody Willis out of the police department here in the city."

"It's a pleasure," the woman said.

Ryan then went on to give Dorothy a very quick overview of everything that had gone on.

"My, my," Dorothy said. "That all sounds quite disturbing."

"What did this guy look like? Did he give you a name?"

"He was very fit, athletic-looking. He's maybe thirty years old or so? I really couldn't tell, if I am being honest with you guys. He had dirty blonde hair. Average height, I think."

Ryan pulled up a photo on his cell phone.

"Is this him?" he asked.

Dorothy pointed a crooked finger at the phone. "Yep, that's him, all right."

Same man who killed Whitney and Allen...

"Had you ever seen this man before he came in today?" Ryan asked.

"Never seen him before in my life."

Ryan nodded. "And sorry but you didn't say if he gave you a name or not...?"

Dorothy palmed her face. "Oh, goodness, gracious me! Yes, yes. He said to call him B.B.? I'm not certain how he spelled it. B-e-e-b-e-e? Just plain B-b? I really couldn't tell you."

B.B...

That was all Ryan needed to hear from the woman for now. He asked a few more questions about what B.B said and about his demeanor, hoping to maybe get a better feel for his motive. However, she wasn't able to give him much. He thanked her, got her contact information, and then asked her to leave and close up shop. It was out of the ordinary for Dorothy, but she'd had a shock and Ryan was persuasive. She wasn't going to argue with an FBI man, anyway.

Once she was gone, Ryan stared at the box in his hands. It was small. A perfect cube.

"It's *really* light," Ryan said.

"I still don't trust it," Willis said with an uncertain look on his face.

"It can't be a bomb or anything like that. If he wanted us dead, I have a feeling we would be dead already. He wouldn't have taken his sweet time putting all of this together or putting up new paintings in a dry-cleaning facility just to kill us. I've dealt with a lot of serial killers in my life. They're wired differently. They're also unpredictable. But I've seen enough of them to know that this is exactly what it looks like: a game. A game he wants to play. A game he knows we *have* to play with him."

Willis didn't say anything. He merely gave Ryan a single nod. That was all the approval Ryan needed from him. With that, he tore open the box.

CHAPTER SEVENTY

Celeste Ventana lived in a tiny, one-bedroom home on the west side of the city. The house was in a large subdivision where the majority of houses were the same size as Celeste's. Along with the bedroom, there was a bathroom, a kitchen, a living area, and a covered back porch where she kept her washer and dryer. It was a cute little home. She kept it very tidy too. Every counter, floor, table, chair was spiffy clean.

John was impressed, to say the least. He now sat in the living area in one of the two leather chairs there. Celeste sat in the other. They had been there for a good while now. John was getting anxious. Before they left police headquarters, Celeste texted Viviana and asked if she worked today. Viviana replied, saying that she had started work at midnight and would finish by ten in the morning. Celeste then told her she'd love to have lunch or dinner with her, and Viviana agreed.

So, here they sat. Watching. Waiting. Waiting for Viviana to return to her house, which was directly next to Celeste's. The front of Viviana's house could be seen perfectly through a set of windows in Celeste's living room.

It was just a few minutes after nine o'clock. They had about an hour, give or take, given that as a waitress at a 24/7 pub, Viviana could either get released from work on the early or late side depending on how busy the night had been. The plan was for them to confront Viviana the moment she started to walk from her car to her front door. John had asked Fox to join them, but he politely declined, saying he needed to get some other things done while they were away. His decision seemed a little bit odd to John, but he didn't think too much of it, concentrating instead on the stake out. Fox was a young, awkward detective, who was bound to make young, awkward detective decisions. Nonetheless, John had felt that Fox would have jumped all over the opportunity to question their *first* true suspect in the case.

Waiting for Viviana, John and Celeste made small talk. She was a fascinating person. She was originally from the DC area where her father worked as a tour guide at the Capitol building and her mother ran a family-owned restaurant just outside the National Mall area. Both parents had since passed away from cancer. Celeste was an only child and the only family she had were one set of grandparents, two sets of aunts and uncles, and three cousins. She wasn't close with any of them. She had joined the MPD as an intern during high school. Celeste was an incredibly bright student, confiding proudly that she was a Presidential Scholar, the most prestigious honor that can be achieved by an American high school student. On the side, when she had time off from work, she helped run a charity organization called "Bedz for Kidz". She was single, lived alone, and had already paid her small house off.

When John asked what had become of the family restaurant, Celeste explained that it was passed on to her after her parents passed away. In her mother's will, it stipulated that Celeste could choose to sell the establishment if she wanted in order to fully pursue her career in law enforcement. So, she did just that, and was able to fully pay for a home of her own, as well as put a good amount of money into savings.

"It all worked out," she said. "Even after they left this earth, they still found a way to bless my life greatly."

"They sound like they were some great, hardworking people. And from what I can see, the apple didn't fall too far from the tree. You seem like a great woman, Officer Ventana. Please understand that I mean that in only the most professional of senses. You're super impressive as an officer *and* as a person."

Celeste smiled shyly. "I see myself as pretty average, but thank you. That truly means a lot to me."

John returned the smile and nodded. His mind then wandered to Fox. He kept thinking back to the Detective's surprising decision to not come along.

"What do you think of Detective Fox?" John asked.

"Tyrique?" Celeste asked in between sips of water from the bottle in her hand.

"Yes."

"He's a good detective. He's a really smart and enthusiastic guy. Why?"

"I don't know. I'm just having random thoughts. I get paid to overthink."

Celeste tilted her head to the side. "Expand on that."

John shrugged. "Just a question; a question I want answered truthfully."

John winked at Celeste. She rolled her eyes.

"You got me."

"So, what exactly can you tell me about Detective Fox?"

Celeste's face changed. "You want me to be honest with you?"

"Yes, please. I want your honest opinion."

Celeste breathed in. "Alright…here it goes…"

CHAPTER SEVENTY-ONE

The great unveiling of the box's contents didn't appear to be worth the tense anticipation prior to its opening. Inside were two tightly rolled papers labelled with a fine tipped, black, permanent marker: "1" and "2". Ryan pulled them out one after the other.

"This is odd," Willis commented.

Ryan pulled the rubber band off the first roll and then carefully unrolled the paper. It read:

- Aloha
- Peach
- Tarheel Bay
- Evergreen
- Old Dominion.

- Paintings-1-2-3

That was it. A plain sheet of paper with a jumble of random words typed in a straight line down the paper. Ryan handed the first paper to Willis. He then unwound the second paper. It was a plain sheet, aside from one small, typed paragraph directly in the middle of the sheet. It looked to be a definition copied straight from a dictionary:

CRUCIFIXION / (ˌkruːsɪˈfɪkʃən) /

: method of putting to death by nailing or binding to a cross, usually by one's feet or hands; widespread form of CAPITAL punishment in the ancient world.

Ryan shook his head as he handed paper #2 to Willis. Taking the sheet from Ryan's grasp. Willis then handed the first one back to Ryan. Ryan stared down at paper #1. His mind was reeling.

Aloha...Peach...Tarheel...Bay...Evergreen...Old Dominion...

"What is all this gibberish?" Willis asked, looking perplexed.

Ryan gave a slight shrug. "I don't know yet."

"What about that t-shirt?"

Ryan grabbed the shirt off the desktop and tossed it to Willis.

"It doesn't mean anything," Ryan said. "At least I don't think so. It just serves to makes the whole box deal look much less suspicious. That's my feeling."

Willis was carefully looking over every square-inch of the shirt, even turning it inside-out.

"I think you're right," Willis confirmed.

"Do me a favor and pull down those photographs," Ryan said, keeping his eyes locked on the first sheet of paper.

Willis did as he was told and set paper #2 into the small box. Ryan continued to study sheet #1, reading its words over and over again in his head. At the moment, they made zero sense.

Soon enough, Willis had all three frames tucked under his right arm. Ryan set the other paper back into the box and helped Willis lay out the frames side-by-side on the floor. Ryan crouched down. To his left was the photograph of the Graceland Mansion, in the middle was the photo of Bobby Knight, and the picture to the far right was of the Grand Ole Opry

Willis stood with his hands on his hips. "This is completely ridiculous."

Ryan didn't respond. He retrieved the two rolls of paper, then again crouched down in front of the photos, reading the papers over and over again.

"As for the paper labelled with a '2', it's easy to see what he wants us to understand," Ryan said, handing the first roll to Willis. "Within the definition, he highlights random letters in bold. The 'c' in cross, 'a' in usually, 'p' in widespread, so on and so forth. Together, those letters spell out 'capital'. Then he obviously didn't think very highly of our problem-solving skills, so he made sure to add to the definition and bold and capitalize the word 'capital'."

Willis nodded in agreement. "I caught that too."

"But it's labelled with a '2'. So, it must be the second clue. The key to solving this guy's puzzle is figuring out what this first page is trying to tell us."

CHAPTER SEVENTY-TWO

Ryan flipped over the photos to find that they were similarly numbered. There was a big "1" drawn on the back of the Bobby Knight photograph, and "2/3" was written on each of the others.

"They each have both a two and three on them?" Willis questioned.

"They must be interchangeable," Ryan said. "All of this put together is some sort of message."

Ryan shifted the pictures in numerical order from left to right and placed them back upright. He rose to his feet, stroking his chin.

"These photos are all of iconic things from two different states. Indiana and Tennessee," Ryan thoughtfully stated. "Knight is an Indiana legend. Graceland Mansion and the Grand Ole Opry are Tennessee icons."

Willis nodded.

"Both the Grand Ole Opry and Graceland Mansion are in Tennessee..." Ryan pondered. "I guess that's why they must be interchangeable...probably..."

Lightbulbs were going off in Ryan's head now. Willis said nothing and let Ryan continue to work.

"These random words…" Ryan said, straightening the paper labelled with the "1." "What is the first thing you think of when you hear 'Aloha?'"

"Shoot, Hawaii, I reckon."

"Right. And what fruit is Georgia famous for?"

"Hmm," Willis pondered. "Georgia peaches, correct?"

"Right again. Are you a basketball fan?"

"Definitely."

"College?"

"Yup."

"So, answer me this: what's North Carolina's mascot?"

"The Tarheels."

Ryan nodded. "Those are the things I think of when I hear 'Aloha', 'peach' and 'Tarheel'. But that still leaves the last three words. So, I was thinking, wait, if the paintings signify different states, then these words probably do too. Hawaii is nicknamed 'the Aloha State'. Georgia is nicknamed the 'Peach State'…"

"And North Carolina is the Tarheel state," Willis concluded.

"*Exactly.* Now what do we have left? Bay, evergreen and Old Dominion. Massachusetts is known as the Bay State, Washington is the Evergreen State, and…"

"Virginia is the Old Dominion State," Willis finished.

"Bingo. That gives us Hawaii, Georgia, North Carolina, Massachusetts, Washington, and Virginia, in that order."

"Yeah, but what is that supposed to tell us?"

Ryan shrugged slightly but still looked to be in deep thought. "Hopefully I'm on the right track here…I'm just trying to put it together now…the pictures stand for Indiana, Tennessee, and Tennessee again. This clue, this riddle, has got to be state-themed. Now I'm thinking about the second paper. *Capital.* What are the capitals of these states…? Here, let me grab a pen."

Ryan walked around to the other side of the desk and retrieved a pen from a drawer. He returned and flattened the second paper on the desktop, then wrote each state down on the paper, one on top of the other.

"The capital of Hawaii is Honolulu," Ryan said, then wrote down 'Honolulu' next to Hawaii. "Georgia's capital is Atlanta."

He continued until all nine states were accounted for.

Honolulu, Atlanta, Raleigh, Boston, Olympia, Richmond, Indianapolis, Nashville, Nashville again.

"What do you think this means?" Willis asked.

Ryan tilted his head to the side. He couldn't figure it out. He was stuck now.

"I don't know," Ryan said, relaying his thought to Willis.

Willis opened his mouth to speak, but Ryan excitedly cut him off.

"Wait," Ryan said, "years ago, I came across a killer who was into puzzles that were sort of like this. He loved using riddles, clues, puzzles, you name it. A few of the puzzles involved determining a sequence of words, and then by using either the first letter or last letter in each word, a new word or phrase was formed. For example, 'rotten old bananas' would translate to '*rob*' if you use the first letters, or 'city fro tofu' would translate to '*you*', if you use the last letters of each of those words. I don't know if I explained that very well, but do you see what I mean?"

"Yeah, I do," Willis said, "I know exactly what you're getting at."

Staring down at the paper before him, Ryan mouthed some incoherent words, and then asked, "Does Harbor…*Harbor Inn* ring a bell?"

CHAPTER SEVENTY-THREE

"Tyrique is different," Celeste said, trying to find the right words. "He's unique…mysterious even? It's slightly hard for me to explain. For one thing, he's an extremely young detective. It was a real surprise to many of us when he showed up out of nowhere as this young, hotshot guy. He has an incredible mind. The guys get to playing chess and checkers sometimes and Tyrique destroys all of them. He makes them look plain silly. So, he does have a real talent, and I mean that. He has a very gifted mind, for sure."

"And yet?" John pried.

Celeste looked uneasy. "I…I don't know. There's something about him. There's something that's just a bit off."

John nodded and allowed Celeste to continue.

"I haven't had too many encounters with him that would make me not trust the guy," she continued, "but he gives me a weird feeling sometimes. I don't know if that even makes any sense."

John nodded again. "I totally get it. I've had that feeling about people before."

"This may sound petty but he acts really strange about his phone. He acts like a paranoid teenager with it. It's so weird! I'll walk into a room where he's by himself and see that he's on his phone. Then, the moment I walk in, he jumps and quickly puts it away. This has happened on a number of occasions. He's young and quirky, so it could be nothing. But the thing that really made me start to wonder about him, is when I was out with a cousin of mine one night for dinner and I saw Tyrique in an alley. This was just recently, about a week ago. I walked by and then had to step back so I could take a second look. At first, I couldn't believe my eyes, but it really was him. He was with someone in a hood. They were exchanging something. Tyrique froze, his eyes got big when he recognized me. Then he turned away quickly and ran off.

"Listen, I'm not full-on accusing him of being a dirty cop. It's not that at all. *But* it was weird, really weird. It left a bad taste in my mouth. Neither one of us have brought it up, and things have just been awkward between us ever since, if you weren't able to tell."

John cocked his head to one side. "I honestly didn't notice?"

"Then I guess we played it off well," Celeste said nervously.

"He might have a drug addiction of some sort. That's what it seems like to me. If so, he's constantly having to nurse that addiction."

Celeste shrugged. "That's one thing I thought of…but…I just don't know."

John leaned forward. He knew she wasn't telling him something.

"Celeste? What aren't you telling me?"

Celeste looked extremely uneasy now. She looked clearly conflicted with herself, trying to determine if she should say what she was holding back.

"*Especially* if it could be imperative to moving forward with our case, you have to tell me," John said forcefully. For some reason, he had a feeling that it could be.

Celeste finally made eye contact with John.

"I didn't tell you who I saw under that hood," she said.

John leaned forward even more. "Who did you see?"

Celeste swallowed and looked back down at the floor. "John, it was Viviana. I saw Tyrique with Viviana that night."

CHAPTER SEVENTY-FOUR

Ryan and Willis arrived at Harbor Inn just after nine-fifteen. It was a historic place in Cleveland, standing as the oldest bar in the city. As Ryan opened the front door, the sound of upbeat polka music flooded his ears. Inside, some people were jabbering at the bar while others were dancing about. It seemed awful lively for an early morning.

Ryan stepped up to the bar, Willis close behind. The bartender stepped up in front of them.

"Welcome in fellas, what can I get for you?" he inquired.

The man wasn't short yet wasn't exactly tall either. He was completely bald, with beady eyes, and a Roman nose. His beard was cut into a short, red, goatee, and he had large gauges through both earlobes.

Ryan showed the man a photo on his phone. "Did this man happen to come by here this morning?"

The bartender leaned on the bar. "Yep, sure did. Odd guy, but nice enough, I guess. Why? What's up?"

"He's a person of interest in our investigation. I'm Ryan Turner with the FBI. This is Detective Kody Willis."

"Oh!" the man exclaimed.

He stuck out his hand and shook Ryan's.

"Nate Frock," he said.

"Good to meet you," Ryan replied.

"So, this guy's a bad dude, huh?" Nate asked.

"You could say that. Definitely not the best guy in the world," Ryan answered.

"Man. There was something weird about him, you know? One of those people that just gives you a weird vibe. The guy came in holding a big, framed photograph and an envelope. Said he was with some sort of religious group? Seemed wacky, but then again, we're all for that sort of thing here. He gave me the envelope which had a few hundred dollars in it. Then he asked if he could hang up the photograph somewhere in return for the cash. I said, 'Sure, dude, anywhere you want.' I didn't see any issue with it. And that was the sum total of the conversation I had with him. He hung up the photo, and as quickly as he had wandered in here, he was gone."

Ryan nodded. "Where's the photograph?"

Nate pointed toward the front of the bar. "He hung it right there. Right by the front door."

"Thanks," Ryan said, shaking the man's hand. "I think that's all the information we need."

Ryan and Willis quickly turned away, heading back toward the front door. Slightly confused and still in shock about the conversation, Frock straightened himself up and got back to his work.

Ryan jerked the picture off the wall and gazed down at it. It was a photo of a small yacht tied off to a dock. The side of the boat read "Calypso".

Ryan flipped the frame over. On the back side, written in marker was:

Tick tock. Time is ticking. With each minute, Jepson's life you're forsaking. Find the Calypso. Give it a try. If you fail to do so, Garrett Jepson will die.

"Oh, fantastic, now he writes poetry," Willis muttered underneath his breath.

"Do you know where this location is?" Ryan asked, turning the photograph back over.

Willis gazed down at the picture, slowly nodding his head. "I think so...looks like the docks by Lakewood Park, on the bank of Lake Erie."

"How quickly can we get there?"

"Quick enough. Fifteen minutes, give or take a few."

Tucking the painting underneath his arm, Ryan swung the front door open.

"Let's get a move on," he said.

"I still don't have a good feeling about all this," Willis said, following closely behind Ryan. "Maybe this is the final point in his trap. Maybe he was leading us up to this point all along."

Ryan opened the right rear door of Willis' car and threw the photo in. "I guess there's only one way to find out."

CHAPTER SEVENTY-FIVE

9:30 a.m. Jack Grimes walked into the same Ritz Carlton he had entered the day before, pulling a suitcase behind him. Dressed like a bellhop this time, he strolled right through the lobby, made small talk with a maid on the first floor, sneakily stole her key, and then made his way up to the twelfth floor. He hoped the room was empty this time. It just had to be.

However, as Grimes knocked on the door to room 1205, there was an immediate answer from inside the room.

"It reads, 'Do not disturb'! Are you stupid?"

Grimes looked at the little sign hanging from the doorknob. The voice wasn't wrong, but the whiny voice made his blood boil. It was the same woman from the day before.

Does she ever leave this place?

Grimes could feel his heartrate rapidly increasing. He closed his eyes. He breathed in, then he breathed out. Slowly. Deliberately. He thought of his "happy place". He thought of himself painting on a large canvas underneath a beautiful peach tree. He could hear the running of water from a stream to his right. Birds chirped overhead. In his happy place he was alone. The way it should be. The way he liked it.

Grimes's breathing steadied and his heartrate decreased, until he was back to normal. Grimes knocked again.

Breathe. Control it.

"Are you deaf!?"

Grimes could hear some rustling coming from inside the room now. He knocked again. The television inside suddenly went mute.

"That's it," Grimes could hear the voice mutter with extreme annoyance.

Loud, hard footsteps approached the door, then stopped.

Grimes pulled his cap down to shield his face slightly, and then stood with his hands clasped behind his back. He wore a fake smile on his face.

The door cracked open. "Get that stupid look off your face. What do you want!?"

He hoped that the woman hadn't recognized him. It didn't seem like she had yet.

"I have a package for you," Grimes said, maintaining his smile. "I believe it's a gift."

The woman groaned. "Okay, whatever, give it to me."

Grimes took a step closer to the door and as he did, the woman opened the door wider. That is when he took his shot. He wouldn't need to use the maid's master key after all.

Grimes had never really been into sports. As a child, he never had the chance to be involved in them. That said, it didn't mean he wasn't athletic. He was sneakily athletic. He was strong. He was quick. Before the brunette woman could even react, Grimes was through the door and had a hand wrapped around her throat.

She immediately lost her balance and fell flat on her back. Grimes kept his grip tight around her neck and lowered himself to the floor with the falling woman. The door slowly slid shut behind them. On her way down, the woman tried to cry out, but no sound escaped her crushed throat. Hitting the ground, she flailed her arms in front of her, trying to scratch Grimes's face. Grimes's reach far exceeded her own and she never had a chance at making contact with him. Within a split second, she no longer was able to move her arms, as Grimes pinned them down with his knees.

The woman squirmed underneath him, but all 105 pounds of her couldn't budge beneath Grimes's weight. Grimes weighed an easy 200. He had a slight belly but wouldn't necessarily be described as "fat". He was solid.

Grimes's heartrate was through the roof, far from his normal 57 or 58 beats per minute. But he didn't care. Not right now. He was seeing red. This woman had gotten in his way not only once, but twice now. And she disrespected him, dehumanized him. He wouldn't have it. Not today.

Grimes had already known what he was going to do before he had even entered the room. He knew he would kill her, and he knew exactly how.

Throughout his life, pets had always been hard for Grimes to keep. He expected perfection. He expected routine. He expected it not only from himself, but from his pets as well. This was why he had never been able to keep a dog. The moment they pooped or peed on the floor, chewed up the couch or a shoe, or randomly chose not to eat when they were supposed to, Grimes would snap. He wouldn't have it. Because of them and much research, he had become confident in his ability to break a neck. He had lost count long ago of the number of dogs he had killed by way of snapping their necks, but the number was large. The process was quick, effective, and most importantly, not at all messy. Exactly as Grimes preferred.

The woman beneath him was frail. Her neck was much frailer than the neck of many of the dogs he used to own. It would be easy, effective, and not messy. There was a process to it, though. It wasn't as easy as the movies made it out to be. He had learned that right away with the first few dogs that he owned.

There were basic principles. There had to be an emphasis on the use of torso muscles to augment the weaker muscles of the hands and arms. Movement of the victim's body *must* be minimal to gain the right leverage against the vertebrae, no matter how small and frail the victim was. The neck is very flexible, so solely bending the neck alone is inefficient. Neither is simply twisting the neck. Instead, a combination of the two *must* be used. It is a necessity to both bend and twist simultaneously. With that, the chin is a useful point of leverage. It can be utilized as a lever to enhance the twisting pressure.

The woman's face was now turning a shade of deep purple. Her mouth hung open. Grimes released her throat and the woman gasped for air. As she did, Grimes shoved one hand under her chin and the other behind her head, and then did what he had done to so many of his "misbehaving' pets throughout the years.

Grimes stood to his feet and turned to open the door behind him. He retrieved his suitcase from the hallway. Not a soul was to be seen in the hall.

Perfect.

Grimes rolled the suitcase through the room, dragging it over the top of the lifeless body that was now lying in the middle of the floor.

"Excuse me, ma'am," he said, as the bag drug over the woman's pale face.

Grimes set the bag on the bed and opened it up. He smirked as he gazed at the bag's contents. It was go-time.

CHAPTER SEVENTY-SIX

At a few minutes past 9:30, Ryan and Willis jumped out of the car. They had arrived at the docks near Lakewood Park. There were various boats tied off to the docks, and many were out on the water, as there always were on Lake Erie. Ryan and Willis trotted toward the cluster of boats that were anchored.

"If the boy really is here, do you think we're too late?" Willis asked as they trotted along.

"Can't say," Ryan replied. "We're closing in on the three-hour time frame that The Crucifier gave us, but we can't know how exact he was really being. We're about to find out."

As they came up onto the docks, Ryan was already scanning the boats, reading the various names plastered on the hulls.

The Drunken Lady, Flying Dutchman, Jupiter, Baby Moon, Riff Raff...

Lots of boats with random names plastered on the sides of them, but none named Calypso so far.

"Look!" Willis exclaimed. "I think that's it."

Ryan quickly turned his gaze to where Willis was pointing.

There it is.

He couldn't see the name "Calypso" from the angle where they stood, but Ryan knew it was the boat they were searching for. It looked exactly like the one in the picture from Harbor Inn.

Ryan set into a jog toward the boat and Willis followed closely behind. Sure enough, there it was: "Calypso" written on the starboard hull of the large yacht.

The two eased their way onto the deck of the vessel. So far, they didn't see anything out of the ordinary. Nothing on deck, nothing in the cabin. Then they both stopped in front of the hatch in the middle of the boat, next to the cabin. Ryan took out his gun and motioned for Willis to open the hatch. Willis bent down and pulled up on the door. It wouldn't budge. He tried a second time. Same result.

"The thing is locked, or stuck, or something," Willis said.

Ryan set his gun on the deck and pulled on the hatch with Willis. Still nothing. It wouldn't budge.

Ryan scooped up his Glock, then stood to his feet. "I'll be right back."

He remembered seeing a fire axe in the boat's cabin when they were searching around in it. Using the butt of his Glock, Ryan broke the glass that contained the axe, and pulled the axe off its rungs. He then returned to the hatch and immediately began taking swings at it. Splintered wood flew everywhere. Ryan chopped a hole into it just big enough to stick his arm through. He tossed the axe on the ground, then stuck an arm through the hole and found the latch on the inside. He slid it open and pulled the hatch door upward.

Ryan pulled the door completely off, and then set it down on the dock. He and Willis then made eye contact, before cautiously descending the stairs below the deck. The moment his eyes were below deck and able to see what was inside, Ryan saw him. The kid had shaggy blonde hair, was short, in his mid-late teens. The boy Ryan could now see below deck perfectly matched the description he and Willis had been given. It was Garrett Jepson.

CHAPTER SEVENTY-SEVEN

Almost fifteen minutes before ten, Viviana Newport's car pulled up in front of her house. Viviana was dressed in a short, checkered skirt, long tube socks, white tennis shoes, and a baby blue, collared shirt.

John jumped to his feet. "Okay, let's go."

Celeste also jumped up. "Give me one second."

She trotted out of the living room area and into her bedroom. Within a few seconds she came back out.

"Sorry, had to grab something," she said.

John didn't mind and he didn't question her as to why she needed to make a sudden detour into her room. He reached the door and stopped when he put his hand on the door handle. He turned to Celeste.

"Listen, you're going to be okay," he said. "Wherever this mess takes us, wherever it takes you, I'm going to protect you. *Nothing* is going to happen to you. I promise."

Celeste didn't reply but just nodded as John opened the door.

He felt terrible for her. He, himself, was still shaken up about what Celeste had said.

Does Fox have something to do with The Crucifier? Does he somehow play a role in all of this?

Celeste had explained to John that she didn't want to tell anyone about it. Previously, she had chosen not to because she had seen her colleague and her neighbor/best friend behaving suspiciously in a dark alley. It shook her up for personal reasons. She wanted to ignore the fact that two people whom she knew well might be involved in drugs or something else of the sort. But now it was more than that. When she realized that Viviana was somehow involved with The Crucifier, it scared her to death. The game changed then.

She realized that not only was Viviana involved in the recent murders, but Fox might have been as well. She also knew good and well that every officer, detective, and agent who had closely investigated the recent murders had all ended up dead. She knew that if she opened her mouth, she too would receive their same fate. In fact, she couldn't believe that they had let her live this long after she saw them both that night. She reflected that since the footage of Viviana with Simmons and Lee had been discovered, her life was now even more so in danger. Fox knew that Celeste would now start connecting the dots. He would have told Viviana immediately. Then whoever was in charge of them would've been notified too. Or maybe one of them *was* the orchestrator of it all…but the one thing Celeste was convinced of was that it would only be a matter of time before someone came for her, before her own life would end. The fear in her eyes was real as she opened up to John.

John kept trying to convince himself that it was all a matter of coincidence. He liked Fox. Maybe he wasn't dirty…but he knew better than to go against a gut feeling, than to give a potential person of interest the benefit of the doubt. Plus, it made total sense that there would be someone on the inside…John knew this had to be the one explanation for how each investigator had ended up dead, thus far. There *had to be* someone on the inside.

John exited the door with Celeste close behind. She didn't bother to shut the door behind her, and it hung open, blowing back and forth in the humid, morning breeze. John hit the corner of Celeste's house and walked across Viviana's small front lawn. Viviana was at her front door now, fumbling with her keys.

"Viviana Newport," John called out.

The woman froze then turned around. A look of shock crossed her face, but it was immediately replaced by a big smile.

"That's me," she answered.

Her eyes darted to Celeste then back to John. She was trying to play it cool, but John could tell that internally, she was freaking out.

"My name is John Drexel, I'm with the FBI. May we have a word with you?"

"Of course," she said. "Celeste, it's nice to see you. Is everything okay, you guys?"

John was now no more than ten yards away from Viviana.

"Yeah," he replied, "we just think you may be able to help us with a case we're working on."

"Little ol' me helping with a big case, huh?" Viviana replied. "I don't know about that, darling, but I can sure try. Come on in."

Viviana unlocked the door and walked inside. John gestured for Celeste to follow her as he brought up the rear. Turning to close the door, he swept the streets with his eyes, but found nothing and no one out of the ordinary.

So far, so good.

CHAPTER SEVENTY-EIGHT

They walked through an extremely tiny kitchen and then into a small living space.

"Please, please, sit down," Viviana said, ushering John and Celeste to her couch. "Make yourselves at home. Anything I can get you, dears? Celeste, I know you like my homemade sweet tea?"

Celeste was attempting to show that she wasn't uncomfortable, that nothing was wrong, but she wasn't playing it off very well. It was written all over her face that she was nervous.

"Uh-um, yes, please," she stammered.

"Coming right up," Viviana replied.

John looked beside himself at Celeste. She had her right hand on her thigh. Her hand was noticeably shaking. He placed a reassuring hand on hers for a moment, felt her trembling cease, then he pulled away.

Viviana arrived back with a glass of tea in one hand and ice water in the other.

"I figured you really were thirsty, but were just being polite," she said.

Ryan took the water and thanked the woman, and Viviana then handed the tea to Celeste.

Viviana sat across from the couch in a rocking chair. She immediately began rocking back-and-forth.

"So, just exactly how can I help you two?" she asked.

John spoke up. "Have you ever heard of The Crucifier?"

"Oh gosh, my goodness gracious! Why yes, yes, I sure have. Who hasn't heard of him? Makes me sick even thinking about all that's gone on."

"I'm going to cut to the chase with you," John said, leaning forward and clasping his hands together. "We saw you on video leaving a van at Cash for Cars. That van was used by The Crucifier. Do you have any sort of explanation for this? If not, we will have to bring you in, Ms. Newport. There's a whole pile of evidence against you right now."

Viviana stopped rocking. Her face went pale. She stared blankly at John, words struggling to escape her mouth.

"Ms. Newport, we're going to have to bring you in for questioning. You can come of your own free will, or by force. The choice is yours."

"The van…" she spat out. "It…I-I-I have-I have an explanation. I do. I do. I knew there was something wrong about that whole deal. I just knew it…"

"Ms. Newport, what are you saying?" John asked.

Viviana was shaking her head wildly. She jumped to her feet.

"The van…I was paid to take it there! I needed the money!"

She was now in tears. Her eyes were already puffy. She ran her fingers through her thick hair, still shaking her head.

John rose to his feet. "Ms. Newport, I'm going to have to ask you to calm down. Sit down. Talk to us. Tell us what happened?"

"Vivi, we can help you," Celeste chimed in.

Viviana plopped back down into her rocking chair, then immediately shot up again. She put her index finger up in the air.

"Wait, wait, wait, darlings," she said, with a hopeful energy. "I have proof! Oh, my goodness! I've got it. Just, please, give me one second."

She started to walk away but John's voice stopped her.

"Stop!" he commanded, taking a couple of long strides toward her. "Sit. Down. You need to relax. You're a person of interest, and you're acting erratically. I can't just let you jump up like a crazy person, spout random things out, and then leave. Talk to us."

Celeste stood up now too. "If you're in any kind of trouble, whatever is going on, we can help you. I promise. Please, just sit down."

Viviana's shoulders relaxed. She took a deep breath.

"I'm sorry," she said, as she sat down, breaking into a sobbing fit. "I'm so sorry."

John stepped back to the couch and sat down. "It's okay. When you're ready to talk to us, let it out."

Once she controlled the sobs, Viviana let out a deep breath. "I should have known. It all seemed so fishy to me, but if I'm being honest with you, I've actually been involved in a lot of sketchy things in my life. It was just another job, another way to make some extra money. Guys, I'm a waitress at a pub. I barely get by. Anything helps."

"Slowly and carefully explain to us what happened," John commanded.

"A man approached me when I was out for lunch. I walked out of the restaurant and *bang* he was right there in front of me. I admit, he seemed pretty sketchy, and he said he needed me to get rid of a van for him. He said he would give me one hundred dollars on the spot if I just parked the van in a particular place for him. Trust me, I was really leery about the whole deal. I'm a smart gal, and as any smart gal would do, I kindly declined. Then I tried to walk away from him, yet he was persistent. He grabbed me by the shoulder, and it felt like he looked right through my very soul with his cold, lifeless eyes. It scared me half to death, you guys! It sent chills up and down every inch of my body and not the good kind of chills either."

"So, then you just agreed anyway?" Celeste asked, incredulously.

"Oh no, no, not right then. Like I said, I'm a smart gal, Celeste. You know that too. And although I'm small, I can fight back. The guy was puny, and even though he freaked me out, I could have fought and stood my ground."

"Then what happened?" John asked.

"He…he said that if I didn't…" Viviana looked directly into Celeste's eyes. "Then Celeste Ventana would die."

CHAPTER SEVENTY-NINE

Against the wall directly across from the steps was Garrett Jepson. He was hogtied and gagged.

With his gun out, in position to lift and fire at any moment, Ryan cautiously moved down the steps.

"Is anyone else in here?" he asked.

The boy replied by shaking his head and making a grunting sound. Ryan scanned the room. There didn't appear to be anyone else.

"Is there anything in here we need to be worried about? Are we safe to come down?" Ryan asked.

Jepson replied with a simple shake of the head and a muffled "yes."

Ryan made his way down the steps, still alert, ready for anything. As he came up on the kid, he went down to his knees, pulled out his knife and cut the boy's hands and feet free. Jepson then took it upon himself to jerk the gag out of his own mouth.

"My name is Ryan Turner, I'm with the FBI," Ryan said. "With me is Detective Willis. It's Garrett, right? We're going to get you out of here."

He then went on to cut the duct tape free from the boy's face and pulled the gag out of his mouth.

Jepson rolled over onto his back, then stretched out his arms and legs.

"Thank the heavens," he said. "The dude was right. You really did come."

What?

"We really did come?"

Jepson sat up and put his back against the wall. "Yeah, man, you really did. I didn't know if the crazy dude was pulling my leg, or what. When he took me, I thought he would just kill me."

Ryan looked at Willis, then back at Jepson. "What are you talking about?"

"Some guy took me. Called himself B.B. or something weird. He was a creep, obviously. Taking a seventeen-year-old kid, like, what? I was kept tied up in the back of some van or something…"

"Wait," Ryan interrupted. "When were you taken? Actually, let's back up. Before you answer that, we need to get the heck out of here."

Before Jepson had time to disagree or concur, Ryan grabbed the kid by the arm and drug him to his feet. The three hurriedly walked up the stairs leading up out of the hatch. No one bothered to close it behind them, and they ran off the boat's deck and to Willis' car. Ryan, all the while, kept his eyes peeled, taking in his surroundings. Once they reached the car, Willis jumped behind the wheel, Ryan in the shotgun seat, and Jepson in the back. Jepson, much to Ryan's surprise, seemed physically and mentally healthy. He didn't seem particularly phased at all. Everything somehow looked to be okay with him.

"Just drive," Ryan commanded Willis. "I don't care where to."

Willis nodded, shifting the car into gear, then quickly accelerating.

"Garrett," Ryan said, "as I started to ask a second ago, when were you taken? And give us a rundown of what happened up to this point."

Jepson cleared his throat. "Last night, when I was on my way to my buddy's house, this van pulled up next to me. I was on my bike. It happened so fast. I lost control of the bike and ate asphalt, man. Then all of a sudden, I had a bag over my head and was thrown into the van and my legs and hands were tied up. Some man told me to be quiet or else he would slit my throat. I about pissed my pants, man. I didn't say a word. Stayed in there all night. I don't know where they finally parked the van, but when they did, we must have stayed in that spot for hours. I even heard someone snoring at one point. He snored ridiculously loud! Like some kind of beast. He needs to see a doctor, or something."

"Garrett, please stay on track," Ryan ordered.

"Sorry, sorry, sorry. Anyways, I guess that's where we all spent the night? Kind of strange. Weirdos sleeping in a van. Oh, yeah! I think there were three of them, but I don't know that for sure. Doors kept randomly opening and closing. Then, after hours and hours, we pull up to this here place. The bag gets pulled off my head, and I see this creepy dude in front of me. He's the only one left there. Well, I guess if he wasn't holding a kid hostage in a van, he wouldn't have been all that creepy because he seemed like a normal-ish kind of dude. Anyways, he told me that he had rented a boat and was going to leave me in it. He said I was going to be fine, that he wouldn't hurt me. He told me that the police would come for me soon…"

"So, you hadn't been on that boat very long?" Ryan asked.

"Nah, maybe two hours, if that?"

"Wow…carry on."

"So, he cut me loose and told me to walk with him to the boat he rented. He said he just needed to put on a show. He reassured me over and over again that he didn't want to do me any harm, and I would only get hurt if I didn't cooperate, blah, blah, blah. So, I cooperated! Never argue with a crazy person, am I right? I walked with him onto the boat. He took me below deck, took off a backpack that he wore, and removed a bundle of rope and tape from it. He cut a small piece of rope and put it tightly into my mouth and taped it there. Then he hog tied me. He said he would lock the hatch just to make things seem more legitimate, but again reassured me that nothing was going to happen to me. He said something weird a few times along the lines of me not being a part of the ultimate plan, not being a chosen one."

Ryan couldn't believe what he was hearing. "He didn't hurt you? He's not planning on hurting you? Nothing like that?"

"Nope, evidently not. As weird as it may sound, he was a man of his word."

Ryan shook his head. "I don't get it. What was the point of all this then?"

Jepson shrugged. "Who knows, man. There're crazy people out there everywhere, and I do mean everywhere. The guy must have just had a lot of screws loose."

"You didn't know this guy?"

"Nope, said he went by B.B. I didn't know him, though. Ain't ever seen him before in my life."

Ryan kept shaking his head. "So, that was it...? And you said something earlier, 'You really did come?' What did you mean by that?"

Jepson cursed. "My bad! That's totally my bad. Yeah, once he tied me up, he said that in a few hours a man named Ryan Turner would come and save me. I thought he was just making all that crap up. At that point, I still wasn't fully sure whether he was really going to let me live or kill me right then and there, or what. But sure enough, a Ryan Turner did show up. So, as it turned out, the crazy, weird dude was telling me the truth."

"Something's not right about all this," Ryan said, turning away from Jepson, looking straight ahead now.

"You're telling me," Jepson commented.

"This man you're talking about called us earlier this morning. He's wanted for murder. In fact, he's a wanted serial killer, Garrett, not just some crazy guy. He told us he had a boy named Garrett Jepson and that the boy had three left hours to live. He gave us a set of clues to solve that eventually led us straight to you. At this point, his three-hour deadline is all but up and you're still here."

Jepson's face had changed. His entire demeanor had now changed.

"Wow…" he said. "Wow, wow, wow! I didn't know it was all this deep. Wow!"

"It's 'that deep'. Are you sure he didn't do anything to you that might cause you harm?"

"I know for a fact he didn't," Jepson said confidently. "Especially now, with what you just told me, it sounds crazy that he didn't, but, yeah, I'm totally fine."

Ryan ran his fingers through his hair and down the back of his neck.

Why would he do this? There's always a reason.

"Is there anything else you can tell us about this B.B. guy?" Ryan asked. "Anything else he said, did, or didn't do? Anything at all?"

The boy was lost in thought for a moment and then by the newfound spark in his eye, it was obvious that a light bulb had gone off in his head.

"I can't believe I forgot!" he exclaimed.

"Forgot what?" Ryan asked.

"The one thing he said to be sure to tell you. Right before he left me on the boat, he turned around and told me to tell you something."

Ryan gestured with his hands for Jepson to continue. "Well, get to it, kid."

"My bad. He said to tell you that you should've stayed in DC, and that you're going to wish you told John goodbye. Does that make any sense to you at all?"

Ryan said nothing. It made perfect sense.

John...

CHAPTER EIGHTY

Ethan Jordan was a Democratic Senator from California and currently the Senate Majority Leader. He was 59 years-old, had salt and pepper colored hair, and was a couple inches over six-feet-tall. Senator Jordan was a proud man, though he hid that side of himself from the rest of the world. Above all else, Jordan loved power. He loved his last ten-plus years in the Senate. He loved even more the newfound fame that had led to him taking over as Senate Majority Leader. This important position had also led him to a potential 2020 Presidential run. In current exit polls, he was the number one democratic candidate. It was simple to him, and he didn't understand why other candidates didn't understand how to play the game. He had three simple rules, which he always followed: one, find any way possible to bring in a surplus of campaign funds, whether legal or not; two, give the people what they want to hear, but don't be *too* radical; three, pay off important leaders from both sides of the political aisle---past and present---to endorse you.

So far, he had done all three perfectly and still had lots of campaign time left to go. It felt good getting out of the gates fast. It also felt good knowing most of those running against him were radical and incompetent. He would never say it to anyone, because it delegitimized his thus far successful campaign, but the competition was simply weak. A monkey could win the Democratic nomination for this upcoming election.

Senator Jordan now sat in his DC office, located in the Russell Building. He had just finished meeting with three refugee families that he had invited into his office. He, of course, had made certain that several specific media outlets would be there, and after his meeting with the refugees, he made sure to let the reporters know the *exact* story he wanted them to run, and *exactly* what he wanted them to say. Jordan knew that he had 90% of the country's national media wrapped around his finger. They ate up everything he said as they bowed down to him. Everything he did and said was considered gospel, and he was able to instruct them to run whatever story he preferred. As a politician, he couldn't have been in a better place.

He sat behind his personal desk, with his legs propped up on it. He sipped from a cup of coffee in his hand, which his personal assistant, Angelina Sousa, had just brewed for him. Angelina was absolutely wonderful. Not only did she make the best coffee in the world, she was also drop-dead gorgeous. He would always say that it was her impressive resume that inspired him to hire her, but her resume wasn't truly all that impressive. It was her dashing good looks that he was instantly drawn to. He was pretty sure that she knew that too, and she seemed more than okay with that knowledge.

As great as the morning had been so far, for some reason, Jordan wasn't feeling very well. He was hoping that it was just a matter of the last couple busy weeks catching up with him. Over the past month and a half, he probably averaged a mere four hours of sleep per night, and a few nights included no sleep at all. The various illegal pills that he took helped, but still the lack of sleep affected him. The human body needed sleep. So, that's what he was contributing to his current stomach pain, sweats and fatigue. He had been feeling fine all morning until just now.

Senator Jordan swung his legs off the desk and hunched over. The pain in his abdomen was suddenly worsening now. He pressed a button on his desk to call Angelina. In no time, she was quickly running through his door and came to his side.

Even in his current state, he was able to appreciate her beauty. She had been out for the last week, or so, on sick leave. Today was the first day she had been back for quite some time. And it was definitely nice having her back.

Angelina was a tall woman. She was built too. She attributed it to daily workouts spent in the gym. She was a powerful looking woman. Some men may not find that attractive in a woman, but Senator Jordan did. And her face…it was almost heavenly. Otherworldly. Perfect. It had a certain glow that was indescribable. She had long, wavy, jet black hair. Her eyes were a dark, ocean blue and piercing. She had full, red lips and a perfectly straight set of white teeth. If there was ever a living Greek Goddess in the flesh, it was undoubtedly Angelina.

"You look amazing," Senator Jordan managed to say in between abdominal spasms.

Angelina blushed while shaking her head, but there remained traces of visible worry written all over her face.

"What's wrong, sir?" she asked, placing a hand on his forearm.

The Senator gagged and covered his mouth. He pointed demandingly at a trash can that sat in a corner of the room. Angelina rushed to the can, then brought it to Senator Jordan. He instantly vomited into it. Angelina turned away, doing her best to fight back her own gag reflex.

"I'm so sorry that you're seeing me like this," Senator Jordan said, with his head in the can. "This is absolutely disgusting."

Angelina walked behind the Senator and placed her hands on his shoulders. "No, no, hush. You're going to be okay. You have no reason to apologize to me."

Senator Jordan lifted his head up slightly. "You know, the Republicans would jump all over me if they saw how touchy-feely you are with me sometimes. They'd surely try to bury my campaign over it."

"Oh, please," Angelina said, as she rolled her eyes while rubbing Senator Jordan's shoulders. "There's obviously nothing weird between us. Just because you're a great looking guy, with an assistant that's young, single, vibrant, beautiful, smart…"

With his head still lowered into the trash can, the Senator chuckled. "Yeah, yeah, and that's exactly my point, Angie."

Angelina smiled sweetly and took the can from Senator Jordan. She looked him in the face.

"Sir, you really don't look too good," she said with a look of concern. "You're pale as a ghost."

"My head is spinning now too. Ugh. I need to go home, right now, Angie. I don't remember the last time I felt this awful."

Angelina nodded. "Yes, I understand! You need to take care of yourself. You stretch yourself way too thin sometimes. I'll get you home, okay? I'll take you myself. Your security can sit this one out."

Senator Jordan looked up at Angelina. He sure wasn't about to argue with that. In fact, if this is what would happen every time he got sick, maybe he would try to get sick more often.

My heavens, you're beautiful.

"You really don't mind?" he asked, just to sound polite.

"Of course not! It's the very least I can do. And besides, extra quality time with you isn't something we always get outside of the office."

The Senator smiled. "Thank you, Angie."

"Let me inform everyone about what's going on, and that we're closing up shop for the day. Then I'll get you home, okay?"

"Sounds great."

Angelina smiled her heart-stopping smile, then began to close the office's door behind her.

"Angelina?" Senator Jordan called out.

Angelina turned around. "Yes?"

"It's nice having you back."

Angelina grinned. "It's good to be back, sir."

CHAPTER EIGHTY-ONE

Ryan stared blankly at Garrett Jepson. His whole world was spinning rapidly off its axis. B.B., or whoever he was, had *wanted* Ryan to come to Cleveland. He had wanted Ryan to arrive here when he did. He knew Ryan would attempt to rescue Jepson. And knew that he would eventually find the boy. He *wanted* Ryan to find him. B.B. never meant Jepson any harm. It was never his intention. The boy was just a small part of the bigger plan. A distraction and a game. A way to mess with Ryan. But also, a power move. It was a way to show who was really in control.

He knew Ryan and Willis would solve the puzzles, and he knew that if they somehow didn't, then it would work out perfectly as well. He was just buying time. He was keeping Ryan away from DC for as long as possible. Away from DC, away from the centralized scene of the murders, away from John and talking to him. But for exactly what reasons? Ryan couldn't put his finger on that part it yet. All he knew was that this killer had been two, no, more like three steps ahead of them this entire time. Even the DC officers' discovery of the missing van was all a part of it…it left John there, it brought Ryan here alone.

Ryan swallowed.

This isn't good…this isn't good at all.

Ryan snapped out of his trance at the sound of both Willis and Jepson calling his name. Jepson put a hand on Ryan's shoulder, jerking Ryan back into reality.

"You good, Mr. Turner?" Jepson asked.

"This was all part of his plan," Ryan said quietly. "G-Man was a hundred percent right…. this *was* a trap. Just not in the way we thought it could be…"

Willis looked over at Ryan with concern written all over his face. "What do you mean? Aren't we good? What's the matter?"

Ryan shook his head slowly, staring outside the passenger-side window. "No. No, we're not good. We're not anywhere near good. That psychopath wanted me to come here. He wanted me in Cleveland."

"What do you mean?" Willis asked.

Ryan ignored the question. He was mostly thinking out loud now.

"He wanted me here. He wanted me to go after Garrett and wanted me to find him too. He wanted me away from DC."

"Mr. Turner," Willis said, "If I'm being honest, you're scaring me. Are we safe? What do we need to do now?"

Ryan looked over at Willis. "Yes, we're safe here. For now, at least. The problem is what's going on DC at this very moment. That's our real problem."

Ryan pulled out his cell phone.

"And what's going on there?" Willis asked.

Ryan shook his head. "That's the thing...I don't know. But whatever it is, I'm stuck here and there's no way for me to stop it. I walked right into the trap...I need to call my brother."

Ryan found John's contact in his phone and called him.

The phone rang and rang and rang...then rang some more. No answer. Ryan ended the call before the voicemail recording started and tried calling again.

Same result.

He texted John and waited a few minutes for a reply.

Nothing.

He then called again.

Same result.

His heart was pounding. Willis kept saying things and asking questions, but Ryan inadvertently ignored all of it. He couldn't even hear Willis' voice. He was thinking of Simmons and Lee and what had happened to them, how they had died. Ryan ran his fingers threw his hair and down the back of his neck. He was sweaty now. His mind was racing in every which direction. John had to be alright. He just had to be.

Ryan called his brother again. This time when it went to voicemail, Ryan left a message.

"John, I ran into a big problem here. A big, big problem. You need to call me. I'm heading back to DC now. I'm going to get there as soon as I can. There's something conspiring there, and I don't think you're safe. Please, get back to me as soon as possible. I love you, man."

CHAPTER EIGHTY-TWO

"He said Celeste would die?" John asked in disbelief.

"Yes…" Viviana answered, with tears running down her cheeks.

John cocked his head to the side and looked the Viviana up and down. She was blankly staring down at her feet.

"So, after that, you just agreed?" John asked.

Viviana nodded. "That's when I gave in. He gave me the instructions and then said if I told anyone about what happened he would kill me too. He said he'd been following me for quite some time, and that he always has eyes on me. But, like, why me? I just don't understand. Why me?"

John hadn't anticipated the conversation going in this direction. He was taken aback. It seemed legitimate. But still, he couldn't rely on Viviana's words alone. It was her story, and just because she was emotional didn't mean she was telling the truth.

John nodded his head slowly. "Listen, we still need to take you in. We need to get you to talk to us more about this and we will need you to identify this man for us. Okay? We can get a sketch artist there at the station, but we need to take you there. If what you're saying is true, neither of you two are safe here. So, regardless, you'll be far better off in our custody."

Viviana covered her face with her hands and shook her head slowly. "Why is this happening to me…?"

"Ms. Newport, it's going to be alright," John reassured. "We just need you to come with us. Okay? Please."

Viviana looked up. She had somewhat calmed her emotions now.

"Okay," she said, emotionlessly. "I just really need to grab something really quick. It might help my situation. It might be the one bit of evidence to support my story."

Before John could reply, Viviana hopped to her feet and quickly walked to her bedroom.

John jumped up. "Ma'am, hold on! I have to go with you. Stop!"

Viviana didn't stop. She seemed to have zoned him out. Understandable, though, in a way. She was going through a lot. A million thoughts must have been going through her head.

John quickly trotted behind her and followed her into the bedroom. He stopped in the doorway. Viviana went to the wall opposite of the door and began to dig around in a dresser. Instinctively, John put a hand on the gun at his side. The woman dug crazily through the clothes in the drawer that she now had her head stuck in. Socks, underwear, shorts, pants, t-shirts flew everywhere. She seemed to be taking an awfully long time finding whatever it was that she was looking for.

"I know I put it in here somewhere," she muttered to herself. "I *know* I did."

John's sixth sense began to kick in and he didn't know precisely why. It was that feeling he always got when something was awry, when something was wrong, or when someone was watching him. He didn't know why it had suddenly come over him, but he couldn't shake it.

"Ms. Newport, please hurry," he instructed. "Just what are you looking for, exactly?"

"Just give me a moment," she snapped, irritably.

Now John was getting irritated. He took a step further into the room. He started to speak again, but just as he opened his mouth, he felt a sharp, stabbing pain in the back of his neck. He slapped at the source of the pain and contacted a syringe of some sort sticking out of his neck. The needle in his neck sliced downward, tearing open the tiny hole that the initial injection had caused. In shock, John realized whatever had been in the syringe had already entered his system. His eyes became heavy. His legs were weak. His vision blurred. He could now see Viviana walking toward him with a sinister smile on her face. He tried to turn and swing at whoever was behind him, but instead was pushed in the back by the perpetrator. His wobbly legs crumbled underneath him, and he fell flat onto his face. He could feel his chest constricting. He couldn't breathe. His head was pounding.

The last thing he saw were Viviana's feet directly in front of his face. The last thing he heard was Celeste's voice coming from behind him.

"I'm so, so sorry, John."

CHAPTER EIGHTY-THREE

Over 200 miles away in New York City, a room on the 12th floor of the Ritz Carlton near Battery Park, was being blown apart by an onslaught of explosives set by Jack Grimes. Soon, Kuron Taylor would arrive on the scene with Lieutenant Strodderbeck. They would watch in disbelief as firefighters fought to put out the flames that engulfed larges sections of the 10th, 11th, and 12th floors.

Simultaneously, over 200 miles away, at another address in New York City, a little girl named Kayleen Turner was kicking a soccer ball in her family's backyard after eating a pancake breakfast, made by the hands of her mother, Laura Turner. With Kayleen, ran around a little three-legged dog named Tripod.

Almost 400 miles away, in Cleveland, Ohio, Ryan Turner was making frantic phone calls to Director Felix, Detective Fox, Kuron, John over and over again, and even Laura. Nearly 400 miles away, Ryan's heart was aching and was filled with sincere prayer that everything would be okay. Soon, he would re-board the private plane that brought him to Cleveland earlier that morning. Soon enough, he would arrive back in DC, only to find that he was too late.

Meanwhile, here and now, Senator Jordan and Angelina Sousa sat inside the Senator's home, neither one of the two personally acquainted with Jack Grimes, Kuron Taylor, Felicia Strodderbeck, Laura and Kayleen Turner, or even Ryan Turner, himself. They didn't know what was going on 200 miles away in New York City, or 400 miles away in Cleveland. They were completely focused on the here and now.

Senator Jordan's stomach pain had begun to ease, and he was more than thankful for that. As he began to backtrack in his mind, he realized that the stomach pain had started shortly after he took his first drink of coffee this morning. It must have been due to spoiled creamer, or something like that. He thought about calling Angelina out on it but decided against it. They were on good terms right now, and it felt like he was dreaming, in the sense that this beautiful woman was *actually* in his home. Oh, how he had dreamed of bringing her home with him one day. And now here she was.

If she wasn't working for him, if he wasn't running for president, he would've already asked her out, maybe even married her by now. She was the perfect woman. A lot younger, yes, but he knew there was something special between them. And, furthermore, he knew that she knew it too. He saw the way that Angelina looked at him every so often, heard the way she talked to him, the way she was always there to comfort him and lift him up when he needed it. He looked over his shoulder at her now as she stood in the kitchen with her back to him, warming up a pot of canned chicken noodle soup. She was so elegant, so beautiful. She was a living Goddess.

His wife, Martha, had passed away just over a year ago after a massive heart attack. It broke his heart at the time. But looking at Angelina now, he knew that maybe, just maybe, this young woman had been put into his life for a reason. In this moment, he thought that dropping his presidential campaign and maybe even his Senate position for the sake of an open relationship with Angelina. To him, it was worth it. He knew he wasn't a good man, yet it's who he was. He knew that he was mixed up with some bad people and with some even worse things, but again, it's who he was. Truth be told, he actually *loved* that side of himself, as evil as it may have been.

Would I ever come clean to her about who I really am?

The question journeyed through Senator Jordan's mind as he watched her.

No, I wouldn't. I couldn't.

He knew he couldn't ever bring himself to tell the whole truth, to leak who he really was. He had kept that side of himself hidden from the entire world. He had kept it from Martha throughout their entire marriage. He knew with a surety that he could keep his inner demons hidden from Angelina too. With all that said, he also knew he had to tell her how he felt before she left him today. He *had to* know for himself if she felt the same.

CHAPTER EIGHTY-FOUR

Angelina Sousa had her own secrets as well. She also had her reasons for wanting to be in the Senator's home. It had been a long time coming and here they finally were.

Angelina stirred the soup on the stovetop. It smelled *wonderful*. She hadn't eaten this morning, due to the knots in her stomach that came from the anticipation leading up to this very moment. She thought about possibly eating a bowl of the soup, herself. Besides, it was her all-time favorite soup. It reminded her of her childhood.

However, she decided against it. What would be the point, anyway? Her time here was going to be busy. There would be no time for eating a bowl of chicken noodle soup.

She used the serving spoon in her hand to transfer scoops of the soup into a large ceramic bowl, then she turned off the burner and retrieved a soup spoon for the Senator. She looked in Senator Jordan direction and caught him gazing at her over his shoulder. He immediately turned back around and tried to play it off like he was stretching.

Angelina smirked. She almost found it cute how big of a crush he had on her. But still, it was pathetic. So very pathetic. She knew that he thought he hid his feelings well too. It was obvious since the moment he hired her that he had strong feelings for her. It creeped her out at times, yet she played along. She played her part because she had to, and she knew it would come to an end eventually. She was just thankful for the degree she had gotten at the University of Maryland so long ago, and was thankful for her physique and good looks, since, without both, she wouldn't have ever gotten into the position she was in now.

Senator Jordan wasn't only oblivious to the fact that Angelina had secrets and inner demons of her own, and that she knew he had feelings for her, but he was also oblivious that there was now a big white van parked in front of his grand mansion. It was unknown to him that it was Angelina who had given the driver the code to come through the gates.

Angelina walked into the enormous living room area where the Senator sat. He laid back in an expensive recliner. The ceiling hung 14 feet above the room. A 160-inch flat screen TV was installed on the wall. A pool table sat in the middle of the room between the seats and the TV. Arcade games and a bar were on the other end of the living space. There was no way he'd been able to afford the home from his old salary as an elementary teacher and even his new job as a senator. It was well beyond impossible. It was hilarious to Angelina that no one had ever called him out on it. She thought the Republicans would have by now, but many of them were dirty in so many different ways too. Government, Washington, politicians, they were all crooked. It was all one gigantic, never-ending mess. And she despised it.

"Here you go, sir," Angelina said sweetly, handing the steaming bowl of soup to Senator Jordan. "I hope it tastes okay. And please don't burn yourself, it's still pretty hot."

The Senator took the bowl in his hands. "Thank you, my dear. You're an angel."

Angelina smiled and patted the Senator on his thigh.

"You're so very welcome," she said. "I'm going to clean up the kitchen. I'll be right back. Now don't you go anywhere."

She winked at the old man and he winked back. "Oh, I won't. Not in this condition."

The kitchen was already pretty clean. It didn't really need her attention; however, the excuse gave her some more time to think about her approach, more time to think about how she would go about her next steps. She rinsed out the pot under the large kitchen sink then made her way back to Senator Jordan.

She had made up her mind. She could have chosen the easy way about it. She already had what she needed. It was tucked deep inside her pocket. A split second, one simple movement was all it would take. But she wasn't one to take the easy way, or the quick, time-saving route. Angelina enjoyed dragging things out. She enjoyed the lead up, the anticipation. This was why she loved the work she had been doing. It had become a part of her. In fact, it *was* her, just as much as her name was Angelina Sousa.

CHAPTER EIGHTY-FIVE

Angelina returned to Senator Jordan and sat in a recliner next to his. In between the two seats was a coffee table. On the table was the Senator's bowl of soup.

"Aw," Angelina said sticking her lip out, "is that really all you can eat?"

Senator Jordan shrugged. "Sorry, Angie, that's all I've got."

Angelina frowned. "You poor thing. I'm so sorry! Here, I'll take the bowl back to the kitchen for you."

The Senator put a hand up. "No, that won't be necessary. Just sit and relax, Angie. You've already done plenty for me today."

"I do enjoy taking care of you. I mean that. I would do anything for you."

Senator Jordan blushed. "I need to be honest with you...I can't believe I'm saying it now, given my current physical situation, but I've been wanting to tell you this for a while."

Angelina held up a hand. "You hush, because there's something I've been wanting to tell you too. And I've kept it in for way too long already now, Ethan."

The Senator said nothing. Angelina had his full attention. She didn't call him by his first name very often.

She slid out of her chair and knelt at Senator Jordan's feet. His chest was heaving in and out.

"I love you, Ethan," Angelina said softly, placing her hands on his knees. "I have never cared about someone the same way I care about you. And I know the age difference thing is weird, and I know you're this big-time, super important person and all, with all the fame and I'm just little me. And I know this is so out of the blue…"

The Senator leaned forward and placed a finger against Angelina's lips. Her skin crawled at the man's touch.

"Just stop there…stop right there, Angie…Angie, wow, I can't believe this."

He leaned back in his chair. Surprise, happiness, pride covered his face.

"I want you, Angie," he said, leaning forward again. "I need you. I mean, I love everything about you. I love everything that you are. You also mean more to me than I can even explain. I've been waiting for this moment for so long. You have no idea."

He placed a hand over one of Angelina's and looked deeply into her eyes. Angelina took her other hand and placed it on top of Senator Jordan's. She patted the top of his hand before slowly pulling it away, and then moving it down to her pocket. The Senator caressed her other hand with his fingers. He began to slowly lean in for a kiss. Angelina wanted to puke at the sight of his lips closing in on hers. Before he could get his face any closer to hers, Angelina pulled the syringe from her pocket and used the side of her leg to slip the cover off the needle.

"I love hearing you say that," she said, "because, trust me, I've been waiting for this moment for so long too. *You* have no idea."

The moment she finished her last sentence, Angelina shoved the needle deep into the Senator's right thigh, just before his lips touched hers. Senator Jordan jerked back as he screamed out in pain. He lashed out at his leg and Angelina leapt to her feet. A menacing smile crept onto her pretty face.

"Ah! Ah! What did you do? Angie, my dear, what did you do to me?"

Angelina's smile widened. "*Don't* call me dear. And I've always despised it whenever you call me Angie."

The Senator's eyes went wide in fear. "What are you doing!? I...ah! Ah! I can't feel my legs."

"The more you freak out and squirm about, the faster the chemicals will set in. So, please, keep acting irrational. All you're doing is helping me."

"I can't move! What have you done?"

Angelina crouched back down in front of the man. "It's all very simple, Senator. You see, I injected you with a chemical mixture that has curare in it, which is a muscle relaxer. Not only can the substance act as a muscle relaxer, but it can do so in an extreme sense, ultimately causing paralysis. Through injection, it's absorbed through the blood. If you had, say, taken curare orally, then you wouldn't be experiencing the same effects that you are now at this moment. This is because curare compounds are large and hard to pass through the digestive tract and into the blood stream. If I could've put it into your soup, I would've. I know, this is a bit of a violent and harsh way to go about drugging you. I almost feel sorry."

"I can't move my arms now!" Senator Jordan cried out. "Or my neck!"

"Yes, that's correct, you can't. And lucky for us all, it's just a matter of time before this toxin will keep you from being able to talk too because, you know, talking involves the use of muscles. Although, unlucky for you, do you know what this toxin doesn't paralyze? It does *not* shut down your pain receptors. So, those will be fully responsive. You won't have to worry about them not working properly."

The Senator's eyes darted back-and-forth yet he didn't say a word.

"Oh, perfect," Angelina said. "Looks like it has fully kicked in already. I'll be right back, Senator Jordan. Now don't you go anywhere."

CHAPTER EIGHTY-SIX

When Angelina returned, she wasn't alone. Helping her carry a large wooden cross through the massive, metal front doors and into the mansion, were two people covered in black from head to toe. Their names, unknown to the Senator, were Helga and Friona. They carried the cross through the doors and set it directly inside the door.

Senator Jordan's eyes were locked in place. He stared straight ahead. He was oblivious to what was going on next to him and to who had just walked in.

"Oh, my dear Ethan, we're back," Angelina said.

Although it was Angelina, it wasn't her voice that the Senator heard. This new voice was deep, eerie, garbled, and made Senator Jordan's skin crawl.

"Don't be scared, it is I," Angelina said, approaching Senator Jordan. "It is I, the woman you love, Ethan Jordan."

Angelina dropped down on her haunches in front of the Senator's feet, leading him to grunt loudly. She now wore a mask. The mask was white, covering her entire face aside from her two cold eyes. The voice modifier caused the mouth area of the mask to bulge outward. A gold cross hung around her neck.

"What changed, Ethan?" Angelina asked. "I thought you loved me?"

She stood and grabbed the arms of the chair that Senator Jordan sat in. She used the arms to keep her balance as she leaned forward so that her face was a mere inch away from the senator's. She tilted her head to the side.

"*This* is who I am. *This* is what I am. You said that you love everything about me, right?"

She leaned in, putting her face next to his.

"*Fear,*" she said into his ear. "It is normal to experience this. Soon, your fear will turn into pain, and then soon after that, the only sensation you'll want to feel is that of *death*. You will want it. You will accept it."

The Senator continued to grunt, unable to speak. Angelina pulled back slightly and ran a finger down the man's face. She then stepped back and began to pace around the chair.

"This moment has been a long time coming, Ethan Jordan. I almost wish you were able to speak again. But at the same time, you would just blabber nonsense, as you always do. Right now, I can speak to you without interruption. Soon, though, the chemicals will wear off and you'll be able to talk, but it should be awhile until that occurs."

Angelina spun the chair around to where Senator Jordan could see the cross lying on the floor. Standing, one on each end of it, were Helga and Friona. The Senator groaned loudly.

"Beautiful, isn't it?" Angelina asked. "Your Judgement Day has finally come, and I am the judge, the jury, *and* the executioner. You really thought all this time that someone wouldn't find out what you have been doing, what you are involved in? Especially being someone with a platform such as yours? You really didn't think it would catch up to you? You're hurting people. You're destroying innocent lives. Martha might have been stupid, but I'm not. *We* are not. We knew what you were doing, so I decided to work for you, gain your trust, get established, and really make sure that you were the sick, dirt bag we believed you to be.

"It was beautiful how everything worked out. How you hired me in the first place. How you actually fell in love with me." Angelina laughed an evil laugh. "Hmm, so pathetic, isn't it? But even how you brought me here today. It was all destiny. It was all a matter of the universe catching up with you and punishing you. Fate is what brought me straight to you."

Angelina crouched down in front of Senator Jordan again.

"Friona," she called out, "bring me the blade."

Friona walked up like a soldier with fluid, deliberate strides. She stopped next to Angelina and held out her hand in which she held a long, jagged blade. Keeping her eyes locked on the paralyzed man, Angelina took the blade into her right hand.

"Such a beautiful weapon," she said, stroking the sharp blade. "So many different people's blood has spilt onto this blade. Yours will make a wonderful addition."

Angelina stood, then made her way behind the recliner. Standing over Senator Jordan, she used the blade to cut into the man's forehead. It sliced through the skin like butter. She cut a long, straight line from his hairline down to where his eyebrows met. She then cut a horizontal line in the middle of the first wound to create a perfect, bloody cross on the man's pasty, white forehead. Streams of blood ran from the wound, coating his eyebrows a thick red color, and running further down into his eyes, then down his bony cheeks. She wiped the blood off the blade using the Senator's shirt, then walked back to where the man could see her through his blood-covered eyes. She crouched down again.

"I hope you don't feel special," Angelina spat, "because you are not; however, you are the first to see me without the mask. None of the other sinners have had the privilege to experience that."

Angelina set the blade on the floor and reached up with both hands to remove her mask. As she threw the mask down, her pearly white teeth gleamed. Though it was her same beautiful face, there was something different about her. Something different about the look in her eye. Something dark. She wasn't the same person as she was before she put on the mask. She was something else entirely.

"As you should know, you are not the first, Ethan Jordan," she said, in the voice Senator Jordan was familiar with. "And you will not be the last. You *are* one of the main perpetrators, one of our main targets. So, this is a big steppingstone in our work. I do thank you for that. Your death brings us so much closer to our final destination. It brings us that much closer to our work's completion. Until your people turn themselves in and reveal who they truly are underneath the fluff and the fakeness and the lies, people will continue to die. Our work is *inevitable. My* work is inevitable."

"Who…are…you?" Senator Jordan muttered, his words almost unintelligible.

Angelina smiled a wicked smile. "Looks like your words are already coming back. Well, Ethan Jordan…"

She grabbed the armrests of the chair and leaned in close, her nose almost touching the Senator's. She looked directly into his eyes. A tear streamed down both of his bloodied cheeks.

Angelina's teeth gleamed like white diamonds. "I. Am. The Crucifier."

Dear Reader,

So, you've reached the end of Turned Around and must have endless questions regarding what has happened up to this point, right? I'm here to tell you that those questions *will* be answered. Ryan Turner *will* return. You may be wondering if I'm going to answer any of those questions in this letter…and I'm sorry to inform you that, no, I won't be doing that here. So, with that said, will you have to wait until Part II of Turned Around to find those answers? Yes…yes, you will. And trust me, it'll be worth the wait.

I write this letter at the conclusion of this story, for a few reasons. One: once again, I wanted to let you know that this is not the end of Ryan Turner's pursuit of The Crucifier. Things will only get more exciting, heart-wrenching, jaw-dropping, and twisted. The story has only just begun. It will be well worth the wait.

Two: I wanted to inform you that this story was meant to be much longer. My previous plan with this project was not to stop the storyline where I did. Instead, it was going to be one lengthy novel, rather than two parts. However, in 2019 I received a mission assignment to serve in Spain for two years. I received this calling through the Church of Jesus Christ of Latter-Day Saints and reported to the mission on July 10, 2019. Due to this new journey in my life, I had to put my writing career on a brief hold (key word here is *brief*) and decided it might be a good idea to split up the story and be able to release the first part as soon as I got back home from Spain. I returned about 3 months ago, and this is why the final product of Turned Around is just now being released.

Three: from the bottom of my heart, I want to thank you. You are the reason I do this, the reason I spend late nights working on my craft, and the reason I decided to get another book ready to be released the moment I returned home from my missionary service. Your support is what helped me make Turned Around possible. For that, I cannot thank you enough.

I hope you enjoyed Turned Around. Again, the world of Ryan Turner will be back and better than ever. I also have a few other projects in the works that I am incredibly excited to share with you in the near future. I can't wait to release them for you and wish I could have had them finished by now, but at the same time, I am very humbled and blessed to have had the opportunity to serve the people in Spain over the course of the last two years. It was a life-changing experience. And who knows, maybe my experiences there will one day be composed into a book…we'll just have to wait and see!

Always,

Jorrell Mirabal